# THE LIVES OF
# DIAMOND BESSIE

# THE LIVES OF
# DIAMOND BESSIE

*A Novel*

JODY HADLOCK

Published by SparkPress, a BookSparks imprint,
A division of SparkPoint Studio, LLC
Phoenix, Arizona, USA, 85007
www.gosparkpress.com

Published 2022
Printed in the United States of America
Print ISBN: 978-1-68463-117-9
E-ISBN: 978-1-68463-118-6

Library of Congress Control Number: 2021914905

Formatting by Kiran Spees

For Charlie
and
Bridget

In memory of
Fred McKenzie

ROMEO
And we mean well in going to this mask,
But 'tis no wit to go.

MERCUTIO
Why, may one ask?

ROMEO
I dreamt a dream tonight.

MERCUTIO
And so did I.

ROMEO
Well, what was yours?

MERCUTIO
That dreamers often lie.

ROMEO
In bed asleep, while they do dream things true.

MERCUTIO
O then I see Queen Mab hath been with you.

*Romeo and Juliet*, Act 1, Scene 4

# 1

Forgiveness means letting go of the hope for a better past.

— Lama Surya Das

*Buffalo, New York, December 1866*

I had been with the Sisters of Our Lady of Charity of the Refuge for four months when I finally drew up the courage to speak to the Mother Superior. The silent period was in effect, but I couldn't wait any longer. As I approached her office, my body, weighted with a swollen belly, grew heavier. Before I could change my mind, I steeled myself and knocked on her door. After a terse *"Entrez,"* I entered. When the Mother saw me, she frowned.

"Why are you not at the laundry, Elisabeth?"

The Sisters, who had come from France to establish an order in Buffalo, had given me a new name upon my arrival. It still made me cringe. "Reverend Mother, I wish to write a letter to my mam."

"That's not allowed."

I had expected to be denied my request but it stung nevertheless. "Why not?"

"You must let go of your past," Mother said impatiently, her brows knitted, "so you can start a new life."

All the penitents, as we were known, were forbidden to talk about our pasts, our homes, our families. We couldn't even reveal our real names, but that hadn't stopped my friend Genevieve and me from confiding in each other.

"Your *maman* knew that when she sent you here," Mother said, "because of your… transgression." Her eyes rested on my sin.

"But—"

Mother's eyes narrowed and, after a moment of tense silence, she asked me what I would write to my mother.

I clasped my hands together to still their shaking and hoped my voice wouldn't fail me. "That I wish to go home."

"Your family doesn't want you." Her mouth curled slightly as if she enjoyed the cruelty of her words.

"That's not—"

Mother's posture stiffened. "Our Lady of Refuge is your home now."

I lowered my head and uttered my next words slowly. "I don't belong here."

"You think you're too good for the Sisters and your fellow penitents?"

"No," I said softly.

She tapped the Bible on her desk. "It is vanity to be proud."

"It's—"

"How dare you talk back to a Bride of Christ," she snapped. "You have fallen from Grace and can only be restored to purity in God's eyes if you carry out your atonement in the proper spirit of remorse— without complaint."

We'd been told we would be rewarded when we'd done our penance, with what no one knew.

I stood there meekly as Mother went on. "The work you do in the laundry helps wash you of your sins. Do you know what happened to *Jezabel*?"

Before I could answer she leaned forward, her voice rising with her agitation. "She was thrown over a balcony and eaten by dogs. If you do not do your penance, you will perish in the fires of Hell and remain there for all eternity."

"How long," I started, nearly choking on my words. "How long will it take to get redemption?" The last few words came out barely above a whisper.

"What makes you think you're so special you'll ever enter Heaven?" she thundered, bolting out of her chair and ushering me out of her office.

Dismissed and demoralized, I went to the laundry.

At supper, I expected to be denied a meal and forced to kneel on the floor, as other penitents were made to do for speaking during the silent period. But nothing happened.

For the next two days I slept uneasily, fretting over my visit to the Mother, fearful of what my punishment might be.

On the third day, Sister Agnes came to my dormitory before dawn. The creak of the door woke me. A few other girls stirred from their slumbers but remained quiet. As I rose, Genevieve caught my eye. My friend's look expressed sympathy and terror for me.

After dressing, I followed Sister Agnes down the stairs. I slowed my pace, knowing where she was taking me. "Mother Superior is waiting," she barked.

When we reached the basement room to which I would be banished, Mother stood outside the door in her stiff white habit, white scapular, and black veil as dark as her heart.

"You would really put someone with child in there?" I asked the Mother with as much defiance as I could bluster.

She glared at me. I had insulted her decency. Now I would really pay. "Get inside, you impudent thing," Mother said.

I felt a kick in my abdomen. Was my baby as distressed as I was? I took a step back, placed a protective hand on my belly. "I will not." As much as I feared the nuns, my fear of being locked away so near to giving birth was greater.

Mother's dour face clouded, a storm gathering. "Now," she hissed.

When I didn't move, Mother said to Sister Agnes, "Get this insufferable wretch inside."

The Sister took me by the elbow. "Elisabeth—"

"That's not my name!" I screamed and shook my arm free.

Sister Agnes was as thin as a communion Host, but the Mother was stout and used her heft to shove me toward the dark room. I stumbled. My arms and knees hit the stone floor first, and then I felt the thud of my belly. Slowly, I rolled onto my side. As I groaned, Sister Agnes stepped over me and grabbed my dress. Mother straddled me and they pulled me into the room.

Mother closed the door and locked it, leaving me in pitch black. I clutched my stomach, fearful the fall had injured my unborn daughter. I was sure I would have a girl, just as my older sister, Hannah, had shortly before I'd been sent away for my unpardonable sin.

Slowly, I heaved myself off the floor and inched forward. A rat scurried across my path. When I found a wall, I slid my back down it and folded my knees until they rested on my swollen belly. Without a coat or blanket, I shivered in the damp cold. It seeped into my nose, my throat, my bones.

After a while the door opened. Dim light from the kerosene lamps in the hallway allowed a glimpse of a tray. As one of the nuns pushed it inside, I lunged on my hands and knees toward the door before the darkness closed in on me again. The tray held a cup of cooled tea and stale bread, which I greedily drank and ate.

I didn't have my rosary beads, but I said the rosary over and over again anyway. When I wasn't praying, I was planning my escape. The convent's stone walls weren't high enough to keep me from getting out.

Long after I lost count of my time in the basement, I felt a pop and warm liquid seeped between my legs. At first I worried I had lost control of my bladder—the chamber pot left for me was nearly overflowing—but then I felt a spasm, so sharp I doubled over. As more of the fluid gushed onto the floor, I crawled to the door and banged and screamed for help until I lost my voice and my hands ached.

Agonizing pain came in waves, each one bigger than the last: crashing, rolling tides, like the waves that had battered my family's crowded ship on our voyage from Ireland to America. Then, I'd been at the mercy of the sea and the captain; now I was at the mercy of the nuns and God. I closed my eyes. When I opened them I was separated from my laboring body, floating near the ceiling looking down at myself. Was I dead? I was writhing in agony below, so I must be alive. Where I hovered there was no torment, only peace and calmness. It was only when I began to worry that I needed to be with my body to bring my baby into the world that I went back to the savage throes of childbirth.

When it was over I collapsed in relief. My body throbbed but unbridled joy soared within me when the nun who had rescued me from the basement placed my precious daughter in my arms. "Should I start nursing her now?"

The Sister hesitated. "No, let's wait."

I assumed she knew best. After a short time she took the baby so I could rest. Exhausted, I fell asleep. When I woke, nightfall had come. I was alone. I drifted into sleep again. In the morning the nun who ran the infirmary returned. She handed me a cup of ergot of rye tea. I took a sip and asked for my baby.

She wouldn't meet my eyes. "You need to rest."

Another sip of tea and then more firmly I said, "I want to hold my baby."

"She's being taken care of," the Sister replied and turned to leave. I grabbed her arm.

"I want my baby. Now."

She shook loose of my hold and left the room. The Sister's behavior was upsetting. Of course as a new mother I wanted to hold my child. Was she sickly? When I'd held her, she hadn't appeared to be anything but the healthiest infant. If something had happened in between giving birth and her being taken from my arms, why would they hide that from me?

Later in the day Sister Agnes came.

"Please bring Hannah back," I said.

She gave me a quizzical look.

"I named my baby after my sister."

She started to say something, then hesitated and stopped.

"Please, I want to see my baby," I pleaded with her.

She straightened as if bracing herself. "She's been taken to St. Vincent's."

I stared at her, confused.

Her next words stunned me to my core. "It's an orphan asylum."

I bolted upright. "What do you mean? I can take care of her."

Sister hesitated, pursed her thin lips. "It's for the best."

"Bring me my baby," I said, my voice sharp and high as I fought back the hysteria rising inside me.

"I can't… she's already gone."

"What do you mean?" I threw off the bedsheets. "She's *my* baby."

"Elisabeth—"

"Stop calling me that. My name is Annie."

I choked down a sob, then let it come forth. My body wracked with despair.

The nun in charge of the infirmary returned, hastened by my screams, and instructed me to stay in bed. With all the strength I could muster I pushed them both and stood. Sister Agnes lost her balance but the other nun stood her ground. I clawed at her, drawing blood. When Sister Agnes regained her footing, they pinned me down and held me until I stopped struggling.

Venomous bile filled me. The nuns had taken my name, my dignity, and now my baby. The convent wasn't a refuge; it was Hell, and I would no longer remain a prisoner.

# 2

After two days in the infirmary I was told I must return to my work in the laundry, where I'd slaved for hours on end six days a week, cleaning filthy linens from the hospital. My body still ached from giving birth, so much that I could barely stand, but I did not argue with the nuns. All I could think of was leaving the convent and finding Hannah.

That night, back in the dormitory, Genevieve lifted the covers and slipped in beside me. We weren't supposed to visit each other's beds, but the girls regularly broke this rule. The nuns held our words captive during the day; at night they rushed forth in furtive whispers.

I told Genevieve of my plan to escape, thinking I could convince her to join me. The thought of having someone by my side eased my fears.

She shook her head. "I've been out in the world. It's not a nice place."

After her father left, her mother had forced a twelve-year-old Genevieve to dance at a concert saloon to help support the family. It was a local detective who, horrified by the sight of a young girl on the stage, brought her to the nuns.

"Do you know where you'll go?" Genevieve asked as she tucked a strand of loose hair behind my ear and smoothed my short auburn locks. All penitents had their hair cut upon arrival, just as soon as we'd been given a new name, a bath, and an ugly dress to wear. We were told it was a means to help bring us into a state of Grace.

"Somewhere in town, I suppose. I can't go back home."

Genevieve's eyes grew wide. "Oh no, you mustn't stay in Buffalo. The nuns will go looking for you and they'll involve the police. They'll bring you back here. But first, they might let you stay a night in jail."

As much as I hated to admit it, Genevieve was right. If I went to the orphanage, I would be caught and brought back to the convent, under stricter rules. That would be a worse fate. Mother Superior would undoubtedly throw me back in the basement. I shuddered as I recalled the cold hard floor, the rats scurrying across it.

The morning of my planned getaway, I woke with a fever, hot and lumpy breasts, and a dull ache in my abdomen. I longed to stay in bed, but I didn't want to wait another week for the wagon that delivered supplies to the convent on Saturdays. It was the only time the back gate was opened.

Before I left my village of Canton in far upstate New York, I'd given my mam most of the money I'd earned working at the men's clothing store on Main Street. The rest, six dollars, I brought with me and hid underneath the porcelain statue of the Virgin Mary in the corner of the dormitory. As the other penitents filed out of the room, I quickly retrieved my savings and hurried to get in line.

By the end of the week we always moved more slowly, which irritated the Sisters, but it gave Genevieve, who had agreed to help me escape, and me a chance to break away as we crossed the yard to the building that housed the workrooms.

We hid behind a shed, shivering in our thin coats, and watched as Sister Agnes opened the gate. As the wagon pulled onto the grounds,

Genevieve approached her. I feared for my friend. She would be punished severely once the Sisters discovered my absence. But she insisted she wanted to do this for me.

I peeked around the side of the shed. The wagon shielded me from view. The driver was perched in his seat, his back to me. I crept toward the open gate and could hear Sister Agnes admonishing Genevieve as I slipped past them.

Once I had boarded a streetcar and paid my five-cent fare, I sank onto a bench and clutched my stomach, praying the pangs would subside and that the nuns wouldn't find me. As the horse-drawn car plodded along, I wondered if I should have walked to the train depot, but I didn't think my aching body could handle it.

The small brick depot, warmed by a wood-burning stove, was nearly empty. Suddenly self-conscious about my drab, grey convent dress and short hair, I approached the ticket booth with trepidation. The elderly gentleman on the other side barely acknowledged me.

"Where to?"

"One ticket to Rome, please," I replied, remembering that was where we switched trains when Sister Agnes had escorted me from Canton.

"That'll be three dollars and seventy-six cents."

I gulped. That would leave me only two dollars and nineteen cents. But what choice did I have? I couldn't stay in Buffalo. Reluctantly, I handed over the money.

To focus on something other than my fear and my feverish aches, I browsed the dime novels in the book stall inside the depot, while keeping a watchful eye out the window. It seemed like forever until that loud clanking bell, coupled with the shrill whistle, signaled my train's arrival. I went outside to the platform, anxious to board as soon as possible.

When I traveled with Sister Agnes from Canton to Buffalo, we'd sat in the ladies' carriage. That was the first place the nuns would look for me. And though they would never enter the men's coach, it would look suspicious if I tried to sit there. Would they look for me in the third-class passenger car? I wondered, uncertain which railcar, if any, might best protect me.

The conductor yelled, "All aboard!" I glanced around again and froze. There was Sister Agnes, walking toward the depot with a policeman. I scanned the length of the train and spotted the mail carriage. Without hesitating, I proceeded toward it and boarded.

The mail carriage was empty save for a table, several canvas sacks with brass locks, and a pile of wooden boxes stacked up in a corner. I rushed to hide behind the boxes as a man entered the car. I could hardly breathe for fear of what would happen if he discovered my presence. He shuffled through the mail, whistling as he worked.

When the conductor called for final boarding, the man in the railway post office shut the door. The space dimmed but light shone through the windows along each side of the car and the skylights in the ceiling. Suddenly, I heard his footsteps come toward me and, as he leaned over to grab one of the canvas bags at my feet, our eyes met. He was young, in his early twenties perhaps, and his placid expression surprised me.

"What'cha doin' in here, miss?" he asked me, no hint of anger in his voice.

I was about to speak when the door opened. The mailman motioned for me to stay quiet and stood to address the visitor.

"Mornin' officer," he chirped. "What can I do for you?"

I stifled a gasp.

"Have you seen a young woman, about sixteen years of age, in a grey dress?"

I held my breath. Would he give me away?

"No, haven't seen anyone."

"Sorry to bother you," the policeman said. "Have a good day."

The door shut, but I remained on edge. What if the mailman thought better of it and changed his mind before the train left the station? His footsteps came toward me again. He squatted down in front of me. His hands were clasped, his elbows resting on his knees.

"You're from the convent, aren't you?"

I jerked my head up. "How did you know?"

"One of my sisters was sent there."

I leaned my head against the wall. My body relaxed.

He stood and held out a hand. As he pulled me to my feet, I winced. "Are you unwell?" he said with concern.

"I'm fine," I said, too embarrassed to admit the truth even as the cramp in my abdomen continued to worsen.

The train started to move and I nearly lost my balance. The young man caught me. "Perhaps you should stay seated," he said, returning to the pile of the mail he'd been sorting.

I nodded, relieved to settle myself back on the floor. The swaying of the train lulled me to sleep. He woke me at the first stop. "Miss, it's probably best if you go sit in the ladies' car now. It'll be a lot more comfortable for you."

He helped me to my feet and I followed him to the door, but I was reluctant to exit. What if the police had sent word by telegram to the next station? The postal agent noticed my hesitation. He leaned outside the door and glanced around. "It's okay, you're safe." I thanked him and stepped onto the platform.

Once I'd settled into the ladies' car, my thoughts turned to my final destination. I wouldn't stay in Rome; it wasn't far away enough from the Sisters for me, and I didn't know how far north I could get with the little money I had. Canton was out of the question for the time being. I wouldn't go there without Hannah or without my family's permission. The last time my sister and I had spoken, she had refused to convince our mam to let me stay in Canton, denouncing me for the shame I'd brought to the family. Our priest had advised Mam to send me to Buffalo and, without my da, who died when I was ten years old, the Father's word was final.

Wherever I landed, I wouldn't have anyone to help me. I would be a stranger, with no family, no friends, no convent walls to protect me. The relief of being away from the Sisters was tempered by the fact that I had no idea what to expect once I arrived in my new town. I hadn't considered what I would do for food and shelter.

In Rome, I still had no idea where to go. I looked helplessly at the ticket agent, who grew more and more impatient by the second.

"Well, miss, I haven't got all day." He pointed to the others in line behind me.

I considered the other stops on the line. Gouvernour was close to Canton, but that was where the father of my child lived and I didn't want to go there. "What about Watertown?" I said. The town wasn't too far from home.

"That'll be a dollar thirty-eight."

I handed over two dollars, took my change and my ticket, and mumbled thanks as I walked away.

When the train arrived at Watertown and it came time for me to disembark, it took great effort for me to stand. In addition to the ache in my abdomen, I felt feverish and my legs shook so badly I feared they would buckle. Yet, somehow, I held steady and began to walk as if I knew where I was going, though I hadn't a clue.

I followed the flow of passengers into a tall red brick building near the depot, down its long hallway and into an opulent lobby.

"Welcome to the Woodruff House," a male clerk said to a couple that approached a long counter along a wall. I lingered as they registered with the hotel but flew out the door when I heard the clerk inform them of the nightly rate.

Canton's one main street was lined with modest, mostly one-story buildings. Here, structures as tall as three, four, and even five stories towered over the square in which the hotel was situated.

The afternoon light was waning, and what little warmth the pale winter sun offered would soon dissipate. As I walked around the square, contemplating my next move, a lamplighter called down to me from his ladder. "What'cha doin' out 'ere all alone, miss?"

The man jumped off his ladder and walked toward me. "I'm meeting someone," I said cautiously.

"Who're ya meeting?"

"That's none of your business. I must be going."

The man quickly closed the distance between us and grabbed my arm. "Why are ya in such a hurry?" His body reeked of unwashed skin and his breath of rotten teeth. "Why don't we go for a drink and a little fun?"

I managed to tear myself free. "Leave me alone," I hissed as I ran away, his sinister laugh trailing behind me.

At the edge of the square, the scent of fresh pumpernickel and sourdough beckoned me. I couldn't waste my last eighty-one cents, but I hadn't eaten all day. As I neared the bakery, I felt a wetness between my legs. Lifting my dress, I saw a crimson red stream pooling down my thighs. Then everything went black.

# 3

Through half-opened eyes I made out the blurred figures of two women hovering over me. I was lying on a table beneath a pile of quilts. I felt the warmth of a fire blazing nearby. The familiar scent of ergot of rye tea reached my nose. I tried to sit up but a hand gently pressed me back.

"Miss, you need to lie down."

"Where am I?" I said, slipping back into sleep before I could hear the response.

When I woke again, the same woman was still by my side, but I had been moved to the most luxurious bed I'd ever slept in. I glanced around the room. My convent dress was draped over a chaise. I put a hand to my chest; I still wore my chemise. The woman, who had a homely but kind face, helped me sit up. She put a cup to my lips and warm liquid coursed through me.

"Where am I?" I said again.

"My landlady's house. What's your name?"

"Annie."

The woman smiled. "That's my name, too. But everyone calls me Mollie."

Before I could ask why, she asked me where I was from.

I blinked back tears. "Canton. But I was most recently in Buffalo." I didn't want to tell her why.

"Who's Hannah?"

"My sister." I wanted to say that was also the name I'd given my daughter but I could not form the words.

As I took another sip of tea, Mollie touched my arm gently. "When did you give birth?" she asked, no hint of judgment in her words or on her face.

I stopped drinking and lowered the cup away from my mouth. "How did you know?"

She took my tea and set it on a nightstand. "Your stomach is still swollen. And some of the afterbirth hadn't come out."

I made a face. I had no idea what she was talking about.

Mollie removed the damp cloth from my forehead. "It caused a bad infection," she explained as she set a fresh rag into place. "You were in such a state. We called a doctor. He said it was a good thing we found you..."

I placed a hand on one of hers and peered into her hazel eyes. "Thank you. I don't know how I could ever repay you."

She put her other hand, damp from the washcloth, over mine. "What kind of person would I be if I left you lying in the street?"

At first nothing disturbed me and I slept soundly for the next few days. But as I began to improve, the liveliness of the house kept me awake. Women's voices echoed in the hallway during the day, and at night, men's voices too. Throughout the evening the house bell rang constantly. Laughter and music and singing floated upstairs as a door downstairs, I assumed to a parlor, opened and closed.

When I had recovered enough to leave my room, I put on the wrap Mollie had left for me and ventured into the hall. The other doors were shut. *Perhaps the boarders are at work*, I thought, my spirits lifting with the hope that maybe one of them could help me find employment.

Downstairs, the housekeeper was dusting the furniture in the parlor, a large dimly lit room that reeked of liquor and cigar smoke. A more enticing smell emanated from the back of the house, so I made my way to the kitchen where the woman who had helped Mollie tend to me hovered over the cast iron stove.

"It smells good in here," I said, announcing my presence.

The cook's hands flew to her chest as she whipped around. "My Lord, you startled me!" She spoke with a foreign accent I didn't recognize.

"I'm sorry."

She waved me off. "You must be starving. You haven't eaten in days. Sit."

Her manner was brusque but kind. She ladled stew into a bowl and set it before me at the table. Forgetting my manners, I ate it greedily.

"Where is everyone else?" I asked between bites.

"It's too early for these girls."

"Too early?"

She chuckled. "You don't know what kind of house you're in?"

"This is a boardinghouse, is it not?" I said, though the sounds that echoed through the house at all hours of the night suggested otherwise.

The cook's heavy frame shook as she laughed heartily at my expense. "Honey, this is a joy house."

I tried to hide my shock. This must be the kind of place my priest in Canton and at the convent had railed against.

As I headed back upstairs, an older woman, more matron than maiden, emerged from a room behind the staircase.

"I see you're feeling better," she said. "I'm Mrs. Harding."

By her demeanor I surmised she ran the house. I wondered where her husband was but didn't dare ask. "Yes. Thank you for taking me in."

"You're welcome to stay as long as you'd like. Did Olga give you something to eat?"

"Yes, thank you."

And with that Mrs. Harding took her leave. "I'm going to run some errands. Please tell the others I'll be back this afternoon."

Upstairs, the girls were stirring.

"Which one is Mollie's room?" I asked a girl who was just opening her door.

She pointed but shook her head. "I wouldn't knock yet, she's probably still asleep."

I heeded her warning.

"I'm Nora," she added, walking past me to the landing rail. "Olga, I don't smell any coffee! Are you making some?" she shouted.

Olga replied with what I imagined was an expletive in her native tongue. Nora looked at me, rolled her eyes, and we both giggled. She retreated to her room but left the door open, so I followed.

Nora's bedchamber was virtually identical to mine but piles of clothing were strewn across her four-poster bed and floor, bottles and brushes of varying shapes and sizes cluttered her vanity, and a stack of books lay alongside her chaise. I sat down and picked one up.

Nora reached for a hairbrush. "You like to read?"

I nodded. I'd brought my collection of dime novels with me to the convent, but Mother Superior had confiscated them upon my arrival. "There will be none of that in this holy house," she had told me, holding up my copy of Ann Stephens's latest, *The Gold Brick*, shaking it as if trying to dislodge a demon from between its covers. "Habitual novel reading leads to nervous disorders, and, in a state of mental intoxication, wayward conduct is sure to follow." Sneering at my protruding belly, she had added, "I believe you know this to be true."

"Take it, if you'd like," Nora offered. "Take as many as you want."

I hadn't read anything in a long while and yearned for a new escape. I grabbed three books and examined them. The frontispiece of George Thompson's *Venus in Boston: A Romance of City Life* depicted a woman on a settee leaning over to kiss the man seated next to her, a small dog observing them from the floor. I had never seen such a sensational drawing in a book and didn't quite know what to make of it. What kind of novel was this? I found myself intrigued.

"Thank you. I'll return them soon."

"Take your time," she said, setting her brush down. "I'm going downstairs to get some coffee."

I ventured over to Mollie's bedchamber. She answered my knock with a corset in hand. While she dressed, I sat at her vanity. Among the array of bottles was one for laudanum. My mam often used the opium tincture to calm her nerves, especially after my da died when I was ten years old. Sometimes I feared she used too much.

I pushed that distressing thought out of mind and picked up a pocket-sized black book, the *Chicago Sporting and Club House Directory*. "What's this?" I said to Mollie.

She glanced at the book. "It's a list of the best parlor houses in Chicago. One of my callers forgot to take it with him." Then she declared, "I'm moving to Chicago."

Before I could ask when, she said, "What happened to your baby?" and turned around. I went over to her to tie up the back of her corset.

"The nuns took her from me."

"Of course." She sucked in her stomach as I started lacing. "Why did you leave Buffalo?" Mollie's tone was inquisitive not judgmental, but the agony of having my baby taken from me was still too fresh. I pulled the string harder. "I couldn't stay at the convent one more day."

"I can imagine. I wouldn't want to live in such a place." She shuddered dramatically.

"There, all done." I patted her back and made my own declaration. "I plan to get Hannah back."

She gave me a quizzical look as she reached for her hoop crinoline.

"I named my baby after my sister," I explained.

"Ah. What about your family back home?"

My face must have taken on a grieved look because Mollie quickly added, "Forgive me for prying."

She opened her armoire. I held the bodice she handed me while she donned a skirt and ran my hand over the rich, dark green silk. Mollie's clothes were much nicer than the calicos I'd worn in Canton. I had looked forward to wearing the latest fashions when Leslie and I married. Thinking of him further soured my mood.

Mollie smoothed her skirt. "I used to work at one of the factories. There were a few women who had babies. They hardly spent any time with them because they worked so many hours."

She took the bodice from me and slipped her arms into it. "The lucky ones had families who could help."

"And if they didn't?"

Buttoning her bodice, she said matter-of-factly, "They did whatever was necessary to survive."

I didn't ask what that entailed, but I imagined working in a brothel was one of the choices. I would never resort to that.

# 4

Six weeks after Mollie rescued me, I stepped outside Mrs. Harding's house, ready to start my life anew. I gingerly navigated around the snowdrifts, but slush still managed to seep into the worn soles of my shoes. As I approached the square, to my right I observed a row of long, low buildings by the river. Some of them spewed black smoke.

It had been easy to obtain a position at the men's clothing store in Canton. Surely it would be easier here, with so many businesses. The thought that I could soon earn enough money to get Hannah back lightened my step.

But my experience in Canton didn't matter. Every shopkeeper eyed me disapprovingly, turning me away when I couldn't give a reference. Late in the afternoon, on the third day, my options nearly exhausted, I entered a covered shopping arcade. Soft daylight poured through the second-floor ceiling made of small glass squares. I was so mesmerized by it, I nearly bumped into a gentleman exiting a set of stairs.

Several stores as well as an art studio lined the ground floor. A help wanted sign hung in the window of Baker & Chittenden, Tobacconists. I paused at the entrance, mustering the courage to enter. The heavy pungent smell reminded me of my da and his ever-present pipe.

A tall man carrying a stack of cigar boxes in from the back room noticed me. "May I help you?"

The way he eyed me made me pull my coat tighter. "I'm looking for work," I said warily.

"What kind of experience do you have?" he asked, setting the cigar boxes on the counter.

I told him about my job with Mr. Storrs and then lied. "I'm recently widowed."

He moved closer. Peering down at me, he said, "You look rather young to be a widow."

Heat rose in me, not fever, but a blush of shame, as if he knew what I had done.

"I need some help in the storage room," he offered.

Trying to still the quaver in my throat, I said, "What kind of help?"

"I'll show you."

"How much can you pay me?"

"That depends." He ogled me again.

The hair on my skin stood on end. I took a step back. "Thank you, but I should go." As I turned to leave, he grabbed my arm.

"What are you doing?" I cried. "You're hurting me!"

The man started to pull me toward the back room, his breath hot on my neck. "I'll show you what I want."

Unable to wrench away from him, I pretended to stumble, hoping he would loosen his grip. He only held me tighter. Just then, the jingle of the door's bell forced the man to release me, and I rushed past the startled customer entering the store.

I returned to the house, still shaking. Mollie was out. Nora's door was open. She glanced up from filing her nails when I entered and wrinkled her brows. "Are you all right?"

When I told her what had happened, she sighed. "Respectable

women don't work at those kinds of places. It's not a proper occupation for a woman."

I thought of Nora's "occupation," and how improper it was, but kept quiet.

"Besides," she said, "you'll never get a job in *that* dress."

My dress from Our Lady of Refuge had been washed, but no amount of cleaning could remove the ugliness. I'd always hated the itchy woolen dress and the shame I felt when I wore it.

"I would let you borrow something," Nora added, "but you still have the problem of supplying a reference."

Remembering Mollie's comments about the mothers she used to work with, I asked Nora if the factories would require a reference.

"You want to be someone's slave?" Nora rolled her eyes and pointed her nail file at me. "How much do you think you'll earn making shoes or working in the mills?"

I didn't want to admit that I hadn't thought about it so, with forced confidence, I said, "I'm sure it would be enough to live on my own."

Nora scoffed. "Darling, the most you'll make is a dollar-and-a-half a week. And guess what? Room and board costs more. Besides, they'll also ask for a reference."

"Maybe not with her looks," Kate said as she entered Nora's room and threw herself down on the bed.

I thought of my days at the convent slaving away long hours in the laundry with no pay. Bitterness crept into my voice. "How does a woman live on those wages?"

"She doesn't. Those jobs are for girls who live at home," Kate explained. "Or if they're on their own, they meet men at assignation houses."

"At what?"

"A place where men and women meet to have sex."

My jaw dropped.

"I do hope you're not trying to persuade this poor girl to become a public woman," Mollie, who had just returned, chided the others from the doorway.

"She's already a fallen woman," Nora said, looking at me pointedly. "And once that happens, honey, there ain't nothing you can do to get back up."

"If it ain't you, it'll be another girl," Kate chimed in. "Do you want to be the one on the street?"

"You could always go to the workhouse for the poor," Nora suggested.

"She'd be better off in a jail cell," Mollie said with the disdain of someone who knew from experience.

"Besides, you won't find a fancy, rich man at a factory," Kate added. "Only a lowly manager, and he'll probably want to take advantage of you." She was about to say something else but Mollie's glare stopped her.

I had to find employment somewhere, anywhere. Maybe I'd have better luck finding work in a bigger place. "I could go to New York City," I said hesitantly.

Nora laughed. "Honey, you'd be eaten alive. You wouldn't be able to find a job, at least not a respectable one. When I was there the newspapers had advertisements saying, 'No Irish need apply.' The stores too." She set down her nail file. "Men will use all kinds of tricks to lure innocent girls like you into places you'd rather not be. Have you read that book I loaned you, *Venus in Boston*?"

I shook my head.

"It's about a pretty but poor fourteen-year-old girl who sells apples to help her family survive—until a lecherous old man has her kidnapped and brought to his mansion so he can deflower her."

I was glad I hadn't started reading the book. Horrified, I said, "I shall bring it back to you at once."

Nora threw her head back and laughed raucously. "George Thompson and others like him write books about life the way it is, not sappy fairy tales."

As I was about to protest Nora chirped, "But don't fret, the girl is rescued, her virginity intact. Now *there's* a fairy tale ending!"

I bit my lip. My options were rapidly narrowing. "I could work for a family," I said, more brightly than I felt.

"You want to be a Bridget?" Kate said.

"A what?"

"A Bridget is the term for an Irish domestic servant—and it's not meant in a nice way."

"Most of the household servants in America are Irish girls," Nora chimed in. "With your looks, you'll have the master of the house trying to take you to bed your first night. The wife will hate you. And her spoiled rotten children will—"

"They wouldn't let her near the children," Kate interjected.

"Why not?" I glanced around, waiting for an answer. It came from Mollie. "Most of the wealthy families are Protestant. They would never allow a Catholic to help rear their children."

Nora drew another bleak picture. "You'll go to work as some uppity woman's servant, sleeping in their attic with the vermin, hot in the summer, freezing in the winter. You'll marry an Irish laborer, and next thing you know, you'll have ten children and run a boardinghouse to help your family make ends meet."

"I'll do no such thing," I said, raising my chin. "I plan to marry a rich man."

I ignored the girls' skeptical looks and went back to my room, deflated. It seemed a woman could only survive in this world with the help of a man. And no reputable man wanted a woman who'd borne a child out of wedlock. Even if I claimed to be a widow, I still wasn't as desirable. It seemed I was out of options.

# 5

'd made up my mind, but I couldn't get myself to knock on Mrs. Harding's door. As I tried to draw up the courage, the door swung open. She paused before addressing me. "Do you need something?"

I stared at her, paralyzed. But the thought of holding Hannah again galvanized me. "Do you have a minute?"

She motioned for me to follow her to the parlor. We sat in silence as I convinced myself that this was the right path for me. I took a deep breath and said, "I wish to board at your house." My voice broke on the last word, and with it, my spirit.

Mrs. Harding arched her eyebrows. "You do understand what that means?"

"Yes, ma'am."

She eyed me. "Will your family make trouble if they find you here?"

They would be horrified, but I would never tell them. "You needn't fear any trouble, ma'am."

"Very well. I'll explain the house rules."

I straightened and gave her my full attention.

"The one rule you must follow at all times is to perform your art. You can't refuse a guest." Her use of the word "art" almost made me laugh.

"You're here to please our guests. You must maintain a pleasing manner and do everything in your power to keep them happy."

She paused to let me take this in, searching my face, I supposed, for any signs I might not be up to the task. I feigned a calm demeanor but my insides churned like a bucking horse.

"Don't hurry them, and be sure to wash yourself from the basin after each caller, rearrange your hair and gown, and come downstairs. One may offer you a bottle of perfume, which you are allowed to take. If so, thank him. And if a gentleman gives you any extra money, you may keep it. But half the agreed upon fee belongs to the house."

After each guest? How many would I entertain each night? I had ever only been with one man, and I was in love with him. I wanted to run from the room, run as far away from Mrs. Harding's as I could. But I wanted Hannah back even more. I would do whatever it took to provide for her.

"Yes, ma'am, I do," I said when Mrs. Harding asked if I accepted all the rules.

"One more thing," she said. "You'll borrow a dress from one of the other girls until you can buy yourself a new one. You don't want to start off in debt."

My stomach knotted even more at the realization that I was to start right away.

Back in my room, the large bed dominating the space took on new meaning. With Leslie, our trysts in the threshing barn were always hurried, on the rough loft floor, the excitement heightened for fear of discovery. Here, I would have to take my time with strange men, in a bed meant for sacred, marital love.

In preparation for the evening ahead, I soaked in an oak tub and then seated myself at Mollie's vanity. She arranged my hair as best she could given its length. I noticed the initials "CH" on the silver-plated brush.

"Whose is this?" I asked, my curiosity getting the better of me.

She hesitated. "Why do you ask?"

"Those aren't your initials."

"It belonged to an old friend. Her name was Cora."

"Was?" I looked at Mollie in the mirror. Another hesitation.

"She's not living here anymore, that's all I meant," she said.

I sensed there was something she wasn't telling me. "Where did she go?"

"That's not important," Mollie said cryptically. It was clear she didn't want me to pursue the matter anymore. I broached another subject that had been on my mind.

"How do you… how do you keep from…?"

Mollie paused. Our eyes met in the mirror. She understood. "We cleanse ourselves after each caller," she said. "And if it does happen, there's a concoction you can make to induce a miscarriage. But…"

I waited for her to continue. When she didn't, I turned to face her. "But what?"

"I didn't want to tell you, after everything you've been through…"

I grabbed her hand. "What?"

The longer she went without saying anything, the more worried I became.

"The doctor," Mollie started. She stopped and took a deep breath. "He doesn't think you'll be able to have more children."

"Oh," I said, lowering my head and letting go of her hand. My body shook as I took in this unwelcome news.

Mollie tried to lighten the mood. "Let's finish getting you ready," she said as she dipped a brush into one of the many colorful containers on her vanity. But as she reached for my face, anger overcame me. "What are you doing?" I barked, grabbing her arm.

"I was going to paint your face."

"Absolutely not." Neither my mother nor any of my sisters had ever worn rouge, no respectable woman did. I could perform my job, as disrespectful as it may be, without it.

"But the men like it."

"I don't care."

Mollie blinked. I softened. "I'm sorry. I didn't mean to hurt your feelings. This is difficult for me."

She set down the brush. "I understand," she said.

I hadn't wanted to ask Mollie why she had come to Mrs. Harding's, but now I pried. "How did you end up here?"

She walked over to the window and gazed out for a moment then turned back to me. "My parents threw me out when they discovered I was no longer a virgin. I ended up at the workhouse and found work at the shoe factory, but it wasn't enough to support myself. I started meeting men at an assignation house and that led me to Mrs. Harding. It's different when you're just starting out. It takes some getting used to."

For a moment I almost lost my nerve, the urge to run gripping me once more. But whatever I would have to endure would be worth it to cradle Hannah in my arms again.

"You're young and beautiful, and men will swarm to you," she said, placing her hands on my shoulders and peering into my eyes, her expression solemn and motherly. "Whatever you do, don't ever be fool enough to work the streets."

Olga brought me a pair of silk stockings so delicate I feared I might rip them when she handed them to me. In her broken English—she had, I learned, emigrated from Rumania—she told me to encourage guests to buy as much liquor as possible; alcohol, not the bodies on offer, was the main source of income for the house.

After fastening my stockings with pink rosebud garters, Mollie helped me slip into a baby-soft pink silk gown and ivory-colored slippers.

Mrs. Harding looked me over and approved of what she saw. "Now you just need a name."

I groaned. "Why can't I use my name?"

"It's bad luck," Nora explained.

They began throwing out suggestions, all of which made my skin crawl.

"I was given the name Elisabeth in Buffalo," I interjected.

The girls gasped.

"You can't use the same name as the madam," Nora said.

"How about Bessie?" Kate offered. The other girls nodded their approval. I had known a Bessie in Canton. It was popular among the Irish. I eyed Mrs. Harding.

"Bessie it is," she declared.

# 6

Mollie's firm grasp kept me steady as we descended the stairs, though my heart beat faster than the brisk clip-clop of the carriage horses outside. Piano music and lilting voices spilled from the parlor into the hallway while doubt and nausea swept over me.

"There she is," Kate announced as I stepped into the parlor.

The talking ceased. The men stared. I lowered my eyes, raised them, and surveyed the room. I wanted to rub my temples to stop them from throbbing but feared it would seem impolite.

Mrs. Harding took my elbow as if she were picking up a piece of bone china and steered me toward the only gentleman in the room who seemed to be unattached. He was short and paunchy. "I'm pleased to introduce Miss Bessie Moore."

To me she said, with a gesture toward my first caller, "This is Mr. Augustus Sweeney. He's one of Watertown's most respected businessmen."

I managed a weak smile. "Pleased to meet you, sir," I said, wondering why he would visit a brothel if he was so respectable.

"Please, call me Augustus." He gave Mrs. Harding a pleased look, to which she nodded and then moved away. Mr. Sweeney and I stood in awkward silence. I didn't know what to say to this man who was closer in age to my father than to me. It hadn't occurred to me to ask the other girls how to converse with callers. He must have sensed my uneasiness. "I understand this is your first night."

My cheeks flamed. "Is it that obvious?"

He chuckled. "Don't worry, I'm a regular. Mrs. Harding knows she can trust me to be good to her girls."

His reassurance calmed me, but only briefly, as visions of what he would have me do to him gripped my thoughts.

"Would you care for a drink?" He stopped the butler and ordered whiskey for himself and a glass of wine for me before I could even answer the question. I took a cautious sip. It tasted bitter and sweet at the same time, and, within moments, soothed my nerves.

The parlor walls, which I hadn't paid attention to before, were lined with paintings, mainly hunting scenes. But it was the depictions of naked girls dancing that caught my eye.

Mr. Sweeney winked at me. "Elizabeth has an interesting art collection, doesn't she?"

I blushed, forehead to forearm. "Forgive me. I shouldn't have let my eyes wander."

The butler handed me another glass of wine, with a look clearly meant to remind me that we were forbidden to drink too much in front of our guests. We were there for their enjoyment, not ours.

"What is your business?" I asked, wanting to delay the inevitable trip upstairs.

"Threshing machines."

My mind flashed to the threshing barn, to the last time I'd seen Leslie, when I'd told him I was carrying his child and he had informed me that he was engaged to another woman. I lowered my glass without taking a sip. Mr. Sweeney asked if I was familiar with the farming equipment, which separated wheat husks from the grain.

"Yes," I said, ducking my head slightly.

His eyes expressed puzzlement. "Are you all right?"

"I'm fine." I fought back tears. "It made me think of home."

"Where is home?"

I immediately realized my mistake. I needed to keep the conversation light, focused on my guest's needs.

"Nowhere interesting," I said demurely. "Shall we go upstairs?" I blurted, hoping to avoid another intrusive question.

Mr. Sweeney grinned. I cringed inside. With as much confidence as I could muster, I hooked my arm around his and tilted my head coyly. I tried my best to take the stairs with self-assurance, though I was light-headed and wobbly.

When we reached my room, Mr. Sweeney took off his jacket and held it out. I laid it over a high-backed chair, along with his waistcoat and pants.

As I slipped off my gown, I remembered Kate's advice to pretend I was an actress. If I played my "role," I would get through this, I told myself. I removed my corset and started to take off my chemise.

"Wait," Mr. Sweeney said. He inched closer to me and removed my hair piece. My thick hair was still shorter than what men desired, but he didn't seem to mind. He murmured something and kissed my neck. His hands were smooth like Leslie's. I pushed my former lover from my mind as Mr. Sweeney slipped the straps of my chemise off my shoulders. The lingerie dropped to the floor and he gently lowered me onto the bed.

As I had done when I gave birth to Hannah, I left my body and floated to the ceiling. My time in Buffalo seemed another lifetime already. Hovering on the ceiling, detached from my body moving beneath a stranger, I told myself I could endure this, if it led to getting my daughter back.

Afterwards I lay still, thankful it was over, and worried whether I'd performed my "art" well. Mr. Sweeney rose and I helped him dress as I had been told to do. As he left he placed something on the washbasin. I walked over to clean myself and there was a five-dollar gold coin gleaming in the darkness.

It weighed more than I expected. I'd never made this much money in an entire week, let alone in one day. I wondered how many such coins I would need to attain my goal of being reunited with Hannah. How many men would I need to sleep with? The thought quelled my happiness over the coin.

# 7

In the beginning Mrs. Harding steered the gentler clients to me, the ones who didn't want anything kinky or out of the ordinary. They were mostly middle-aged married men seeking some excitement in their otherwise dull lives. Sometimes they just wanted someone to talk to. I thought my reserved nature, which they mistook for shyness, would deter them; instead, my callers found it intriguing. As much as one could, I was becoming used to entertaining different men nearly every night of the week.

One evening, when the bell rang, we rushed to the top of the stairs per usual, eager to peek at our potential dates. But this time, the housekeeper turned off the gas lights downstairs.

"What happened?" I whispered to Mollie.

"Must be someone important."

In the darkness below Mrs. Harding welcomed the visitor. A deep, resonant voice responded. Once Mrs. Harding and the gentleman had entered the parlor, the housekeeper turned the hallway light back on. I grew more curious. Businessmen from all over the state frequented Mrs. Harding's house, and we all knew them by name. Who was this mysterious guest?

I assumed one of the more experienced girls would entertain this caller. But, to my surprise, Mrs. Harding came into the hallway and called my name. The other girls pouted, their jealousy evident. Their reaction told me this man would pay a much higher price.

When I reached the parlor, Nora leaned over the railing and whispered, "Don't have too much fun." The others giggled. I blew them a kiss, squared myself in front of the parlor door, and straightened my shoulders before entering.

Before me stood a distinguished-looking gentleman. He was middle-aged, like most of my callers, but taller and more handsome. I didn't have to summon a smile. One came to me naturally, not only because of his looks but because there was an air about him, which put me at ease. I'd been introduced to enough men that I could tell when one approved of Mrs. Harding's selection for him.

When we were seated, James Morris peered into my eyes with a directness I found disarming. It wasn't piercing or threatening; on the contrary, his gaze was inviting, tantalizing.

"How long have you boarded here? I haven't seen you before."

"Seven months."

"It's been too long since I was here last," he said, winking at me.

I leaned closer to him. "Where is your home?"

"Syracuse. I operate a salt mill."

"Family business?"

"From the time I was twelve, I worked in the salt mills. Decided I would own one someday."

While the butler served our drinks, I observed James. The other women at Mrs. Harding's always focused on a man's face and general physique, but I had developed a habit of studying the hands of every caller that roamed my body. Were they rough or smooth? Would their touch be firm or gentle? Would they caress my skin with the confidence of an experienced man or the tentativeness of a shy one?

James's broad palms appeared rough from his days at manual

labor, but he had long, elegant fingers and well-groomed nails. Like most callers, he wore a wedding band. But, in his case, I almost sighed aloud in disappointment.

After the butler left, James handed me a glass and sank back into the sofa. On instinct I moved closer to him. He set down his glass and then mine and drew me to him. My skin tingled. I pulled back slightly. He raised his eyebrows. In amusement? No, his look was an inquisitive one. I blushed.

On our way upstairs, James told Mrs. Harding he would stay the night. I relished the thought of not having to entertain anyone else. On a busy night I could have three or more callers. I would spend as much time as possible in my room before coming down again, long enough to gather my courage to entertain another gentleman, but not too long to earn a reprimand from Mrs. Harding.

With every other man I wanted it over as quickly as possible, but from the first night it was different with James. His firm hands slid over my body like a blessing instead of a curse.

For the first time I didn't think of Leslie when I was with another man. I realized this after James left the next morning. Lying in bed, I felt oddly peaceful. Maybe I had finally put that part of my life behind me. Then, like a splash of cold water, I realized I hadn't thought of my child either. How could I so easily put her out of mind? She had been the driving force of every minute of every day at Mrs. Harding's. I consoled myself with the reminder that I was waiting to hear from my sister. I had sent her a letter and hinted at the possibility of coming home if she and Mam would forgive me for bringing shame to our family.

When her response finally arrived, I raced upstairs to my room and tore open the envelope. I smiled when I read that she was expecting a second child. Wouldn't it be wonderful, I thought, for my Hannah to grow up with her cousins? But, as I read on, I learned that was not to be.

> *As flattered as I am that you have named your baby in my honor, with one child and another on the way, not to mention Mam's health, we can't in good faith take on the responsibility of also caring for you and your daughter. Wouldn't she have a better life with a family where there are two parents, or at the orphanage under the constant care of the Sisters? I know how difficult it is to rear a child under the best of circumstances. I can't imagine doing so alone, especially as an unwed mother.*

The rest of the letter blurred beneath my tears. I set it on my lap, reeling from the rejection. My sister didn't use the word "shame," but she didn't need to; it was in the tone of her letter. Reluctantly, I had to admit her feelings were valid. The day before I'd left Canton, Mam had sent me to the meat market for a plate of beef. She'd let out my dress as much as she could, but I couldn't fit into my corset anymore, and the drawstring in my drawers had stretched as far as it could go. I'd carried a shawl to hide my belly.

At the market, my mam's dear friend Honora stood a few paces ahead of me. I clearly remembered what she'd said to a woman next to her: "What is Mary going ta do now that her daughter has disgraced herself and her family's good name?"

"Mary hasn't been the same since Matthew died, God rest his soul," the other woman said. I recognized her from our church. The two women had crossed themselves before Honora continued, "Aye, she hasn't taken an interest in anything in years. No wonder the girl went astray." With a harumph, she'd added, "I should have warned Mary. Annie is too handsome and high-spirited. 'Twas bound ta happen."

Savoring their smug judgment, the two women had turned to leave, packages in hand, and Honora's eyes had met mine. As she passed me, she drew back her skirt. Stunned, I couldn't move. I had never encountered a woman who had swept aside her dress to avoid contact with me, had never imagined it could happen. I had become an outcast in my own village.

James kept coming to see me. That eased my distress. At first it was once a month, then every two weeks. It was obvious he was falling in love with me.

"I've never lost my head over anything," he'd told me. "Not in business, not in my personal life. Until I met you."

He would never leave his wife, this I knew. But in the farthest recesses of my mind the seed of an idea was forming.

# 8

James and I were lying in bed, my head resting in the crook of his arm. The solitaire diamond ring he'd given me caught the moonlight as I played with the hairs on his chest. My mam owned only one piece of jewelry, the traditional claddagh ring: a pair of hands holding a heart topped with a crown, representing friendship, love, and loyalty. James had given me so many pieces, I needed a jewelry box for them all: seed pearl earrings and a matching necklace, cobalt enamel earrings with a star motif, a coral flower brooch, a tortoiseshell pique pin inlaid with gold, and two rings—one with a cluster of small diamonds, and the large solitaire, one for each hand. I adored them all.

James stroked my arm. "I've been thinking," he said.

"Oh?" I let my hand rest on his chest and enjoyed his caresses, a purring feline in his arms.

"I'd like to set you up in a house, in Syracuse."

This is what I'd been waiting for, what I'd been working towards. As a kept woman in my own house, I would be isolated, unable to be seen in public with my lover. But I would have my little girl. Or so I hoped.

"What about Hannah?" I said cautiously, feeling my goal within my grasp.

James stopped petting my arm. "I thought the nuns were raising her. Do you even know if she's still there?" His tone was measured. He knew this was a sensitive topic. "She could be with a family by now."

I sensed in my heart that my little girl hadn't been adopted, but I had not inquired. I did not want to return to Buffalo until I was ready to leave with Hannah.

I peered up at James. His eyes were fixed on the ceiling.

"If she's still there," I said, "I would like her to live with me in Syracuse."

His expression didn't change but his body tensed. I didn't move, didn't speak.

Finally he said, "You haven't seen her since she was born. She won't remember you. Besides, I don't think it would be a good idea for a man to come and go in her presence."

James already had his own family. He wanted me, not another child. The room chilled. I moved away from him. He noticed the change in my mood but didn't say anything.

After he left I moped around. I had been so certain James would welcome my daughter into our life. Or had I? He never asked about her. And I rarely talked about Hannah, either. I knew my little girl was a topic not to be discussed. I couldn't accuse James of being selfish. He wasn't the father of my child. I was a woman he paid for sex, to entertain *him*, not to share my desires. I had wasted time waiting for a dream that would never materialize. His words had stung, but James was right. Hannah didn't know me.

That thought preyed on my mind as my train rattled west to Buffalo. Mrs. Harding and Mollie had tried to keep me from going, afraid a visit to the orphanage would be too upsetting. But my desire to see my little girl had outweighed any objections. I needed to touch her, to hold her. I wasn't planning to take Hannah with me. Not yet.

As the train approached the depot, I gazed out over Lake Erie. I saw my mother, staring at her beloved Ireland as our ship pulled away from Cork Harbor. She had left three dead children in our homeland. How many times had I caught Mam gazing at the bright yellow globeflowers outside our thatched cottage and thought she was only admiring the garden? The beauty, I now understood, wasn't above the earth; it was in what lay beneath the soil.

I went to the nearest hotel, across the street from the depot, and as I waited to register, I did my best to seem accustomed to traveling unaccompanied. It was frowned upon for a woman to stay at a hotel alone, but I had no choice.

The clerk eyed me as I approached the counter.

"I need a room, please."

"How many nights?"

"Just one."

"Name."

"Bessie Moore."

"Mrs.?"

"No, just Miss." I stared at the clerk, not having anticipated this question.

Mollie and Mrs. Harding had impressed upon me the importance of my appearance. Hotel clerks were trained to spot unrespectable women to protect their establishments' reputations. I had worn a tasteful dress, I never painted my face, and my hands were gloved like a proper lady.

Sensing the clerk's hesitancy, I said with a tone of slight haughtiness, "I assume your hotel has a Ladies' Ordinary. As a woman traveling alone, I insist on dining only with other women."

The clerk relaxed. "Yes, of course we have a Ladies' Ordinary, on the second floor down the hall. I hope you will find it to your satisfaction," he said as he handed me the key to my room.

The anticipation of seeing Hannah grew with each moment, so much that I couldn't sleep, and the next morning I only picked at my breakfast. As I walked to St. Vincent's Female Orphan Asylum under the bright morning sun, I kept glancing over my shoulder just as I'd done when I'd escaped from the convent. But no one paid me any mind. I chided myself for being ridiculous.

The nun at the front desk was surprised when I told her who I was and that I wished to see my daughter.

"What is her name?" Her voice held suspicion and distrust.

"Hannah. The Sisters took her from me the day she was born."

"So you were an inmate at Our Lady of Refuge?"

I hesitated but confirmed that I had lived at the convent.

"The Sisters have good, noble reasons for sending the babies here."

I bristled at her comment, but arguing with her would not bring me any closer to Hannah.

The woman studied me as the clerk had. Her eyes fell on the gold cross necklace I wore. I might be a prostitute, but I was also a Christian. She didn't seem impressed.

"Where is your husband?"

Her question startled me.

"I'm not married," I mumbled.

The Sister's demeanor betrayed what she was thinking. Why hadn't I anticipated this? I should have lied. Better yet, I should have worn a mourning dress, then she would think I was a widow instead of what she suspected.

"How can I trust you're actually her mother?" she said coldly.

I was growing impatient. "If I wasn't her mother, I wouldn't know her birthdate, would I?"

When I gave her the date, she opened a ledger, reluctantly, and flipped through the pages. She stopped at one, scanned the page, and then closed the book.

"I don't think it would be appropriate for you to see her," she said.

"Why not?" I tried to keep my irritation at bay.

"She's well cared for here."

"That's not a reason to keep me from seeing *my* child." Neither of our eyes wavered. "I'm not leaving until I see her."

She pursed her lips and, without saying a word, exited the room. I followed her down the hallway and up a flight of stairs. I was taken aback to see how many young children lived at St. Vincent's. I wondered whether any were like mine, borne out of wedlock.

We approached a young Sister seated in a rocking chair, holding a little girl. I searched the child's face for any resemblance. Was this my daughter? I glanced around at the other children, upset I didn't immediately recognize my own flesh and blood.

"Sister Helen," the nun who escorted me said, "Hannah has a visitor."

Delight flooded me. The nuns had kept her name. The icicles that had formed in my breast against the Sisters thawed a tiny bit.

"This is Hannah's… sister."

I clenched my jaw but didn't correct her.

Sister Helen addressed the little girl on her lap. "Hannah, someone is here to see you."

She started to lift my daughter toward me, but Hannah squirmed and buried her face in the Sister's habit.

"I'm sorry, she's not used to being around strangers."

The word took me aback. How could I be a stranger? I had given Hannah life. Couldn't she sense the blood bond between us?

The more Sister Helen tried to make Hannah to come to me, the more Hannah wailed. I wanted to reach out my arms and comfort her. Instead, I stood rooted to the floor, waiting for Hannah to calm down, trying not to show my desolation at being shunned by my own daughter. Out of the corner of my eye I detected a smug countenance on the pinched-faced nun. I wanted to slap her.

"Perhaps I should come back later," I offered.

"I wouldn't advise that. You see how she reacted to you."

Sister Helen's silence spoke volumes; she didn't want me to return, either.

But I was determined. "I'll come back in the morning," I announced. With a quick flourish I turned toward the door and added before either of them could protest, "I'll see myself out."

Outside the orphanage I let my emotions rush forth. Once I collected myself, I strolled around aimlessly until the summer heat overcame me. Seated on a park bench, I took in my surroundings and noticed a young woman in a maid's uniform exit a nearby home. Something about her was familiar. I watched as she descended the front steps and turned in my direction.

"Genevieve?"

She stopped and cocked her head. Then recognition lit up in her sweet face.

"Annie!" she exclaimed and rushed to me, nearly crushing the basket she carried as we embraced. She took a step back. "Look at you."

She admired my stylish getup and my long hair, which was elegantly swept into a bun underneath my feathered hat.

"You're married!" she exclaimed, noticing my rings.

"No, I'm afraid not."

"Oh." She furrowed her brows but didn't pry.

"Where are you headed?" I inquired.

"Running an errand for my mistress. Do you want to walk with me?"

"I would love to but I'm afraid I'm a bit overheated. Will you join me on the bench? I won't keep you long."

"Of course." She sat down and hooked her arm through mine. "I was so worried about you after you left me that morning. Where did you end up?"

I'd never written to Genevieve. We both knew any letters would not have reached her. I told her how I ended up in Watertown, how the women at Mrs. Harding's saved my life, but nothing about the nature of the house.

Changing the subject, I asked her how long ago she'd left the Sisters.

"Six months. I was fortunate to find employment with a family." Genevieve touched my sleeve. Her fingers lingered on the rich silk. It was obvious she envied my clothes. If only she knew at what cost I'd acquired them.

"Did you come for Hannah?" she said.

I turned my head away, blinking back tears. We sat in silence as a nursemaid pushed a stroller past us. "Not yet," I said.

"I assume you wouldn't want her to live with you... where you are now?" She said it without judgment but clearly she knew what I was up to.

I lowered my eyes. "No, I couldn't do that to her."

Genevieve clasped a hand over mine. "Perhaps it's best she remains with the Sisters, at least for the time being?"

My mind agreed with my old friend but my heart struggled.


Back at the asylum the next day, I stood in the doorway to the children's room and watched as Sister Helen read to Hannah. She gazed adoringly at her caretaker. Sister Helen paused her reading and kissed Hannah on her forehead. She was as taken with my child as Hannah was with her.

I left before either of them noticed me.

# 9

James never brought up Syracuse again. Neither did I. We resumed our relationship as if nothing had ever been said, but something had been extinguished between us. He never asked about Hannah, and I didn't tell him about my trip to Buffalo. I resigned myself to my child staying at the orphanage, at least until I could afford to take care of her on my own.

My situation left me in a quandary. I needed to save money, but my new profession also required the appropriate wardrobe. There were so many necessities—silk undergarments, parlor dresses, walking dresses, jewelry. I spent more money on clothes than I had anticipated, and I enjoyed buying trinkets from the peddler who came to our house. Even though they were only material items, they offered some comfort in contrast to my bleak situation.

When I counted the little money left over each month, I grew discouraged. I was wracked with guilt over how much I'd spent and over how much I enjoyed my new outfits. Doubt, too, crept in; I worried I wasn't worthy enough to get Hannah back. Sometimes a faint hope that a wealthy family would adopt her entered my mind, but I swiftly shrugged it off. I was her mother. She should be with me.

Even though I was upset that I couldn't go home, I didn't want to remain bitter toward my sister. I wrote to her and enclosed some money for our mam. She wrote back and thanked me for the help. Her second child was a boy, and she was soon pregnant again.

When another letter from my sister arrived, I was sure it held news about the birth of her third child. A cup of tea in hand, I headed to my room and settled into my chaise by the window. I imagined Hannah sitting at her small writing desk, little ones clamoring for her attention, as she dutifully wrote to me.

Inside, there were two letters. I glanced at the second one, written in someone else's handwriting. I set it aside and read my sister's first.

*September 17, 1870*

*My Dearest Annie,*

*I dreaded writing this letter. I can't in good conscience begin with the trivialities here at home, so I must tell you straight off what has transpired. I received a letter from Sister Agnes. The only address she had for you was here in Canton.*

*Annie, your daughter has passed away. I know how much of a shock this will be to you, as it would to any mother. I am so sorry my darling. How I ache for you when you read this dreadful news!*

*I remain, as always, your loving sister,*

*Hannah*

The letter floated out of my hands. I crumpled onto my chaise and wailed like a bleating, wounded animal.

Mollie rushed into my room. "What happened?"

Unable to speak, I pointed at the letters. She picked them up and, after reading them, hugged me to her chest.

"Good heavens, what's going on?" Mrs. Harding said when she came upstairs. When Mollie told her, Mrs. Harding joined us on the chaise. "The sorrows we women must endure," she said, rubbing my back as I sobbed. Mrs. Harding knew what I was going through; she had lost her only child and her husband.

Mollie went to fetch a glass, put it to my lips, and a warm, bitter liquid coursed through me. Once I had calmed, she read me the letter from Sister Agnes. My little Hannah had developed a fever. A nun—Sister Helen I assumed—had held my little girl as she took her last breath. Sister Agnes, who had never shown me any kindness, expressed hope that this would bring me some measure of comfort. How could I feel anything but bitterness? My child had died and I hadn't been there.

The laudanum Mollie gave me was the only thing that dulled the misery. When she told me I was using too much, I begged for more until she gave in. I wanted to go to sleep and never wake up. I lost track of the days, just as I had done when the Mother Superior locked me in the basement, but this time I also forsook my prayers.

Mollie wrote to James, and he came immediately. But when he tried to take me into his arms, I pulled away and slapped him with all the force I could muster.

"How dare you! Don't you know my little girl is dead?" I screamed, my body trembling with rage and resentment. "Leave before I strike you again. If I could have taken her to Syracuse, she might still be alive."

My accusation stunned him, but I didn't care. I pushed James out of my room and slammed the door. I hated him, hated all the men I'd entertained, and even the ones I hadn't met yet. Most of all, I hated Leslie for being the first man to lie to me, so thoughtlessly declaring his love, yet so easily abandoning me.

Shortly after James disappeared from my life, Mollie found me on the floor, cutting up my finest dress, the rest in a pile at my feet. She grabbed the scissors out of my hands as I moaned about the money I'd spent on frivolous things. "It's my fault she's dead," I cried.

"Remember my friend Cora?" Mollie said, holding me by the shoulders so I was forced to look at her. "When Mrs. Harding gave her notice, Cora decided taking her life was better than ending up on the street. If you don't stop this, I fear you'll suffer the same fate."

I quieted, realizing that Mrs. Harding would rent my room to another boarder if I did not resume my duties. As much as I loathed being a courtesan, I didn't want to leave the comfort and familiarity of Mrs. Harding's home. These women had rescued me, had become my family. I could not fathom leaving them, so I donned my best dress, took a few sips of laudanum, and made my way back to the parlor with a forced grin.

It was short-lived. No longer could I pretend to enjoy entertaining the men who came to Mrs. Harding's. I found it unbearable to listen to them talk about mundane things, to laugh at their jokes, to make them think they were the cleverest, most interesting men I'd ever met. Of course, they could see through my fake smiles, my fake laughter, my false interest, and it became rare for gentlemen callers to seek out my company.

Unable to meet my obligations to Mrs. Harding, I found myself deep in debt. But rather than giving me an ultimatum herself, my madam sent Mollie. My friend was kind but firm.

"Your attitude toward men has become… untenable. If there's anything out of place in this world, it's a prostitute who hates men. This can't continue, Bessie. You'll lose your room and your mind if you don't change your ways."

She didn't have to mention Cora again. I was done with Watertown. But Mollie couldn't have been more surprised when I asked her if she still wanted to move to Chicago. "You would go with me?"

"Yes," I replied emphatically. I couldn't go soon enough.

# 10

The ground had barely thawed, and buds on the fruit trees had swelled but not yet bloomed when Mollie and I departed Watertown. I had been in mourning for several months and, like nature, I needed renewal.

To pay off my debt to Mrs. Harding, I gave her some of my jewels, and in exchange, she gave us a letter of recommendation, which we carried with us. We also brought a copy of the *Chicago Sporting and Club House Directory* and scoured the little black book, which listed only first-class parlor houses. I couldn't imagine a city large enough to warrant such a guide, nor could I fathom that there were enough women to keep all these establishments profitable, though the advertised rates were double what Mrs. Harding charged.

I gripped Mollie's hand as our train approached Buffalo. I'd felt a sense of dread since leaving Watertown. We would have just enough time to visit Hannah's grave. As distressing as it would be, I had to see where she was buried.

The same pinched-faced nun greeted me at the asylum. This time her expression softened when she saw me; mine hardened.

"I want to see my daughter's grave."

The Sister hesitated. "They don't have individual markers. There's a large cross marking the area where the children are buried."

As if that made it any better. How was I supposed to pray over my daughter's grave?

Mollie and I found the cross. Made of stone, it bore the inscription, "In Memory of Our Children." Mollie put her arm around me. I couldn't cry, I was too numb. I'd lost my reputation, my family, my child. At twenty, I knew more about the harsh realities of the world than I had ever cared to learn.

"Oh, look," Mollie said, "there's a white butterfly."

"Where?"

"On top of the cross."

White *féileacáin* were sacred to the Irish, for it was believed they held the souls of dead children. The butterfly flitted around the cross, then flew toward us and landed on my shoulder. I stood stark still, holding my breath. Out of the corner of my eye, I could see its black-tipped wings. It was oddly comforting to imagine Hannah's soul contained in this lovely creature. Some of my sadness began to lift as the butterfly took flight and disappeared into a nearby tree.

We bought first-class tickets for the second leg of our journey. The farther away we got from Watertown and Buffalo, the more my spirits improved. Though I knew this bereavement would always be with me, its sharpness began to dull.

We arrived in Chicago on a cool, breezy afternoon. The brisk air reinvigorated me like a tonic.

The sporting house guide conveniently also listed hotels. We selected one and found an omnibus driver to take us to the Southern Hotel.

After a laudanum-induced and much needed rest, we donned our best dresses and headed to the home of Jennie Williams, a grand affair at 88 Fourth Avenue. An elegantly dressed gentleman opened the door, and I handed him the letter from Mrs. Harding.

"Mrs. Williams is engaged at the moment, but she'll be available shortly," he said, ushering us into the foyer.

If you didn't know this was a brothel, you would believe it to be the home of a wealthy family. Elegant oils of pastoral scenes and refined women adorned the dark walnut paneling, and abutting the mahogany staircase at the end of the long hallway stood a life-size marble statue of a nude woman leaning against a tree trunk, a sunflower drooping from her right hand.

As I admired the sculpture, a man and a woman exited the parlor. The woman, who I surmised was Mrs. Williams, was older than I expected, and austere in her high-necked dress, which accentuated her narrow face and thin nose. She spoke in a well-mannered tone, like a noblewoman in a Jane Austen novel, not a madam, and held herself more regally than Mrs. Harding.

Mrs. Williams nodded to her butler, who walked over and deftly handed her our letter of recommendation before escorting the gentleman out the door. Mrs. Williams read the letter, and then walked over to greet us.

"You were admiring the Clytie," she said to me. "Do you know the story?"

"No, ma'am."

"Clytie, a water nymph, was in love with the sun god, Apollo. When he spurned her, she starved herself and transformed into a sunflower, her face gazing eternally towards the sun."

"It's beautiful."

"It cost me a hefty sum." Mrs. Williams motioned for us to follow her.

She led us to a most luxurious parlor with two white marble fireplaces at either end, mahogany tables overflowing with Venetian glass, and dark red velvet drapes billowing onto the floor. The butler appeared to close the doors but not before an orange tabby slipped through and jumped onto Mrs. Williams's lap.

"You come highly recommended," Mrs. Williams said, addressing me, not Mollie. I sensed Mollie was hurt, but she didn't show it. She was always keenly aware that she wasn't as pretty as other girls. Even with her hair up, it was thin and mousy. And her clothes never fit her well. Her hips were too wide, her shoulders too narrow.

"I don't know if I have room for two more *demi-mondaines* right now," Mrs. Williams said as she stroked her cat.

If the madam wouldn't take us both on, should I accept a room here, or go elsewhere with my friend? I didn't want to leave her in a lurch, but I also needed to make a living. "We would prefer to stay together," I said.

The tabby jumped down and rubbed herself against Mollie's skirt. Mollie always had a way with animals. In Watertown, she was forever feeding strays, much to Mrs. Harding's chagrin. Mollie picked up the cat and set it on her lap. It rolled over and purred.

Mrs. Williams studied Mollie. "Matilda has taken a liking to you." She turned to me. "I suppose I could make room for both of you."

# 11

More than twice the number of girls boarded at Mrs. Williams's house than at Mrs. Harding's, and she ran a stricter bordello than our former madam. We ate supper at four o'clock, to allow us time to digest our food and take a mandated rest before the house opened at eight in the evening.

The other women didn't so much as acknowledge Mollie and me until Mrs. Williams had made the proper introductions. Maud, a former governess, sat to my right. She was the oldest of the boarders and even more regal than our madam. Another woman was an accomplished pianist. Mrs. Williams took pride in her boarders' talents, as if they made her brothel more respectable, but when you're lying on your back, it doesn't matter to the man what you can do outside the bedchamber.

The woman to my left was young, a pretty Southerner named Lottie Lee who, a third girl exclaimed in awe, was related to the general.

"Is that so?" I tried to sound impressed, though Mollie and I exchanged doubtful glances.

"Where do you hail from?" Maud said. "If you don't mind my asking."

"Not at all," Mollie replied. "Bessie and I boarded together in Watertown, New York."

"Watertown?" Maud obviously had never heard of it.

"It's north of Syracuse," I said.

"Near Syracuse?" Lottie said excitedly. "Why, that's not far from Seneca Falls where the very first Woman's Rights Convention was held."

"Lottie is our resident suffragist," Maud chided.

"The meeting was held in '48," Lottie explained. "Elizabeth Cady Stanton and Lucretia Mott organized it."

I hadn't heard of the convention but knew of the two women. They received much scorn in the papers.

"Did you know," Lottie said in a conspiratorial tone, "there are doctors and alienists who think the Great Social Evil only attracts insane women?" Her voice dripped with sarcasm. "They believe we become whores to satisfy our own 'unnatural' lusts."

Maud shot Lottie a look, but Lottie continued. "They think women who become who—" This time Lottie caught Maud's piercing gaze. She paused but then decided to go on, despite her friend's warning. "They think we display hysteria and nervous disorders more than respectable women. The nerve!"

I nodded. We were supposed to be pious and pure. If a woman allowed herself to be seduced, she must be mad.

Lottie went on. "Men demand our services while women declare us pariahs, never faulting their husbands for patronizing our houses, only us. We're Peitho."

"Lottie," Mrs. Williams interjected. "Need I remind you not to speak of these matters in front of our gentlemen guests?"

"No, ma'am." Admonished, Lottie lowered her head.

"Peitho?" I asked Lottie.

"The goddess of seduction, Aphrodite's companion," Maud explained. "Peitho is also the goddess of persuasion."

"That doesn't seem so bad," I offered.

Maud smiled. We would get along famously.


The summer was hot, dry, and windy. Fall soon came with the cloudy, shorter days. Sunday, October 8, 1871 started like any other. A few of the girls stayed in their rooms waiting for the first guests to arrive. The rest of us gathered in the parlor. Some sat around the card table, playing whist; others listened as the pianist practiced a new song. I'd learned pianists in such establishments were always men, usually middle-aged, and were known as "professor." I occupied myself by reading on a sofa, ready to tuck my book behind a cushion whenever the house bell rang. It was always slim pickings on a Sunday, but we had to be ready.

Around ten o'clock, we heard a persistent rapping on the front door. The butler answered, but when he came into the parlor, there was no caller with him. "There's a fire headed our way," he exclaimed. "We must leave now."

The girls stopped their game and the professor quit his piano, but no one moved. Moments later, Mrs. Williams rushed into the room. "Girls, did you hear Oscar?" In her firmest tone, she commanded: "We are all leaving. Now."

"I need to pack some things," one girl whined.

"We don't have time," Mrs. Williams snapped.

"Can't we at least get our coats?"

Our madam sighed heavily. "Hurry."


Outside was bedlam. Fourth Avenue was jammed with people, most empty-handed, moving swiftly south, sheer panic on their faces and in their strides as horse-drawn wagons veered violently through the crowd. To the north, red and yellow flames flared, vivid and lurid against the black sky.

We hurried down Fourth Avenue until we felt far enough away to be safe and found a field where we sat huddled together. Throughout the night, we couldn't take our horrified eyes off the blaze as great columns of fire shot up and rode the wind to the next building northward and then another, a fiery tumbling of dominoes. With every breath, we inhaled smoke and ash, and our dry eyes stung from the floating embers.

When the sun rose the next morning, the inferno still burned far to the north. Black clouds hung over the lake.

As we trudged back to Fourth Avenue, we passed hordes of men, women, and children. Many were families, huddling; husbands with bewildered looks, wives clinging to infants, wailing over their losses, not yet ready to be thankful to still be alive. The homes far south of the city had survived, but those in the city had not fared as well. Most of the houses on our street had burned to the ground, and our worries grew with every step. When we finally reached Mrs. Williams's address, she collapsed, falling into the middle of the ash-filled street. Though covered in soot from the rooftop to the singed ground, the house had been spared by one block. I should have been relieved but I felt only indifference.

At first the house was quiet. But soon after the blaze died out, a steady stream of workers converged on the city: architects, engineers, masons, and of course, confidence men. Everywhere you walked, debris was heaped next to piles of brick, stone, and wood for the legions of construction crews swarming around the burnt district. Mrs. Williams's place once again became a bevy of activity.

From the beginning I'd had plenty of callers, and I also had my regulars. Important guests were assigned to me or to Maud, who, despite being in her early thirties, carried herself in a way that made her desirable to men who wanted not only a body, but a mind as well. Like me, she didn't engage in the kinkier requests from callers. Daisy chains, where men and women lay naked on the floor, their faces muzzling unspeakable areas, and drunken orgies, known as Bacchanalian dances, were out of the question.

During the mean winter months, some of the girls left for warmer climes like New Orleans, so those of us who stayed behind had more callers to entertain each night. The lack of competition was good for Mollie, but I didn't enjoy the extra burden. And after a while I thought I would suffocate in the confines of the house, despite its large size.

When Lottie returned from New Orleans, she talked excitedly about having gone to lectures to hear the suffragist Olive Logan and others speak. Lottie may have been poor shanty trash, but her interest in the movement spurred her to become more educated, and spurred me as well. Her vocabulary broadened, though her pronunciation, with her heavy southern accent, wasn't always perfect. "Who better than women who are marginalized in society to speak up for equal rights?" she would argue. "We're the least likely to be listened to, and we need to demand to be heard."

I went with Lottie to lectures, and Maud often joined us as well. The performance halls in the business district had been destroyed in the fire, but a few on the west side, the Globe Theatre, West Side Opera House, and the castle-like Vorwaerts Turner Hall had survived.

Occasionally we also went to see a dramatic or variety performance, like the Wyndham Company's English production of Victorien Sardou's play, *Nos Intimes*, though I was surprised to learn from Lottie that we had to enter through the Globe Theatre's side door and sit in the third tier, to which Maud objected. "We have tickets for the dress circle," she said pointedly.

I was confused.

"Lottie's talking about the section reserved for *femmes du pave* and others of their ilk," Maud explained to me, her voice dripping with disdain as she referred to the streetwalkers. "A class to which we *don't* belong."

"But we *are* whores," Lottie shot back.

"You may consider yourself one, but I do not," Maud replied. "I prefer to call myself a courtesan, or better yet, a *hetaira*."

Lottie rolled her eyes.

"What is a *heta*-?" I said.

"*Hetaira* means female companion," Maud said, clearly irritated. "They were the highest-class courtesans and the most educated women in ancient Greece. They were articulate and could hold their own, intellectually, with a group of men." She flicked an imaginary piece of lint from her dress as she continued her lesson. "Women were entirely dependent on men, but not the *hetairae*. They were independent and had money."

"I like that title much better," I said, hoping to lighten the mood.

Lottie relented and we entered through the main doors. Eyeing the third tier from our seats, I immediately realized why Maud was so adamant about not sitting there. The gallery patrons drew almost as much attention as the actors onstage with their rowdy and boisterous behavior. The prostitutes weren't there for the performance, but rather to meet customers and make arrangements for the rest of the evening.

I conveyed a silent thank you to Maud as the play began. But I was bothered by her declaration. Why couldn't a woman be married and also have her independence and freedom? I wanted both. I didn't realize I had let out a heavy sigh until Maud glanced at me, inquisitively. I reassured her with a smile and turned my attention back to the performance.

"I want to be a *hetaira*," I confided in Maud once the performance came to an end. "I want to make enough money to leave this life."

She gave me an approving look. "You're well on your way. You dress tastefully, you're well-read, and you don't act like a silly young schoolgirl with the men. There's only one piece of advice I have for you." Maud became the stern governess. "Stop medicating yourself with opiates."

I lowered my eyes, too embarrassed to respond. I hadn't realized it was so obvious. But sometimes it was the only way I could make it through the day, the anguish over my Hannah's death still too much for me to bear.

"I know doctors and pharmacists prescribe laudanum for everything under the sun, but I've seen the deleterious effects it can have. You're too young to let that happen to you." Maud paused. "And your friend, too."

I raised my head. "Mollie?"

"Yes. She has a rather morose nature, and it's worsening. This is a hard profession for most women to endure... more so when their looks worsen with age."

Mollie did seem more haggard than usual, and with the house full of boarders again, she wasn't entertaining as many callers. I thanked Maud for her concern and agreed to curb my habit, and to speak to my friend about hers.

The next afternoon, I paid a visit to Mollie's room. She barely glanced up from the *Godey's Lady's Book* she was reading. I sat at her vanity and noticed a new box—Dr. James P. Campbell's Safe Arsenic Complexion Wafers.

Alarmed, I said to Mollie, "Isn't arsenic a poison?" My da and brothers had used it to kill rats in our barn.

"Not if you take only small amounts."

"Why do you need it at all?" I pressed her.

She set down her magazine. "To clear my complexion, if you must know." Her voice held an edge. "You don't need them, you already have beautiful skin."

I understood her desire to improve her appearance, but I worried for my friend. Lately, her eyes possessed an unusual brightness, and her complexion and her lips were too pale. I picked up her bottle of the opium tincture. "Is it safe to take this and the arsenic?"

Mollie sighed heavily and impatiently grabbed her magazine. "Oh, don't be silly. I'm careful. If it helps, what's the problem?"

I certainly wasn't in a position to judge, given my use of laudanum. Having made my concerns known, from now on I would keep them to myself.

In January 1873, Mollie and I traveled to New Orleans to spend the winter at the city's most exclusive parlor house. Miss Nellie Otis's four-story home boasted four parlors, a winding mahogany staircase in the foyer, satin-covered walls, and of course, the obligatory Clytie, this one a bronze bust of the water nymph's head bursting from a sunflower.

I fell in love with New Orleans, a city unlike no other. We avoided the dangerous and crime ridden Gallatin Alley and Smoky Row, but I was drawn to the bawdiness and revelry of the French Quarter. I'd never been in a place so alive. I felt an undercurrent of something I couldn't describe, as if the city didn't just belong to the living but to something mysterious, otherworldly.

We left New Orleans in the spring just as the city air was perfumed with a fragrant explosion of magnolias, gardenias, and oleanders. In the fall, the country plunged into a financial panic. Despite the depression, Mrs. Williams's house was busier than ever. It always amazed me that the world around us could be falling apart, but men still flocked to us, and the madams and their *demi-mondaines* made a mint. Except for Mollie, who declined my invitation to return to New Orleans after the New Year.

"Suit yourself," I said, but I was troubled over our failing friendship.

When I returned to Chicago in the spring, a letter arrived from my sister. She and I wrote to each other regularly. I had always suspected Mam's health was worse than Hannah would reveal. Now she confirmed my fears. Our mam had been diagnosed with Bright's Disease, a combination of dropsy and inflammation of the kidneys, and her mind was deteriorating. I had to go home.

# 12

The picket fence in front of Mam's home on Gouvernour Street was freshly whitewashed, and the delphiniums in the garden were as lovely as I remembered. As my carriage driver opened my door and helped me alight, I squinted at the screened-in porch. I could barely make out the silhouettes inside. Behind me I heard the familiar flowing of the Grasse River. After the hustle and bustle of Chicago, I welcomed the quiet of my village. Bees droned lazily amid the clumps of Blue Flag Irises and Queen Anne's Lace without the interference of a riot of carriages, wagons, and trolleys.

"Mammy, who's that?" A young girl asked from the porch.

"Annie!" Hannah shrieked. It was strange to hear my real name again after all these years. Hannah ran to me and hugged me so hard I feared a rib might crack. She pulled away and, still holding my hands, surveyed me.

Eight years earlier I had left Canton a young woman, naïve and stubborn. Now I was well-traveled, well-dressed, independent, and still stubborn. Even though the letters Hannah and I exchanged were friendly, the reason I'd left Canton was always between the lines. I hadn't written to let her know about my arrival, preferring to take the chance that she would be happy to see me, instead of being crushed if she had told me not to come. I was relieved at her joy.

I wore my best traveling habit and felt self-conscious next to my sister in her plain calico dress. She had only been outside Canton once, when she worked as a live-in servant with a family in nearby Potsdam. A farmer's wife, she didn't care about keeping up with the latest fashions. I had grown so accustomed to wearing an elaborate chignon, my head felt bare without it.

"My, my, you're as beautiful as ever." Hannah hugged me again.

"How's Mam?" I couldn't conceal my worry.

Hannah's delight dimmed as she took my hand. "Come say hello."

In the years I'd been gone, Mam seemed to have aged decades. She sat in her rocking chair, as always. When I entered the sunroom, her face lit up.

"Tis mo Annaidh?"

"Yes, it's your Annie," I replied in Gaelic before I kissed Mam on both cheeks.

She took my face in her hands. "'Tis glad I am you are home."

Her eyes held a faraway look. She was back on that proud island. My mam, whose family name, McCarthy, traced back to Eoghan Mor, son of the second-century King of Munster; my mam, whose ancestors had lost ownership of their lands to the English in the seventeenth century; my mam, who had left her beloved island, never to see it again, now sat before me, pale, her abdomen, hands, feet, and eyes all swollen.

I glanced at Hannah, whose look indicated we would talk later.

Hannah had four children and another well on the way. Margaret, who went by Maggie, was nearly eight. I remembered the day I'd held her as a newborn. It seemed like yesterday; how the time had flown.

Thomas was six; John, four; and Mamie barely a year old. John hid behind his mother's skirts, but Thomas and Maggie wanted to know all about their Aunt Annie. I didn't envy my sister's life as a farmer's wife; it was hard work. But she had a husband and children who adored her, and for that I envied her.

I had brought gifts for everyone. Sweets for the youngsters, and for Mam and Hannah, pashmina wool shawls and soft kid gloves. "I don't know how I can wear these," Hannah said. "They're too nice."

"Wear them to Mass. You'll be the envy of every woman there."

Hannah's lack of a reply told me that's what she feared.

I handed Mam her shawl. "It's from Kashmir, India."

She ran a hand over the soft wool. "How can ya afford such things?"

"Don't you worry about that mammy."

She eyed the diamond solitaire on my left hand and the diamond cluster on my right. "Are ya married?"

I felt Hannah's eyes on me. "No, mammy." I chastised myself for wearing my rings and gold bracelets, but I hadn't wanted to leave them in Chicago.

"Yer too old not ta be married," Mam said.

I suppressed a sigh. At twenty-four, I was already a spinster.

One morning while Mam was still sleeping, I decided to go for a stroll in the village. I had forgotten how close Canton felt to the sky. Situated in far upstate New York, near the St. Lawrence River, Canton was closer to Quebec than to New York City. As a child I couldn't wait to grow taller so I could touch the clouds. I often wished I could sit on one and gaze down at the townspeople scurrying hither and tither like tiny ants.

Main Street looked the same, though I didn't see anyone I knew. The girls I'd known from church and school would be married with children by now, and most likely at home.

When I saw the L.B. Storrs Clothing sign, I went inside, yearning to see a friendly face. Mr. Storrs was my first employer, and I'd met

Leslie in his store. An amputee, Mr. Storrs hopped around with a cane or crutches and made enough noise that we could hear him approaching long before he could see us, our heads closer than they should be, me blushing and giggling.

Mrs. Storrs was there, but not her husband. She started to smile at me, then just as quickly set her mouth in a tight thin line.

"Hello, Mrs. Storrs, it's Be—" I caught myself. "Annie Moore. You may remember I once worked for your husband."

"Yes, I remember you. What brings you back to Canton?" She said stiffly.

*An odd question*, I thought. The reason should have been obvious. "Visiting my mother and sister."

She didn't respond.

"Is Mr. Storrs here? I wanted to say—"

"He's not here right now. But I'll tell him you stopped by."

She didn't ask how long I would be in town or invite me to return, and I got the distinct feeling she wanted me to leave.

Disappointed, I crossed the road to look at the stores on the other side of Main Street. Stopping for a moment to shield my eyes from the blaring sun, a window signed taunted me. There, in black etched letters, was *his* name, followed by "Attorney at Law." The words on the sign blurred as I stared at it. My throat went dry, my heart pounded, and blood pulsed loudly in my ears as I peered through the window and saw Leslie sitting at a desk, writing.

My hand quivered as I opened the door. Leslie looked up, and our eyes met. He froze, his pen mid-air. I closed the door without taking my eyes off of him. In the years since I last saw him, the man I thought I would marry had lost his luster. He wasn't as handsome as I remembered, or perhaps I was truly seeing him for the first time.

"Annie?"

My body shook so violently I couldn't speak. When I did, I said, "Our daughter is dead."

Leslie continued to stare at me. Did I see fright in his eyes? Did he fear what I might do?

"But you don't care, do you?" I took a few steps toward him. "You wanted me to get pills from a druggist. I refused. But, in the end, you got what you wanted. I had to leave my home, my family, and now our little girl is dead."

"Annie—"

I put up a hand. "Don't speak. I don't want to hear your lies. You deceived me, and now here you sit as if I had never existed."

For the first time I regretted not naming my seducer. Sure, Leslie would have denied being the father of my child, but my silence had let him off the hook. He didn't have to hear a priest say it was most desirable to leave his town to protect his family's reputation. He wasn't sent to a convent for "fallen" men. He didn't have a baby ripped from his arms. He didn't have to resort to unsavory work to survive.

The door opened. "Pardon me for interrupting," a gentleman behind me said.

A look of horror flashed across Leslie's face. I let him wonder about my next words, let him feel the tension that now filled his office. Satisfied I'd made him sufficiently uncomfortable, I replied, my back still to the man who'd entered, "You're not interrupting anything. I've said what I wanted to say." I turned and swept past the confused visitor.

As I walked home, satisfaction filled me. How many times had I dreamed of confronting Leslie? The release made me feel better than I had in a long time.

Mam was sitting in her rocking chair as usual, knitting, the monotonous back and forth of the rocker rails the only sound in the otherwise quiet home. I regarded my mother for a moment, her grey hair pulled back into a severe bun, the crow's feet around her eyes, her slightly downturned mouth.

As a child, even before my da died, I'd sensed a despondency about my mam that I never understood, or, at least, not until I learned she'd lost three children before I was born. Two girls and a boy. By the time my older brother, William, died a year after my da, Mam had fallen into a cocoon of grief from which she never emerged. She still wore black, and the clock on the mantel—stopped after Da's last breath to confuse Satan and give his soul time to reach Heaven—had yet to be restarted. Every year she seemed to withdraw more and more into herself until I feared she would disappear altogether, a ghost receding into the walls.

The next day, Mam and I baked bread together, and I set out with a basket of fresh loaves to take to Hannah, who lived in a cabin three miles outside the village. When I arrived, she was tending the vegetables in her garden where I'd told her my secret. I hadn't expected the disapproval she'd shown me. "Annie, how could you," she'd chastised.

My back had stiffened with indignation. "I love Leslie, and he loves me."

Hannah's reply had been a look I would have expected from our mam, followed by an admonishment. "If he really loved you, he wouldn't have taken such liberties with you."

My sister naturally fit in with society's expectations of women. The model of restraint, she had met her husband before the war and waited four long years to marry him. She was content being a farmer's wife, raising a large brood. She was a saint, and I was but a sinner.

I'd turned my back and kept quiet, taking out my hurt on the beans as I yanked them from the vines.

Inside the cabin, I set down the basket I'd brought and hugged my niece and nephews while Hannah picked up her youngest and sat down in a chair by the fireplace. Once I'd settled in next to her, I asked about Mam. "Is there any cure?"

Hannah shook her head. "Laudanum lessens the pain, but the doctor says there's not much that can be done. The dropsy makes her body swell, as you may have noticed. It's worse in the evening."

I nodded. "Leslie is practicing in Canton now," I said.

"Yes, I know. I'm sorry he wouldn't do the honorable thing."

We sat in silence. I waited for her to say what I knew was on her mind.

"I won't tell Mam how you earn your living. It would devastate her."

I lowered my eyes. In my letters to Hannah, I hadn't wanted to lie, and so I had avoided the subject entirely. For her part, Hannah had never asked where the money I sent came from; she'd only expressed appreciation for whatever I could give. But, of course, she had suspected. Who wouldn't have?

She leaned forward, placed a hand on top of mine. "Isn't there some way you can get out of your situation?"

I had heard of the efforts of the Christian groups who set up a room in their church with flowers and food, ready to receive the unfortunate women into their fold. But they couldn't give us what we needed most: true redemption, acceptance back into society, proper employment, and a livable wage. The truth was, no one wanted us. The temperance women said they did only to honor their Christian values. But they didn't want us in their homes, near their husbands or children. All they had to offer was their religion.

The only way out for women like me was marriage.

# 13

Normally I enjoyed traveling, especially now that I could afford a berth in a luxurious Pullman sleeper. But the elegant surroundings—the walnut paneling, beautifully painted ceilings, and plush upholstered furniture—did nothing to improve my mood on my journey back to Chicago.

The other passengers appeared content with their lives, while I brooded and moped over mine. As I dined alone, a woman and her three young children entered the dining car, and the maître d' seated them at a nearby table. Picture-perfect models of well-behaved children, the two girls and a boy dutifully followed their mother's instructions. One of the daughters appeared around the same age my Hannah would have been. I struggled to fight back tears.

Despite the change in Mollie's attitude toward me, I looked forward to seeing her again. When I arrived at the house midafternoon, I went straight to her room, but she wasn't there. Nor were any of her belongings. I went to Lottie.

"Where's Mollie?"

She closed her book and let out an almost inaudible sigh.

"Is she all right?" I tried not to sound too anxious.

From her perch on her chaise, Lottie said gingerly, "As far as I know."

"What happened?"

"She got drunk one night and couldn't take any callers. Mrs. Williams gave her a warning, but she did the same thing the next night."

I closed my eyes. Frustration and worry replaced my fatigue. "Where is she?"

"At a house in Little Cheyenne."

"Oh, heavens, no," I blurted. Little Cheyenne was the most dangerous part of the city, notorious for its crime and bawdy brothels. It had earned its nickname from the town in Wyoming infamous for its lawlessness. Some of the brothels even had secret panels in the bedchambers so that thieves could empty unsuspecting customers' pockets while the girls entertained them. What had Mollie gotten herself into?

When I arrived at the address Lottie had given me, a glum, sour-smelling man answered the door. I assumed he was the madam's husband or lover. He ushered me into a dingy parlor, which reeked of bourbon and smoke. The sofa and chairs were worn, tired-looking pieces of furniture, and the dust-covered tables had glass stains that any reputable housekeeper would have rubbed. I decided I would rather stand than sit anywhere in the room.

When Mollie entered, I rushed to her, but she winced, a bird protecting a broken wing. I stopped short, surprised at her reaction.

"Why are you here?" she barked.

I ignored her cold demeanor. "I was worried sick about you."

"Why do you care?" she sneered.

"You're my friend. Of course I care."

She shifted her gaze away from me. "Then why did you abandon me?" The hardness in her voice melted into hurt. I ached for her.

"Mollie…" I searched for the right words. I placed a hand on her arm, but she pulled away. "We need to find a way to get you back to Mrs. Williams."

"It won't happen."

The resignation in her voice unnerved me. I peered into her dim eyes. "Why do you say that?" She couldn't give up. She had saved me, and now I would find a way to save her. "You can't stay here. It's not safe."

"Maybe you should have thought about that before—" She stopped and dropped her gaze drop to the floor.

"Before what?"

She shook her head, refusing to finish her thought. Instead, she asked me to leave.

I wanted to close the distance between us, but I couldn't. "If you wish," I replied before seeing myself out.

Back at Fourth Avenue, Mrs. Williams's house felt empty without my friend. I walked over to the Clytie. As I stared at her smooth marble face, I wondered why there was so much sorrow in the world.

Throughout the fall I spent much of my time at the theater when I wasn't entertaining callers. Lottie did much to fill the void. After my annual sojourn to New Orleans, she talked incessantly about an upcoming appearance by the great suffragist Susan B. Anthony. She even had the other girls all atwitter and, after much to-do, Mrs. Williams gave us all permission to go hear Miss Anthony give the Sunday Dime Lecture at the Grand Opera House. Certainly, the fact that Sundays were the quietest day at the house played into her decision. Regardless, we were all overjoyed, and when the doors opened at two o'clock on Sunday, March 14, 1875, we each handed a dime to the attendant and proceeded into the cavernous theater. Within half an hour every seat on the main floor and in the balcony had been taken, and I was pleasantly surprised to see a number of men in the audience.

Miss Anthony was older and smaller than I expected. I had imagined her a tall and austere giant, not the petite, feminine-looking woman before us. She appeared to be about the same age as my mam, though, in addition to the usual signs of middle age, her face was also marked by determination and frustration, hardly surprising given her thirty-year fight for women's liberties.

For the next two hours we sat spellbound as Miss Anthony expounded on the topic of "Social Purity."

*When women are compelled by their position in society to depend upon men for subsistence, for food, clothes, shelter, for every chance even to earn a dollar, this dependence of woman on man gives him the privilege to exact from her a much higher moral code than he is willing to admit for himself, while she is powerless to exact a similar moral attitude from him.*

How well I knew that to be true. Leslie hadn't lost his standing in society. Only I had brought disgrace upon myself, as if I alone was responsible for my becoming an unwed mother. A pang of sadness struck me as Hannah came to mind. I hadn't told anyone at Mrs. Williams's about my child. It was too distressful to speak of, but I thought of her every day.

When Miss Anthony turned her attention to the Great Social Evil and noted the number of prostitutes in the large cities—twenty thousand in New York City alone—there were audible gasps and murmurings among the crowd.

"This army of public women," Miss Anthony intoned, "is continually being replenished by disappointed, deserted, seduced unfortunates. It is a mistake to class all fallen women together, under the sweeping censure bestowed upon them by man. They are angels of purity compared with the males who visit them."

Finally, someone had the courage to stand up for the unfortunate class, to denounce a society that demanded the services of prostitutes while at the same time derided us as pariahs and made us prey to unscrupulous police, piggish landlords, and ambitious politicians who wanted an easy way to refill their coffers.

*We need to lift this vast army out of the temptation to sell themselves, body and soul, for bread and shelter, either in or out of marriage. Girls must be educated like boys to do something useful. Women must have equal chances with men. They must have fair play and, like men, must be eligible to all the honors of society and government. The only possible way to accomplish this great change is to accord to women equal power in the making, shaping, and controlling of the circumstances of life. That equality of rights and privileges is vested in the ballot, the symbol of power in a republic.*

I glanced at the women around me. Some nodded in agreement, but I also knew there were women who agreed that a woman's rightful place was in the home. The notion of equal status was frivolous to them. But they could afford those ideals. They were the ones with rich husbands.

When Miss Anthony said that "virtue and independence go hand in hand together," I thought, *Amen*. But what good would it do me? I had lost my virtue, and I could only have my independence by living as a societal outcast. I contemplated the possibility of women having both. Would there be a day when it became reality?

The speech left me wanting to do something, but what? My circumstances not only limited my options, they also rendered them nonexistent. I left the auditorium feeling simultaneously invigorated and defeated.

I wished Mollie had had the chance to hear Miss Anthony, to realize she had a cause worth living for. I hadn't seen my friend since my visit to Little Cheyenne the previous summer. I remembered her words to me all those years ago in Watertown, when she warned me not to be fool enough to go into the streets. I feared for my friend. I needed to see her again.

This time, the madam herself answered the door. She was gruff and bore the appearance of someone disillusioned with life. Mollie wasn't in, she told me. "She's probably at the opium joint down the street, at the corner." She didn't sound the least bit concerned.

I found the place, in the basement of a decrepit building. It took a few moments for my eyes to adjust from the harsh light of the bright sun to the dimly lit den. An Asian man in white linen stood hunched over a candle, holding a small plate of opium over the flame while his customer gripped a long, slender pipe.

I walked farther into the den and found Mollie slumped in a chair against the back wall, already in a stupor. "Mollie," I said, shaking her shoulder gently. "Wake up."

Her head lolled as she mumbled incoherently. I tried to help her sit up, but her body was dead weight. I couldn't move her.

"You smoke?" The Asian man, the proprietor I assumed, asked me.

"Oh, no." I didn't try to hide my worry. "This is my friend." I turned back to Mollie and took one of her limp hands in mine. She moaned. I squeezed her hand, hoping she would sense my presence. Guilt washed over me. I had failed my friend.

The Asian man hovered around me. He obviously wanted me to leave if I wasn't a paying customer, but I couldn't leave Mollie in this condition. I opened my reticule and pulled out a handful of bills. Before the proprietor could say anything, I shoved them into his hand, and he walked away.

I took my place next to Mollie and watched her while she remained in her drugged stupor. She appeared peaceful one minute, but the next her sleep turned fitful. Her body jerked and she whimpered before moaning out loud, then she calmed just as quickly. When she finally woke, she was groggy, and didn't notice me. I waited for her to fully come out of her opium coma before making my presence known.

"What are you doing here?" she said, confused. "Are you—"

I shook my head. "Your madam told me where to find you."

Mollie's puzzled expression turned to one of consternation. She was obviously miffed at her madam for informing me of her whereabouts. She stood to leave but fell right back into her chair. I offered her a hand. She hesitated but took it. I held onto her as she regained her bearing, and led her out of the den.

When we reached her house, she didn't invite me in. "Please, let me help you find another place to live," I implored. I had saved enough money that I could obtain a room in a reputable boardinghouse for Mollie until she could find employment.

Mollie's response stunned me. "It's too late," she said.

"Oh Mollie, it's never too late. Please let me help you."

The coldness crept back into her demeanor. "I can take care of myself."

Why couldn't she see that she was letting her life slide into a dark place from which she might never emerge? I felt frustrated and utterly helpless.

"I must ready myself for the evening," Mollie said as she opened the door. "And Mrs. Williams won't like it if you're late."

With that, she left me on the stoop.

# 14

On New Year's Eve, Mrs. Williams prepared her special concoction, mixing freshly sliced oranges, lemons, strawberries, and mint with chilled champagne, brandy, and Sauternes—a sweet white wine imported from France—in an elaborate crystal bowl. By ten o'clock, the house was ablaze and every parlor filled with perfumed and cologned flesh, full drink glasses, and lively music. My date for the evening was an actor who went by the name Pug, I assumed because of his nose. He was touring with the Oates Troupe, a group that was scheduled to perform a new French comic opera at McVicker's Theater.

Amidst the opulence of Mrs. Williams's holiday celebration, it struck me how her palace masked the ghastliness of the lives we lived. In Little Cheyenne, the ugliness was prominent, revealing the true plight of the *demi-mondaine*. Just as I started to think about Mollie, my thoughts were interrupted by raucous laughter. Out of the corner of my eye, I espied a gentleman who, on a previous visit, had talked about Wilkie Collins's newest work. I had vowed I would never read sensation fiction after Nora's description of *Venus in Boston*. But the title of Collins's latest work, *The New Magdalen*, intrigued me.

The gentleman came over to me. "Have you had a chance to read Collins's book?"

"I have."

"And what did you think?"

Before I could answer, Lottie spoke up. "What book are you talking about?"

I told her and explained the plot: a former prostitute who can never rejoin society takes on the identity of a deceased woman distantly related to a wealthy, well-respected family.

"If women had more rights, we wouldn't have to resort to this line of work," Lottie stated matter-of-factly.

I cringed, realizing my mistake bringing up the book in front of her. Lottie's caller raised his eyebrows. "What rights do you think women need?" Lottie didn't seem to notice his bemusement or, perhaps, she chose to ignore it.

"The right to vote, for one."

"You think women should be allowed in the polling booth?" His tone held mocking incredulity.

"Yes, and decent wages so we don't have to depend on men."

The man arched his eyebrows. "Don't you make a lot of money here, in this palace?" He scanned the room, waving a hand. "And you don't have to… 'depend on a man,' as you say… Why, you can buy beautiful dresses and travel freely without a chaperone."

Lottie's nostrils flared. "A woman's ability to move about freely comes at the cost of her reputation."

I was thankful Lottie didn't have a glass of wine in hand. She undoubtedly would have thrown the contents into his face.

"Lottie," I interrupted, "Mr. Kensington is absolutely right. We do live well, and although we make our money from men who pay us, we are providing an important service, and it allows us to be independent."

Lottie was speechless.

I turned to Mr. Kensington. "Please excuse Miss Lee. She gets carried away sometimes, but you can see how passionate she is, and from what I hear, she has passion for other, more pleasurable things as well." I winked.

Lottie stood motionless, gaping, until Mrs. Williams entered the parlor. Our madam made a quick sweep of the room with her eyes. She could take in the mood instantly, no wetting of her fingers and raising them to figure out which way the wind blew.

"How is everyone tonight?" my madam asked as she approached our group. "I trust you are enjoying yourselves?"

I placed a gloved hand on Mr. Kensington's arm. "We're having a fine evening, aren't we?"

"I'm not entirely satisfied," Mr. Kensington said.

My heart nearly dropped to the floor.

"I need more whiskey," he said, holding up his empty glass, and we all laughed.

After Mrs. Williams left, Lottie mouthed her thanks to me. No madam would tolerate one of her girls being disrespectful to a guest. I had saved her from being kicked out because I couldn't bear for another friend to suffer Mollie's fate.

At midnight, the pianist played an uproarious rendition of *Auld Lang Syne*, and we sang so loudly I feared the walls would collapse. When Pug and I went upstairs, I had to steady him. He'd had too much to drink, but I'd taken callers to my room in far worse condition.

After removing his jacket and waistcoat, he tugged at his suspenders and let go, so they slapped against his chest. He wobbled as I helped him take off his trousers. I slipped off my dress and undergarments and led him to my bed. I lay down, but he stood at the edge of the bed, hovering over me.

"You bitch, Julia, you're a good for nothin' bitch," he slurred. He flexed his fingers, and then there was a flash of metal. I scrambled for the hat pin I kept by my bed for these occasions, but I wasn't quick enough. Pug swung the knife and nicked the top of my left breast. I screamed. Pug dropped the knife, but before I could move, he lunged at me, grabbed me by the neck with one meaty hand, lifted me clear off the floor, and hurled me across the room.

Just as my head slammed into the wall, the door burst open, and a man shouted, "Leave her alone!"

As Pug turned toward the door, the man sent his fist into Pug's face, and he collapsed to the floor.

"Are you all right?" The man spoke with a German accent, and I detected the familiar scent of Tabarome, with its distinct aroma of bergamot, leather, and tobacco.

I nodded and glanced down at my breast. It was bleeding, but not badly, and my head throbbed.

"What on earth!" Mrs. Williams cried out when she rushed into my room. Pug was still lying on the floor, groaning.

"Someone bring Bessie a blanket and something to clean her wound."

My rescuer, shirtless, his broad muscular arms and shoulders exposed, handed the knife to Mrs. Williams.

"Thank you, Abe," my madam said, and then turned her attention to Pug.

But Abe kept his eyes on me. We stared at one another until Lottie came in with a blanket.

"That man will never step foot inside this house again," Mrs. Williams declared the next day at the midday meal.

The other boarders were still fussing over me, but I wasn't shaken at all. I sought out the young woman with whom my rescuer had spent the night.

"His name is Abe Rothschild," Carrie said.

My eyebrows shot up as I buttered my toast. The Rothschild name connoted wealth and power beyond any ordinary man. Hardly a day went by that a newspaper didn't publish a story about a member of the European banking dynasty.

"Where is he from?"

"Cincinnati."

"Does he come to Chicago often?" I tried to sound nonchalant.

"He's been here a couple of times," she replied. "Always goes up with a different girl. He likes to gamble, from what I hear, and is a bit cocksure."

*What man isn't overconfident*, I thought. I'd entertained countless men who were brash and gambled and drank too much.

Carrie gave me a curious look. "Why are you so interested?"

"I'm always interested in any man who rescues me," I said half-jokingly. "Is he married?" I braced for the answer. The majority of men who frequented brothels were married.

"He wasn't wearing a ring."

"That doesn't always mean—"

"He didn't talk about a wife at home. I think he's too carefree to be tied down."

"Mm. Did he say when he'd be back?"

"No. But he did tell me he's headed to Hot Springs. I've been there, so I asked him where he's staying."

I took another bite of toast to hide my eagerness. "And?"

"The Hot Springs Hotel."

I was leaving for New Orleans soon and was already planning a stop along the way.

# 15

The town of Hot Springs cut deep into the Ouachita Mountains, a mile-long row of low-rise frame buildings nestled in the narrow Arkansas valley. Foot bridges spanned a creek, leading to the entrances of the hotels and bathhouses situated along the east side of the main avenue. The clerk at the Hot Springs Hotel eyed me. But, since my first encounter with the hotel clerk in Buffalo, I knew how to handle myself.

"How much for a week?"

The man's eyebrows shot up. He glanced at the couple waiting behind me, then back at me.

"Seventeen dollars."

I opened my purse and laid the bills on the counter. The clerk grew more alarmed. He peered at the gem on my ring finger. "Is it *Mrs.* Moore?"

"No, just Miss," I said in an even tone.

The clerk shifted his feet. "You'll be staying alone?"

"Yes, of course." I allowed the slightest hint of indignation.

"What brings you to the Springs?"

"Pleasure." I smiled coyly.

The man cleared his throat. "I'm sure you know the hotel doesn't allow any *unregistered* guests." He used the tone clerks take with women of my ilk.

I held his gaze. "Sir, I don't know what you're implying. Perhaps I should speak to the proprietor?"

"I… I… I apologize Miss Moore," the clerk stammered, his taciturn expression giving way to embarrassment. "I'll get your key."

My room overlooked Hot Springs Mountain. Shacks and tents dotted the hillside, where those who couldn't afford the luxury bathhouses went to bathe. As I gazed out the window, I placed a hand on a cold pane. Here I was, warm and well-fed, but I could easily be one of the poor outside. The separation was as thin as the windowpane. I crossed myself.

In the evening, I headed downstairs for supper. I scanned the dining room, hoping to see Abe Rothschild. Couples occupied a few small tables, but the room was mostly filled with men seated at long communal tables; Civil War veterans who flocked to the town in search of relief from the scars of the war in the warmth of the springs as well as in the soothing arms of a woman at one of the town's many brothels.

While I waited for my meal, Abe entered the dining room with another gentleman. He stopped to shake hands with the veterans, thanking them for their service, and took a seat at the table next to mine. Seeing him for the first time in the light of day, I took in his thick dark eyebrows, the broadness of his nose, the way his mustache curled into the corners of his mouth. His youth and vitality distinguished him in the sea of infirmity.

I avoided looking directly at Abe's table, but when his eyes found me, I sensed it. I wondered whether he recognized me, but, before I knew it, he appeared at my side.

"Is this seat taken?"

"Please join me," I said, motioning to the empty chair.

He took a seat and stared at me, making me blush. "You look familiar." He pulled his chair closer. I got a whiff of the same Tabarome scent. "Are you the woman I rescued in Chicago?"

I lowered my eyes. "I never had a chance to thank you properly."

"So you've come all the way to Hot Springs to thank me in person?"

"I'm on my way to New Orleans and decided to stop here for a few days."

He took my right hand. "What a nice coincidence. Or perhaps it's fate," he said with raised eyebrows. His eyes held a glint of amusement. "I'm Abe Rothschild." He kissed the top of my hand. A diamond ring on one of his fingers caught the light. "And you are?"

A quiver ran through me. I glanced around, but no one had seen. Abe was taking more liberties with me than most men would in a public dining room. I found his disregard for what other people thought refreshing. I flashed him my most beguiling smile. "Bessie Moore."

After a few minutes, Abe motioned to his friend at the end of the table. He lowered his voice. "We're going across the avenue to play faro. Would you like to join us?"

"I thought gambling was illegal here."

"So is prostitution."

"Is it?" I coyly tucked my left hand under my chin, flashing my diamond.

Women didn't typically go to such establishments, but this was Hot Springs. We entered a back room where the games were conducted. A few men glanced our way, then went back to their business. I couldn't see the tables for all the men surrounding them, but I only needed to listen to know what they were playing: the clattering of the small, ivory ball racing around the roulette table, the rolling of dice for craps, the shuffling of cards for faro and poker. And the constant clinking of silver.

Abe and his friend, George Ellis, found space at a betting table. George was at least a decade older than Abe, with greasy hair, beady eyes, and an air about him I didn't like. I couldn't put my finger on it, but something about him made me uneasy.

They each bought a stack of chips from the dealer. I stood across from Abe, with the men who either hadn't the money to gamble or had enough sense not to. Occasionally Abe glanced at me, but mostly he concentrated on his card game. His eyes never wavered, his broad-shouldered body remained taut and erect. Some men who patronized brothels were tentative, either from lack of experience or lack of confidence. They needed a woman to guide them. I sensed Abe Rothschild would need no help.

We left the gambling hall well after midnight. As we neared the hotel, we came upon two men engaged in a fight. Without a second thought, Abe and George moved into the gathering crowd. I hung back. I couldn't see the brawl, but I heard the punches.

"What's going on here?" A sheriff's deputy said, arriving on the scene.

I was surprised to hear Abe's voice in response. "I only wanted to help this man even the score," he said. As the crowd dispersed, I saw that he was holding out a gun to one of the fighters.

"The hell you are," the deputy said. "Come with me. The lot of you."

# 16

The next morning I woke thinking of Abe. His boldness hadn't frightened me; instead, I found myself admiring his self-assurance. He didn't hesitate or waver. When he'd made the decision to intervene in the fight, he had stepped forward calmly, with no bluster, just like when he'd rescued me from Pug.

Abe was still on my mind when I left the hotel in pursuit of a bathing gown. As if the doors to all the hotels opened at once, a steady stream of men spilled out into the street and hobbled to the bathhouses. Many used crutches or canes. The ones who couldn't walk were carried on litters. All took with them blankets, towels, and the ubiquitous tin can. Bathers not only soaked in the curative water, but also drank it.

I wandered through the stores, hoping I would see him, and was disappointed when I didn't. After I made my purchase, I spent the afternoon at the bathhouse attached to my hotel, enjoying the soothing steam vapors, my mind continually going back to Abe.

At supper, I engaged in idle conversation with my tablemates, but kept an eye on the entrance until, finally, Abe and his companion entered the dining room.

"Did you have a good night's sleep?" I teased when he reached my table.

"The accommodations were quite pleasant." Abe rested a hand on the back of the chair next to me.

"Please join me," I said. Abe sat down and motioned for George to take a seat on the other side.

Abe didn't act like a man who had spent the night in a jail cell. He didn't seem embarrassed about his arrest. To the contrary, it appeared as though he hadn't thought about it at all.

"Is gambling your only occupation?" I said jokingly.

"Only at night."

"What do you do during the day?" I didn't want to let on how much I had learned about him from Carrie.

"I work for my father's company. He's a jeweler and also has a lace and fabric business. My brother runs the store, and I travel the country drumming up business."

I was familiar with traveling salesmen. They were always on the trains and at the brothels. But most drummers wore sack suits. Abe didn't dress, or act, like a salesman.

"I didn't know the Rothschilds did anything other than banking."

"We're a family of many talents."

I accompanied Abe and George as they played faro again. Back at the hotel, Abe bid me goodnight in the lobby with a bow and a tip of his hat, then stepped closer and huskily whispered in my ear, "Which room is yours?"

"Why do you want to know?" I teased.

He looked at me mischievously and winked as he turned to leave.

When I reached my floor, Abe was already waiting for me, standing at the end of the hallway. He had climbed a set of stairs outside leading to the upper floors, out of sight of the clerks and any guests lingering in the lobby. I opened the door to my room and quickly ushered him inside. We had to be discreet. If anyone saw a man enter my room and reported it to the front desk, I would be kicked out of the hotel.

Sex for hire required putting on an act. I typically blocked out the unpleasantness by pretending to be anywhere other than in my bed with the weight of a stranger pressing down on me. But with Abe, I didn't have to. I surrendered to carnal pleasure as I hadn't since Leslie. My instinct was correct. Abe was experienced, more so than Leslie, despite being younger than him—and three years younger than me.

For some reason, most men believed they were entitled not only to the body they'd paid for, but also to the woman's innermost life. Lying was part of being a prostitute. But when Abe asked what every man who visits a whorehouse wants to know, I let my guard down. My words flowed like an ice flood on the Mississippi. Things kept hidden in my own breast, I now let spill out. I told him about my da, how I'd watched a dark-robed priest administer last rites as my da wasted away from consumption, and about Hannah. I'd lost two of the most important people in someone's life: a parent and a child.

We lay in silence. Abe stroked my hair. Changing the subject, I said, "Tell me about your family," not wanting to spend too much time on myself.

Abe mumbled something about there not being much to say. We drifted off to sleep and he left before dawn. When I woke, there was money on the basin stand. A twinge of disappointment pricked me. I wanted Abe to be more than a caller.

I needed to head to New Orleans, but I extended my stay for a second week. We ate supper together, and afterwards I accompanied Abe as he played faro. Every night he left the gambling hall with a wad of bills, some of which he left in my room in the morning.

One day as I hurried to meet Abe for supper, another guest entering his room gave me a curious glance. The next morning I was still resting in bed when there was a knock at my door. *Perhaps Abe has forgotten something*, I thought as I opened the door. But it was not him. It was the hotel manager. He didn't speak right away, and I started to wonder if he was gathering the courage to engage my services.

He cleared his throat and said, "Miss, I'm afraid I'm going to have to ask you to leave."

"Why?" I feigned puzzlement, fighting a sinking sensation in my gut.

"We've gotten several complaints about your... behavior. It has made some of our guests uncomfortable."

I crossed my arms. "My behavior?"

"Some patrons are threatening to leave if you and your friend don't go."

He said the word "friend" as if it were an unsightly disease not to be mentioned in polite company.

I was a fallen woman, a *fille de joie*, and they didn't want me there.

I packed my trunk and met Abe in the lobby. He hired a hack to take us to the Avenue House, where he easily obtained a room. But when I tried to register, the clerk turned me away. My reputation had preceded me. I couldn't believe how fast word had spread. Abe came to my defense, but his pleas were ignored. It angered me that the same behavior from a man was overlooked, even applauded by his friends and associates, whereas a woman was punished. What gave society the right to endorse this double standard? I finally found a room at the Earl House, a modest establishment without its own bathhouse, which catered to less prosperous guests.

Despite Abe's claim of being a drummer, I hadn't seen him trying to sell goods to any of the stores. He spent all his time gambling, visiting a different establishment every night. One evening, Abe became miffed when a dealer asked George to move his chips so he could see Abe's stack, and his mood soured as he started to lose. Eventually he ran out of chips and stormed out of the room. The dealer laughed and said something about cheaters getting their due.

George offered to escort me back to the hotel. While I didn't care for him, I didn't want to walk back to my hotel alone. But instead of crossing the avenue, George guided me toward a dark alley next to the building we'd just exited.

I hesitated. "Where are we going?"

George put a hand on my waist. I backed away. He had been drinking—not enough to affect his card game—but enough to think he could take liberties with me.

"What's wrong? I'm not good enough for you?"

"I don't know what you mean."

"I think you do." George leaned over and tried to kiss me. I pushed him away.

George's eyes darkened. "Well, well, a high and mighty whore."

I squared my shoulders. "I beg your pardon. How dare you talk to me in such a manner."

Men walked past us, but no one came to my aid.

"I'll talk to you any way I want," George hissed. As he took a step toward me, a fist flashed in front of my eyes and landed on his left cheek, knocking him to the ground.

George rubbed his face, glowered at Abe. "What'd you go and do that for?"

"Leave her alone." Abe extended an arm toward me. I fastened a hand on it. He bent his arm at the elbow, like a gentleman, and we left George lying in the dirt.

When we were a safe distance away and I had regained my composure, I thanked Abe.

"I shouldn't have left you stranded there," he said as we made our way back to my room.

When Abe left the next morning, he didn't leave any money on the basin. I wasn't sure whether it was due to his gambling loss or because he had fallen for me, but I preferred to think it was the latter.

Unfortunately, January was coming to a close and I had to get to New Orleans, or I would lose my room, if I hadn't already. When I told Abe, he tried to convince me to stay. "Is it the money? I'll start winning again."

The idea that this might be the last time I would ever spend with Abe gave me pause. A surge of sadness tugged at me. Before I could stop myself, the words tumbled out. "Why don't you come to New Orleans with me?"

Abe studied me intently. For a moment, I feared I had made a mistake. He grinned and said, "I have some business in Georgia first, but I'll come see you."

As he leaned over to kiss me, I said, "You'd better hurry, my dance card fills up quickly."

# 17

Carnival was in full swing when I arrived in New Orleans. The first ball of the season had taken place January 6, Twelfth Night, in celebration of the Epiphany; but instead of three kings bearing gifts for the Christ child, the Lord of Misrule presided over the merriment in the Crescent City.

I had missed the first month of the New Year and Miss Otis was discomfited. "I thought you would only be a week at the Springs," she said, referring to my hastily written letter. Her expression conveyed both displeasure over my delay and relief at my arrival. But after my time at the Springs, I found it more difficult to concentrate on my callers. The mostly staid, middle-aged men I entertained seemed boring in comparison to Abe, who was bold and brash but also well-educated and charismatic. I tried to put his parting promise out of my mind, but I could think of nothing else.

One quiet morning, I took a streetcar downtown to clear my head. Mardi Gras preparations along Canal Street were in earnest now. At the Custom House stop, I disembarked and headed toward the French Quarter, where the African *marchandes* sold Creole cheeses and warm breads from baskets precariously balanced on their heads. All around me the soft cadence of the French tongue lilted through the mild, slightly balmy air. At first, hearing the language had reminded me of my days at the convent, but the beauty of it soon made me forget the Sisters.

At Café du Monde, I bought a café au lait and a warm beignet and enjoyed the light breeze from the river and the scenic view of Jackson Square. Carriages carrying beautiful, fashionably clothed ladies passed by where I sat. The prettiest ones were always the women of mixed-race ancestry, some of whom boarded at Mahogany Hall, one of New Orleans's busiest brothels.

On my way back, I strolled past the majestic St. Louis Cathedral and up St. Ann Street, hoping to get a glance of Marie Laveau. The Voudou Queen had been infirm for some time, but she often sat in front of her small cottage watching the passersby. I wasn't disappointed. When I looked into her yard, our eyes met. She stood and waved at me. "Come here, my child."

Delighted to have a chance to meet the famous Madame Laveau, I stopped and waited for her at the low picket fence that surrounded her home. She wore a plain calico gown with a brooch fastened around her neck. A bonnet covered her grizzled hair. She reached out a hand and motioned for me to give her one of mine. Her gnarled hand was warm and firm. She squeezed mine and closed her eyes. As we stood in silence, I studied her face. The beauty of her youth was still visible between the life-filled lines.

When she opened her eyes, she peered into mine with unnerving intensity. "Beware the charming man," she said.

I laughed uneasily and tried to move my hand, but she held on to it.

"You must be careful with your profession," she added, without a hint of judgment. I didn't think I bore the mark of a scarlet woman. I never left the house with my face painted like a circus rider, and I only wore tasteful jewelry when out and about. No one would be able to deny I was anything but a lady. How did she know?

She reached into a pocket of her dress, pulled out a small red flannel bag, and placed it in the palm of my hand. "It's *gris gris*, an amulet to protect you."

I felt something inside the bag and smelled incense. I thanked her and tucked the bag in a pocket.

Instead of going back to Miss Otis's, I ventured past Basin Street to Congo Square. At any hour of the day, somewhere in the city you could hear music, whether it be the guitar and violin players who serenaded passersby on street corners, or the piano tunes emanating from people's homes. But there was a different kind of music at Congo Square. You not only heard it, but felt it too; the deep, pulsating rhythm vibrated from the ground up, through your entire body.

In the center of the square, an elderly black man sat astride a large cylindrical drum, his long fingers beating the instrument with a surprising quickness for someone his age. Next to him, a younger man played a small drum between his knees. A third strummed an unusual, long-stringed instrument. Nearby, black women in loose-fitting dresses swayed their bodies to the beat of the music. These people who had once been slaves, who now, even as free men and women, still weren't treated as equals, acted as if they'd always been free. There was a lightness and serenity about them I envied.

Louisianans still lived under military rule. The previous year, the White League had attempted to overthrow the Republican state government and tried to keep Negroes from voting. In response, more federal soldiers had been stationed throughout the city, and the Mardi Gras parades were cancelled for fear of violence from the White League, which had put a damper on my last trip. The heightened tensions of the previous year had eased, though an undercurrent lingered.

You could see it in the steely gazes of New Orleanians whenever they encountered a federal soldier.

As I left the hustle and bustle of Congo Square, I thought I heard someone call my name. Men who patronized brothels never acknowledged the unfortunate class on the street, so I ignored it. But when I heard my name again, I turned and stopped.

"I thought it was you," James said. I almost didn't recognize him, it had been so long.

"What a surprise," I replied, a bit flustered. "What brings you to New Orleans?"

"Business."

I nodded. Of course.

"You look well," he said.

"Thank you."

"Are you living in New Orleans now?"

"I spend my winters here."

"You still live in Chicago?"

"Yes." I glanced around. "Is your wife traveling with you?"

James's eyes dimmed. "Charlotte died two years ago."

"I'm sorry."

"Thank you. Where are you staying?"

I glanced west. "I'm at a house on Basin Street." Most of the city's first-class parlor houses were along Basin, far enough away from the river that we didn't have to worry about the whipjacks—beggars who pretended to be down-on-their-luck sailors—and other sordid sorts. If James knew anything about New Orleans's *demi-monde*, my address told him I still belonged to the underworld.

"I see." We stood in awkward silence for several moments. "Would you mind if I called on you?" he asked. "Tonight?"

"I would be delighted," I said, though truth be told, I wasn't sure. "My madam is Nell Otis. Her house is at 16 Basin."

Walking back, my thoughts again drifted to Abe. It had been almost a month since I'd seen him, and I hadn't heard a word. Perhaps it was for the best, I told myself, but I couldn't help being disappointed.

# 18

A t Miss Otis's, supper was the only time I had to socialize with the other girls. I didn't particularly mind, as they were mostly unfriendly, the permanent boarders resentful towards us seasonal ones. Most of the boarders were still young enough to be called girls. They were catty and vain, and I listened in disgust as they compared notes on their callers' preferred positions, perversions, and their physical defects. I never talked about my callers—I considered it to be in poor taste.

Fortunately, we ate well—steak and potatoes, or gumbo, which I'd never heard of before coming to N'awlins, but had grown to love. We had plenty of fresh shrimp and catfish from the Mississippi, the Gulf Coast, and Lake Pontchartrain, as well as delectable French pastries. A madam wanted her girls to be well-fed. They preferred girls with a little more meat on them than those who were skinny and highstrung. And though Miss Otis was hotheaded and frequently got into rows with her girls, I considered myself lucky to board there.

I no longer joined the girls at the landing at the top of the stairs to peek down at our potential dates, preferring to stay in my room until I was called down. But I wanted to greet James when he arrived, so I descended the mahogany staircase a few minutes before eight. Miss

Otis stood outside the Rose Parlor, wearing an expression of stern disapproval. She motioned to me.

"Is there something else you should have told me?"

I had informed her of James's visit and had no idea what could have happened to cause her consternation. "No, why?"

Motioning toward the parlor, she said, "There's a gentleman here for you, and it's *not* Mr. Morris."

*Could it be?* "Did this gentleman give his name?"

"Abe Rothschild." Miss Otis peered down at me.

I fought to maintain my composure. I had nearly resigned myself to never seeing Abe again, and yet here was. I told my madam about Abe's promise to visit but that I did not know he intended to call on me that night. I didn't let on the hopes I held in my heart.

"Well," she said, "you'll have to tell Mr. Rothschild that he'll either need to engage another girl's services tonight or come back when you don't have a prior commitment."

I didn't want Abe to see another woman, but it would be unwise to say so to Miss Otis. I took a deep breath to calm myself and entered the parlor. Abe's face lit up when he saw me. I grinned in return.

"I thought you had forgotten about me," I teased, though I was more serious than I let on.

Surprise filled his eyes. "You doubted me?"

I shrugged sheepishly. I didn't want to remind him that men didn't often keep promises to prostitutes.

"I couldn't stop thinking about you," he said, moving closer to me.

Blushing, I lowered my eyes. Normally a man's declarations didn't faze me, but Abe's charm unnerved me. I met his eyes again. They seemed to pierce right through me. "When did you arrive?"

"This afternoon. I registered at the St. Charles and came here straightaway."

I stifled a gulp. He was staying at the same hotel as James.

Abe sensed my hesitation. "You don't want to see me tonight?" His voice held a hint of disappointment mixed with disbelief.

"It's not…" I didn't want to tell him the truth.

Abe shot me a wicked smile. "I got here as soon as I could, before anyone else could fill up your dance card."

I told him what Miss Otis had instructed me to say. He took one of my hands into his and peered into my eyes. His held a sparkle of determination. "Who's my competition?"

I stood there speechless, startled again by Abe's audacity. Most men wouldn't pry.

He must have spied a glimmer of fright in my expression. "I know your madam wouldn't allow us to be in the same parlor. As I'm only here for you, do I have your permission to call on you tomorrow night?"

"I would be delighted," I replied, relieved.

As I escorted Abe out, the house bell rang. The butler handed Abe his coat and walked to the door. When I heard the visitor respond to the butler's welcome, my blood ran cold.

"I'm here to see Miss Bessie Moore."

"May I ask who's calling?"

"James Morris." He entered the foyer and rushed over to me.

"Ah, I see you're here to greet me. Forgive me for being late." He kissed my cheek, then stopped and regarded Abe. "Am I interrupting anything?"

"No, no, not at all." I glanced at Abe. His eyes were locked on James. I had no idea what he might do. But Abe just leaned over and kissed me full on the lips. "I'll see you tomorrow," he said, the huskiness of his voice clearly implying what he meant. He donned his hat and brushed past James without a word. Miss Otis greeted James and showed us to the parlor we would occupy. She gave me an approving look as she closed the doors.

As James and I settled onto the sofa he said, "Is that young gentleman a suitor?"

I smoothed my dress and replied nonchalantly, "Oh no, he's just someone I met recently." I didn't want to tell him the truth.

"He's quite taken with you."

That observation pleased me, but I kept it to myself.

Throughout the evening I kept comparing James to Abe. Abe had thick, wavy black hair and dark brown playful eyes that held more than a hint of mischief. James's hair had thinned and greyed, and his eyes had lost their luster. He also wore a Holman's Fever, Ague & Liver Pad. I had seen the device many times. Many middle-aged men wore them to cure a multitude of disorders. But seeing it on James only made me compare him to Abe's youth and virility.

Before James left, he hinted at calling on me again. I half-heartedly welcomed him to do so, noting that I would be engaged the next few days but that I would send word when I was available. The disappointed look told me that he knew why I would be occupied.

Two days later, at noon, a cannon fired along Canal Boulevard, signaling the formation of the Carnival parade for Mardi Gras. Abe and I lay in bed listening to the procession. I rested my head in the crook of his arm. He smelled of whiskey and absinthe from the Sazerac cocktails he'd downed the night before. We'd had an enjoyable evening, but I still didn't know much about him.

"You never talk about your family," I said. "What's your father like?"

Abe's jaw tightened. "My father is demanding. He has… certain expectations."

I suspected Abe wasn't living up to them. It was obvious he didn't want to talk about his father.

Abe rolled onto his side, rested his head in the palm of his hand. "Would you ever run your own house?"

I groaned. Other men had asked me the same thing.

"Why not? You wouldn't have to sleep with strangers… like me," he said teasingly.

It was true that madams rarely entertained callers. They operated businesses, just like Cornelius Vanderbilt ran the New York Central and Hudson River Railroad. But unlike Vanderbilt, brothel madams were not allowed to move among proper society.

"Only as a last resort," I replied, and decided to be bold. "When I'm married, I won't need to, of course."

The corners of Abe's mouth rose slightly, in delight or amusement, I couldn't tell. "Come with me to Cincinnati," he said.

I was taken aback, not expecting this, at least not so soon. Was he serious?

"Where would I live?" I said, lightly tapping his chest. "*If* I go with you?"

"Cincinnati has lots of boardinghouses."

I wrinkled my nose.

"It would only be temporary. My father owns several houses in the city."

I doubted his father would allow a female companion of his son to board at one of his homes—unless we were married.

Playing coy, I said, "I'll think about it."

During the day on Mardi Gras, the brothels were quiet. It was a day to enjoy the festivities along Canal and in the French Quarter. But while the rest of New Orleans settled down at the stroke of midnight to usher in Ash Wednesday, the parlor houses overflowed with men, whiskey, and wine.

Within a few days, Abe announced he had to leave. He grumbled something about having received a telegram from "the old man." It had been sitting at the St. Charles Hotel for two days before Abe returned and retrieved the message. I could tell from his mood that his father would be upset by a tardy reply.

He took me in his arms. "Come with me," he said. We hadn't talked about his invitation again since he first proposed it. He also hadn't said the word marriage. Dare I bring it up? "When are you leaving?"

"Tomorrow."

"I'll give you an answer then."

The corners of his lips curved upward. "You'll say yes. I know you will."

After he left, I went for a long walk through the French Quarter and one of New Orleans's "cities of the dead." St. Louis Cemetery did indeed look like a miniature city, its rows of mausoleums resembling tiny houses. Young boys were always there collecting brick dust for Voudou practitioners, who would spread the scrapings in front of homes in need of protection. Even though I considered the practice silly, I thought it must be nice to feel you had *something* protecting you. Being a prostitute meant being an outcast, always and forever. I'd had nothing, no one, to protect me for years. At twenty-six, I had already lasted twice as long as most *demi-mondaines*. But I wouldn't last forever. Once I grew too old for the best houses, I would be forced into lower-class brothels, like Mollie had been, where I would make less money and mingle with less desirable company. Eventually I'd have no options but to work at the worst brothels and concert saloons or, God forbid, to walk the streets, where the druggists peddled their well-known poisons to fallen women. I had stopped using laudanum, but there was always the chance I could be drawn in again.

When I returned to Miss Otis's house, I sent a note to James asking him to visit that evening. I had made my decision, but I wanted to be sure it was the right one.

"I was afraid you didn't want to see me again," he said when he arrived. We had one of the parlors to ourselves. "It's that young gentleman, isn't it?"

"James—"

"Be careful. He has a reputation."

What man who visited parlor houses *didn't* have a reputation? "Whatever do you mean?"

"I've seen him at the hotel a few times, and I've asked about him. He's a mountebank."

"A cheater? You're going to believe what some stranger told you?" I said crossly, rising from my chair.

"I care about you. I didn't realize until I saw you again how much I've missed having you in my life."

"Now that your wife is dead?"

His face fell. "I suppose I deserve that."

*Yes, you do*, I thought, and conveyed it with an irate look. Deep within me I still harbored resentment over his reluctance to bring my little girl to Syracuse. It could never be the same with James.

# 19

Before Abe returned, I wrote to Mollie and Mrs. Williams to let them know of my change in plans. I restrained myself from telling Mollie of my happiness; I didn't want to be cruel. But it took some effort to shake off the twinge of guilt for not going back to my friend.

While packing, I came across the *gris gris* Madame Laveau had given me. I'd put it in a drawer and forgotten about it. Inside was an odd assortment of items: a pebble, a root of some kind, a talisman with writing I didn't recognize, a tiny bottle filled with camphor oil, and a dried mushroom. I tucked the items back into the bag and placed it inside the drawer again. Perhaps the next young woman who had my room would benefit from its protection.

Abe and I found our boat, a packet steamer, tucked among a line of stern-wheelers and side-wheelers of every size, the boats so close together you could step from one to another. Luggers with their day's haul of oysters passed by the passenger and freight steamers, headed to their own levee.

Animals and cargo crowded the main deck of our boat, along with passengers who couldn't afford a cabin. They would eat food they brought with them and spend their nights on the open deck, laying claim to a box or a bale, with little or no protection from wind or rain—or worse—a fire in the boiler room.

The calliope player struck up his musical instrument, the steamer's shrill whistle sounded, and the boat started to move. A sudden urge to jump back to shore gripped me. The wind picked up. I held onto my straw bonnet and gazed at my beloved city. The tall pointed slate-grey spires of the cathedral at Jackson Square towered over the French Market.

Soon the market disappeared from view, but the church's three steeples were still in sight. We rounded a bend, and for a moment I could still see the center spire before it too vanished in the distance. Tears blurred my vision. Would I ever see New Orleans again? Of course I would, I admonished myself silently. I was being ridiculous.

Abe and I traveled as husband and wife so we could share a cabin. It was the first time I'd ever presented myself as a married woman. It gave me pleasure to do so. I was already relishing the day when it would become a reality.

In the evenings we enjoyed sumptuous meals and Abe gambled. During the day we strolled the promenade or settled into rocking chairs and read novels as the steamer glided up the wide water boulevard past row after row of grand homes, though many had long since fallen into disrepair.

Before we crossed into Mississippi, our boat stopped at the Red River Landing to let off some passengers.

"Where are they going?" I asked Abe.

"Shreveport, and I'm sure some will go all the way into Texas."

"I've always thought of Texas as a lawless, wild place, unfit for civilized society."

Abe laughed at my perception. "Nothing could be further from the truth."

"You've been there?"

"Yes, I had some business in Marshall and Jefferson."

"Perhaps we could go there someday," I said.

Abe smiled. "Perhaps we will."

On the last day of our journey, Abe still hadn't returned from the saloon by the time I dressed for supper. I went to the dining room, where I ate the midday meal alone. When I returned to our cabin, I heard a rustling noise inside. When I flung open the door, Abe was standing there holding my jewelry box.

"What are you doing?" I cried loud enough to catch the attention of a woman down the hall as she opened her door. I stepped inside the cabin and closed the door.

"I only need a piece or two," Abe assured me, as if he were borrowing a cup of sugar. "A few more rounds and I'll have my money back."

His shirt sleeves were rolled up. The last few days he'd been wearing an expensive Jurgensen watch that he hadn't had when we left New Orleans. Now it was gone.

"You can't take my jewelry," I said flatly.

Abe moved closer, put a hand on my arm. "I'll bring them back to you. I promise."

Abe cajoled me until I relented and let him take a brooch with semiprecious stones. It was all I was willing to part with, for in all likelihood, I would never see it again. I always wore my diamond rings and, of course, my gold cross and chain. I had obtained other pieces over the years, assorted jewelry with semiprecious stones and a few pearls, but, like most women, I preferred diamonds.

I didn't see Abe for the rest of the day. But before I retired for the night, I went for a stroll on the promenade and spotted him rushing out of the saloon, yelling, "I'll go to the captain and have you thrown off the boat!" He was so enraged he didn't see me as he flew up the stairs to the Texas deck.

A middle-aged man came out the same door, in no particular hurry. He walked with an awkward shuffle. Curious, I followed him up the stairs but stopped before reaching the upper deck so I could stay out of sight.

"There he is," I heard Abe say. "He's the one who cheated me out of my money."

"You don't say," the captain said. "Did you swindle this young fellow out of his money?" he asked the gentleman.

The man answered in a leisurely drawl, "He's just sore I beat 'im. Fair and square. Owes me a fair amount of money, I might add. Got it right here on this piece of paper."

I cringed. How much was he in debt?

Abe tried to protest but the captain cut him short. "Son, don't you know a professional when you meet one? If you're going to gamble with a pro like Mr. Devol, you better be prepared to pay the price. You're lucky I don't stop at the first landing and throw you off my boat. Now get out of my sight."

As I headed back down the stairs before Abe could see me, I heard the captain add, "And remember, you still owe me for your fares."

I went back to our cabin, fuming, and paced the small space while I waited for Abe to return. When he finally came in, he stopped short when he saw me. He clearly had expected me to be asleep.

"How could you?" I blurted and informed him what I'd overheard.

Abe hung his head. "I'm sorry. Really, I am. I… I thought I would win it back." When he told me how much he owed for his gambling debt, I gasped. It was nearly all the money I had from my time at Miss Otis's.

He looked at me sheepishly. "Will you forgive me?"

I folded my arms and paced the floor. "What are we going to do?"

"We could… I don't know." He fumbled with his hat, looking contrite. "I've messed things up, haven't I?"

*Surely he's learned his lesson*, I thought.

"I have a plan," he said.

I stopped. "What?"

"If you have enough money to lend me, I could pay off Mr. Devol, then we could leave your trunk with the captain as collateral and pawn one of your rings—"

"Pawn one of my rings?" I shouted. Lowering my voice, I hissed, "Are you out of your mind?"

"Please hear me out."

I folded my arms and waited for him to go on.

"We can pawn one of your rings to pay for our passage. I'll take the money to the captain and get your trunk back. And then I'll get your ring." He stepped closer, tilted my chin to meet his pleading eyes. "I promise to make this up to you."

As we approached Cincinnati, I brushed off my disappointment and took in the vista of my new home. Steamboats lined the north bank of the Ohio River. Foot traffic and carriages traversed a suspension bridge that spanned the river connecting Ohio to Kentucky. The city, nestled in a basin like a bird's nest, gradually sloped up from the river to the base of several steep hills. Streetcars inched up the hills like caterpillars on tree branches. Resorts as large as castles dotted the hilltops.

After leaving my trunk with the captain, Abe hired a hack to take us to a pawn shop. It was more difficult to part with my solitaire than it had been to part with my trunk. As I slowly slid the ring from my hand, I reassured myself that Abe would get it back for me.

A few doors down on Race Street was the boardinghouse where I would stay, less than two blocks from the Burnet House, where Abe lived. An Irishwoman in her sixties named Margaret Brickley ran the boardinghouse. She showed me my room while Abe went back to the captain to pay our fares and retrieve my trunk. I barely hid my disappointment at the lodging. The floors needed polishing, the one small rug in my room was faded and worn, the bed small, and the mattress visibly lumpy. The ewer was chipped.

Mrs. Brickley didn't notice my dismay as she nattered on about the house rules and mealtimes. I consoled myself with the notion that I wouldn't be there long. Abe would soon set me up in my own place.

After a grand tour of Cincinnati, Abe went on the road for his father. Left to explore the city on my own, I ventured to the library. If not for the sign and the stone heads of Shakespeare and Benjamin Franklin guarding the entrance, I would have thought the building an opera house with its elaborate stone scrollwork and arched windows. Inside, I stepped onto a checkerboard marble floor in the main hall and peered up at floor-to-ceiling cast-iron alcoves filled with books.

Reading had been my escape for so long. In Chicago, after the fire, the city had opened its first public library, temporarily housed in an old iron water tank. Inside that round, sparsely furnished Book Room, I became Louisa May Alcott's Jo March Bhear in *Little Men*, or Anthony Trollope's Lady Anna, or George Eliot's Dorothea Brooke, a world away from my life as a courtesan.

But I had always been a little uncomfortable in a library, wondering whether anyone suspected my true nature. No longer a *demi-mondaine*, those fears were gone, and I settled into a chair to pore over

John James Audubon's exquisite animal drawings and Pierre-Joseph Redouté's elegant botanical illustrations.

When Abe returned, he paid Mrs. Brickley for my room and board, and ceremoniously handed my ring to me. I'd fretted ever since taking it off my hand, wondering if I would ever see it again, and was relieved now that it was back on my finger. Abe had come through and shown that he was a man of his word. The tiny bit of mistrust I'd harbored since the last day of our trip from New Orleans melted away.

We went to a beer hall in Over-the-Rhine, Cincinnati's German neighborhood, and then walked back down Vine Street to the Atlantic Garden. He bought us beers from the long bar near the front, and we walked upstairs to the billiards room.

"Where have you been hiding this beautiful woman?" A man asked Abe.

Abe introduced me to his cousin David Rothschild, who shot Abe an approving glance and peppered me with questions. David was a few years older than Abe and seemed more like a big brother than cousin.

After a few minutes, David said to Abe, "So, you can't take working for the old man anymore?" He slapped his cousin on the shoulder. "Believe me," he continued, "I empathize."

Stunned, I remained silent as David raised a glass. "To difficult fathers," he toasted.

Abe clinked his cousin's glass with his own. "Hear, hear."

"Why don't you want to work for your father?" I waited until we'd left the Garden to broach the subject and was careful to keep any accusation out of my tone. But I didn't understand why someone would squander such a good opportunity for a stable and lucrative future.

Abe's face slackened. "I told you. My father has too many expectations."

I didn't state the obvious—that his father probably expected his son not to gamble or associate with con men, let alone members of the unfortunate class, like me.

Abe slowed his pace. "My father's upset, so I'm on my own."

"What about my board?" I stopped walking. Abe turned to face me. "Will you be able to pay it?"

Abe grimaced. "I will as soon as I can," he mumbled. "It's going to take some time to establish myself with the new company. It's a good house, one of the larger ones in New York City."

I barely heard him. "I'll be kicked out if it isn't paid on time."

Abe took my hands in his and focused on me so intently I almost looked away. "I promise it won't be long."

I searched Abe's face. Was he sincere? Could I trust him? I was miffed, but I had faced much worse.

# 20

Abe had been gone again for two weeks, and Mrs. Brickley wanted her payment. I had held back a small amount of money, which I wanted to hold on to, but when I couldn't delay any longer, I dipped into my pocketbook.

Another week passed until Abe returned. He was sullen, pensive, and worn out. From long nights gambling more than drumming, I guessed, but didn't pry. Abe didn't say much when I asked about his trip. He had gone down to Texas, then to Alabama and Georgia before returning to Cincinnati, and didn't have much to show for his travels. He barely had enough money to cover my board. "I won't get my next commission for a few more weeks," he grumbled, "and it won't be much."

Abe was hardly home before he left again. While he was gone, I thought about going back to Chicago. Mrs. Williams would welcome me, but I had no prospects for marriage there. Surely Abe would see the error of not working for his father and regain his position. The notion brightened my clouded thoughts.

I went for a stroll in the main shopping district and browsed through the dress goods at H&S Pogue on Fifth Street, then ventured down to Fourth, Cincinnati's most fashionable promenade. It was more crowded. As I navigated through the pedestrians on the sidewalk and admired the storefronts, one sign caught my attention—"M. Rothschild & Co." I peered through the window. A man stood behind a counter showing a customer a lace sample. Was it one of Abe's brothers? I'd learned he had two—Jacob, who was seventeen years old, and Charles, who was twenty and managed this store. For a moment I toyed with the idea of going inside, but quickly thought better of it. It would be best for Abe to introduce me to Charles at the appropriate time.

Continuing down Fourth, I entered Shillito's. The four-story palace was as spacious and grand as Field and Leiter in Chicago. Clerks accosted me everywhere I turned, but I demurred. I didn't have any money to waste.

As I fingered the silks and cashmeres, I noticed a young woman nearby. She was careful not to give herself away, but I recognized the telltale signs. A woman who worked at a first-class house didn't dress or act in a way to draw attention to herself, but even a member of the unfortunate class who blends into society is always a little self-conscious, glancing around to see if anyone is watching her, for it might be a sign someone had become suspicious. We lived under constant fear of discovery and it showed up in our countenance, no matter how hard we tried to hide it.

*It wouldn't hurt to talk to her*, I thought, *to find out where she boards. Just in case.* Before I could change my mind, I approached her. "Excuse me, miss."

"Yes?" she replied, startled, and glanced around. No one was nearby.

"May I ask you a question?"

Her eyes grew wide. Would I expose her in the middle of the store?

"You needn't worry," I assured her. "I only want to ask where you board."

"Where I board?" she said warily.

"Yes."

She furrowed her brows. "Why do you want to know?"

"I arrived recently from Chicago and need to find a new place," I said, making my implication clear.

Eyeing me guardedly, she replied, "I'm at Frank Wright's at 180 Broadway, south of Sixth."

"A gentleman runs the house?"

She laughed softly. "Oh no, Miss Wright is a woman."

I didn't inquire any further. It was obvious from the young woman's dress that she boarded at a first-class parlor house.

"I'm Bessie. And you are?"

"Madeleine." Her voice was prettier than her face, but she had an abundance of rich brown hair, beautiful teeth, and an infectious smile.

"A pleasure to make your acquaintance," I said. "I assume Miss Wright accepts visitors during the afternoon?"

"Of course."

Without thinking, I said, "Please let her know I look forward to meeting her."

As soon as I said the words, I chastised myself. But after Madeleine and I parted, I reasoned that it was prudent to meet her madam. I thought I had left the life behind when I departed New Orleans with Abe, but I also didn't want to end up in the same situation as I had when I left Buffalo.

The next day I took a streetcar to Sixth and Broadway, near Bucktown, Cincinnati's rough Irish neighborhood. Madeleine had apparently informed Miss Wright of my visit, as the housekeeper who answered the door, a woman in her mid-twenties named Alice, immediately ushered me into a parlor.

At one end of the room, a gilt frame mirror hung above the mantel, reaching all the way to the ceiling. Oil paintings lined the walls, and two red velvet serpentine sofas topped with elaborately carved wooden scrolls faced each other in the middle of the room. The sofas sat atop an expensive carpet. A Rococo carved rosewood table stood along one of the walls. Plush chairs were grouped in pairs to allow for more private conversations between the women and their callers.

It didn't have quite the opulence of Mrs. Williams's house, but it was elegant enough. And it was much nicer than Mrs. Brickley's boardinghouse.

The door opened and Miss Wright swept in, followed by a Skye terrier. The dog's silky light grey hair skimmed the floor and flounced, mimicking the madam's dress as she moved across the parlor. I didn't expect her to be so close to my age or so unassuming. Miss Wright's dress and jewelry were tasteful. She wasn't dripping in diamonds like Miss Otis. She had flawless ivory skin and luxuriant black hair, swept back into the obligatory bun at the base of her neck. This madam could shop at Field and Leiter or Carson and Pirie and no one would be the wiser.

"Normally, I wouldn't have accepted your call," she said. "All my girls are recommended; but when Madeleine told me about you, I was intrigued. What is your history?"

Miss Wright nodded approvingly at the houses I'd been associated with in Chicago and New Orleans. We had a casual, easy conversation and I found myself accepting her invitation to board.

My room was exquisitely furnished with a four-poster mahogany bed, a chaise lounge, a washstand and basin, and a fireplace with a marble mantel. I slid my hand down one of the bed posts and sat on the plush mattress. I wasn't happy about living in a parlor house again, but I was glad to be in nicer surroundings. I'd grown used to the finer things in life and didn't want to do without them.

At supper, Miss Wright sat at one end of the dining table, her dog, Jewel, by her side. She was surrounded by several beauties and a gentleman. Joe, I soon learned, was Miss Wright's live-in lover. He kept everyone in line—the staff, the girls, and the callers—and called Miss Wright by what I assumed to be her real name, Louisa, not Frances or Frank, the name she'd assumed when she became a *demi-mondaine*. The real Frances Wright, known as "The Great Red Harlot" because of her many lovers, had been an abolitionist and one of the first women to speak out on the issue of equality, so the name suited our Miss Wright, given her defiance of a system that forced many women into our profession. Women like her and Lottie inspired me and gave me hope.

On my first night I helped entertain a small party of men, who were apparently well known to the other girls. The gentleman a young woman named Elsa had tethered herself to kept looking over at me, obviously bored with her. Elsa was buxom with a tiny waist, but cackled when she laughed, which made the man cringe.

No matter where I moved, I could feel his eyes boring into me. He wasn't particularly handsome. He had a high forehead, narrow-set eyes with pouches underneath, and thin lips.

The professor started playing a waltz. Elsa, apparently noticing her caller's glances, shot me a withering look and pulled him to join the dance.

Madeleine entered the parlor. I caught her eye and she crossed the room toward me. Though we were supposed to be entertaining our guests, I wanted to become better acquainted with her.

"My friends call me Mad," she said.

"You don't look insane," I replied wryly.

"You should talk to some of my callers." She winked and we both laughed.

She was not too far past the "titbit" stage, as newcomers to the business were called. Her parents had left France during the country's potato blight in 1847 and settled in Maryland.

"France had diseased potatoes too?"

"Yes, but I prefer to say my family came to America during the revolution of 1848," Madeleine confided. "It sounds more romantic."

I nodded toward Elsa. "Who's that gentleman?"

"Tom Snelbaker, our chief of police. His father was mayor of Cincinnati."

Of course. The police force here was as corrupt as all the rest. Usually, men of some importance didn't want to be seen in a parlor with other gentlemen, so they were discreetly escorted to and from a girl's room, the parlor doors locked when the gentleman arrived and when he left. But the police chief didn't seem to mind. He was enjoying the attention. I said a silent prayer that he wouldn't ask for my company and reminded myself that I wouldn't be here long.

# 21

"Bessie, you have a visitor," Alice, the housekeeper, announced one afternoon a week into my stay at the Mansion of Joy, as Miss Wright referred to her house. I straightened my dress and checked myself in the mirror before heading downstairs.

All week I'd gone back and forth on the wisdom of coming to Cincinnati, but when I entered the parlor, my reservations dissolved like sugar in warm water. Abe rushed to me, roses in hand. For a moment I was taken back to the barn, when Leslie had dropped the delphiniums onto the floor after I'd told him about my pregnancy. I brushed that thought away and accepted the flowers from Abe. "How were your travels?"

He sighed heavily and avoided my eyes. "It's going to take some time. I'm working on some orders."

"I'm sure it won't take long," I said brightly, but I felt the slightest bit of disappointment.

"I was surprised when I read your note," he said, perking up. "Your boarding here helps tremendously. I was worried about how I was going to pay both your board and mine."

That was it. No apology. No acknowledgment of the sacrifice I had made. A stone lodged in my chest. But somehow I maintained my composure.

"I'm not surprised you landed here," Abe went on with some pride. "Miss Wright runs the best house in the city." He eyed the elegant parlor.

"But," I started, then lowered my head.

Abe tilted my chin to meet his eyes. He seemed confused. "But what?" he said.

"I thought you were going to set me up... in a nice place."

He glanced around the room, waving his hand at the furnishings. "This is a nice place, isn't it?"

Yes, it was, but it was still a brothel, and I was paying my own board. When I didn't answer, Abe said, "Don't worry, I'll be making a lot of money soon. I just need some time."

I thought of the trip from New Orleans, the gambling debt, having to leave my trunk with the captain and pawn one of my rings. But Abe was so charming and persuasive, I knew he'd make a gifted salesman.

"All right," I said.

Abe grinned like the Cheshire cat. I lightly poked his chest with a finger. "But you better keep your promise."

I said it playfully, but I was serious.

Soon after I moved into Miss Wright's, Cincinnati played host to the Republican National Convention. The city's hotels had been booked for months, and the madams had planned well ahead for the influx of delegates and politicians from the thirty-seven states, the District of Columbia, and the territories. Working girls from other cities—Chicago, St. Louis, Indianapolis, Columbus, and Louisville—were already descending upon Cincinnati, inquiring about space at the parlor houses or setting up shop at a hotel.

By Sunday night, three days before the first gavel of the convention, the parlors and ballroom at Miss Wright's overflowed with men hungry for alcohol and flesh. Most of them had wives and daughters, sisters and nieces back home. Their relations would have been appalled to learn of their visitations to a brothel, but a man on the road often seems to forget what he has left behind.

The callers we entertained during the convention were no different than any other crowd, except they talked only of politics. Miss Wright and her staff took great care to make sure the supporters of one candidate didn't mingle with those of another. It was crucial not to allow any rows in a first-class parlor house, lest it earn a reputation as a rough place.

At first, delegates of the favored nominee, Speaker of the House James Blaine, numbered so many they could only fit in the largest parlor. But there were also supporters of New York Senator Roscoe Conkling; Secretary of the Treasury Benjamin Bristow; and Ohio's governor, Rutherford B. Hayes.

As we prepared for the onslaught, Alice called me downstairs. It was earlier than I expected, but I didn't think much of it. Miss Wright was waiting for me at the foot of the stairs. "There's a gentleman who's asked for you."

"Is it someone I know?" Miss Wright would have told me if it was Abe.

"I don't believe so. He's with one of the delegations. I don't think he's had much experience at a house, if any. But he asked for you all the same."

When I entered the parlor, a young gentleman was nervously pacing the Brussels carpet. I had never seen him before. His face lit up when he saw me.

"I met a young chap in the lobby at the Burnet House. He said if I was interested in going to the best parlor house in the city, he knew the best girl."

"How nice of him." I kept a cool exterior, but inside I fumed.

By the end of the week the delegates had rallied around Governor Hayes, and as quickly as they came, they left. I nearly collapsed from exhaustion. I pampered myself with a long, hot bath. When I returned to my room, the housekeeper had left a note. Abe awaited me downstairs. I took my time dressing. When I entered the parlor, Abe rushed over to me.

I crossed my arms.

"I thought you would be happy to see me," he said.

"Why did you send those gentlemen to me?"

"I was trying to be helpful, so you could make more money."

"I thought *you* intended to make more money so I wouldn't have to remain here," I shot back.

Abe gave me a sheepish look. "I'm sorry, I didn't know it would upset you."

Was he that daft? I gave him an incredulous look.

"Please forgive me. I… I don't know what I was thinking."

That was obvious.

"May I stay here with you this evening?" He pleaded with his eyes. "Please?"

I sighed. I had missed his company.

The next morning as Abe prepared to leave, he pulled out his wallet. Miss Wright had an arrangement with her boarders who had love interests. The man could stay one night a week without paying, but more than that and her cut was due. It was up to the woman to decide whether to take her payment as well.

"You don't need to give me any money," I said.

"I was just looking to see how much I have for Miss Wright," Abe replied. He flipped through his bills and turned to me. "I have enough, but it will take nearly everything for the moment. I'm leaving tomorrow to drum up more business. It should be a lucrative trip. In the meantime, would you mind if I borrowed some money? I'll pay you back as soon as I can."

I had made a small mint during the convention and I had been wanting a dress made by Selina Cadwallader, the most sought-after dressmaker in Cincinnati. Mrs. Cadwallader's tailoring had been compared to the House of Worth in Paris. Any woman who knew anything about fashion was familiar with Charles Frederick Worth. It would cost me a small fortune, but I would still have money left over.

I rose and went to the drawer in my vanity and pulled out the box in which I kept my earnings. "I can spare this much," I said as I handed fifty dollars to Abe. "But it will cost you," I added teasingly.

He smiled and pulled me onto the bed.

Madeleine went with me to buy the material for my dress. We could have gone to H&S Pogue or Shillito's to buy the fabric and lace I needed, but I wanted to shop at the store Abe's brother operated for their father. I knew I risked Abe's ire, but I was curious.

Inside, an array of silks, cashmeres, French tulle, and delicate Chantilly and Venetian laces was neatly arranged on shelves and in glass display cases. Madeleine and I waited while a salesman—Charles, I presumed—assisted another customer. He looked nothing like Abe. He was taller and slimmer. When he came over to us and asked what we were looking for, he sounded more refined than Abe, his voice not as deep as his brother's.

"I need fabric and lace for a dress," I replied.

"What kind?"

"An evening gown."

Charles showed me several samples of exquisite silk and satin. I chose gold Chantilly lace, thin gold satin ribbon, a French floral silk of miniature red-orange and yellow flowers on a pale gold background with pale blue vertical stripes, and a bolt of sapphire blue satin.

"To which address should I have this sent?"

"Please send it to Selina Cadwallader. Under the name Bessie Moore."

"Mrs. Moore?"

"No. Miss."

I'd held a tiny bit of hope Abe might have told his brother about me but there was no hint of recognition in his voice.

"You have a brother, do you not?" I blurted.

Madeleine's mouth dropped but she remained quiet.

"Why, yes, I actually have two brothers."

"I met a man by the name of Abe Rothschild, in Hot Springs, and I was wondering whether you might be related."

"I have a brother by that name," Charles said. "I don't know if he's been to the Springs, but I don't keep up with his travels."

After we left the shop, Madeleine and I giggled over my boldness.

When my dress arrived, it was more beautiful than I could have imagined. No one could see me in it and think me anything less than a lady of the utmost refinement. The dark blue satin matched my eyes perfectly. Mrs. Cadwallader had handcrafted a divided overskirt with the satin and gathered it in the back to form a bustle and train. The French floral silk formed the underskirt and capped-sleeve evening bodice. The gold Chantilly lace rimmed the low square neckline and the thin gold satin ribbon was threaded through the lace and tied into a small bow at the center of the bodice. The dress had cost me a small fortune. It was as pretty as any of the fashions illustrated in *Godey's Lady's Book*. I couldn't wait to show it to Abe.

"Do you like it?" I asked him when he came to see me upon his return. I turned around slowly in the parlor, like a queen on a dais, elbows at my waist, palms facing up.

"It suits you nicely," Abe said. I detected a hint of terseness but dismissed it as my imagination. I was thrilled with my purchase and the compliments I was receiving.

"Guess where I bought the material," I said slyly.

Abe's expression went blank for a moment, then his face hardened.

"I didn't say anything. I promise. Madeleine was with me and…"

My voice trailed off as Madeleine grabbed my arm and Abe's and pulled us into a quadrille. He remained tight-lipped as we danced and acted coolly toward me the rest of the evening.

When we retired to my room, the coolness turned to ice. "Why did you go to my brother's store?"

"Why does it matter? I've met your cousin."

"That's different."

I didn't understand, but decided it was better not to ask. I sat down at my vanity to remove my gloves.

"How much did the dress cost?" Abe demanded.

"It's no business of yours. I paid for it with *my* own money."

"You shouldn't spend so extravagantly."

I tossed my gloves onto the vanity. "You're one to talk. You dress as well as I do. Besides," I added, "I must have the proper clothes."

Abe glared at me in the mirror, then came over to me and grabbed my arm so forcibly I dropped the earring I had just removed from my ear.

"You think you're special now that you're the belle of Broadway?"

he sneered, his breath hot on my cheek. "I'm the reason you made as much as you did during the convention."

I wrested my arm from his grip. "How dare you. You have no idea what I have to do to survive."

I turned to face him. "We must entertain men who stink of whiskey and sweat, who leer at us and tell raunchy jokes in front of us, who treat us in ways that would horrify them if we were their sisters or daughters. As the night goes on they become drunker and uglier. They want us to do disgusting things… things I refuse to take part in, but some girls will because of the money or because they don't want to anger the madam."

I rose and so did my voice. "They want us to parade around in costly gowns, or naked, to dance for their entertainment. Not to mention the fines we have to pay, or God forbid, endure a raid and the public humiliation. We must hide and be discreet at all times."

My chest heaved with growing rage. "Do you know why most of us are here? Because we've been betrayed by the men who wanted to enjoy the pleasure of our company, who lead us down the primrose path, promising to defend our reputations, to marry us, but then abandon us because they're engaged or married to someone else. Then they claim they've never known us, or when they do admit their transgressions, they face no repercussions for having 'fallen.'"

Someone knocked on my door. I was obviously disturbing the house, but I didn't care. "We're accused of inviting our downfall. Men pay us attention, flatter us, and before we know it, we're living in the sewer of society. They come in and say, 'Oh, it is a pity you're in such a place. Is there no way to quit it?' When they're the ones who put us here!"

Abe didn't seem fazed by my tirade, which only enraged me more. "There are women here who've been deserted by their husbands and have no other means of support. I've known others who work in a house so they can take care of their ailing parents. It's always only the women who suffer. How dare you chide me for my spending when you gamble all your money away, when you have a wealthy father you can work for."

Abe's eyes hardened into a steely glare. "You know how I feel about my father."

I walked to my door and opened it, startling Alice. I ignored her.

"Get out," I said to Abe.

He stormed past us and I slammed the door shut.

# 22

"Send him away," I told Alice when Abe returned the next afternoon.

But he kept coming back. I sighed heavily when the housekeeper told me he wouldn't leave. "Tell him politely to go to the devil. I won't come downstairs." I started to close the door to my room but stopped. "On second thought, you don't need to be polite."

Not wanting to meet Abe on the street, I stayed inside the house until I thought I would go stir-crazy. After a week I was called down to the parlor early, and found Abe's cousin awaiting me. Had he come to engage me for the evening?

"You needn't worry," David rushed to say when he noticed my hesitation. "Abe asked me to come on his behalf."

"What a nice surprise," I said warily. I motioned to one of the sofas and saw a bottle and two glasses on a table.

"I took the liberty of ordering wine," David explained.

He took a seat and poured a glass for each of us. It didn't surprise me that he was so at ease. Many men treated brothels as social clubs. A visit to one was as much about having a good time laughing and drinking downstairs as it was about having fun upstairs in a bedchamber.

"Abe's quite taken with you."

"Oh?"

He leaned back into the plush cushions. "I'm afraid I've been a bad influence on him. Abe likes to have as good a time as I do." He chuckled. "Maybe even more than I do."

"Do you gamble as much as he does?"

"Does that bother you?"

I shrugged. How could I pass judgment when I slept with men for a living?

David may have come to smooth things over between me and Abe, but in that moment, I realized I had an opportunity. "Abe seems to have a difficult relationship with his father," I said.

"Maier is demanding, no doubt about it. So is my father." He sipped his wine. "Neither one of us can seem to meet their expectations." He said it without the bitterness Abe harbored.

"What happened?" Worried I might be venturing into forbidden territory, I said, "Forgive me for prying—"

David held up a hand. "No need to apologize." He swirled his wine, staring into the glass for a moment before continuing. "Maier wants Abe to work for him, but Abe feels his father is always criticizing him. Which he is. Abe always got into fights, didn't get good marks in school. His brother Charles, on the other hand, is the model son. Did well in school, never gets into trouble, doesn't go to saloons…" his voice trailed off.

"I see."

Miss Wright poked her head into the parlor to give me a look that told me it was time for the house to open.

"Would you like to stay for the evening? I can introduce you—"

"No, thank you, I must be going." David set down his glass and stood, as did I. "Will you give him another chance?"

I nodded. "Tell him to come see me tomorrow."

The next day Abe stood before me, more contrite than ever. "I shouldn't have been so cross with you."

I raised my chin. "I don't like anyone to tell me how I can and can't spend my hard-earned money."

"Neither do I." Abe placed his hands on my arms and gazed at me imploringly. "Will you please forgive me?"

I lowered my eyes. "I'm sorry I went to your brother's store. I…" I forced myself to look at him before proceeding. "Will we ever marry?" There, I'd finally said it.

Abe shifted his feet. His hands fell to his sides. "It's complicated."

"How? No one has to know about… my past. I'm sure David wouldn't divulge anything."

Then it dawned on me. Abe didn't want to introduce me to his family, not because of me, but because his father was disappointed in *him*.

Abe sighed and ran a hand through his hair. "I need some time. I'm making headway in my new position. And with my father."

I thought of what I had given up. I'd made a life in Chicago and New Orleans, but no matter where I lived, as long as I remained a *demi-mondaine*, it wouldn't last forever. I had garnered many jewels but no marriage proposals. It wasn't often someone in my situation met a young eligible bachelor from a wealthy family who frequented brothels and would be forgiving of transgressions like mine. Abe was a rare opportunity. And I did love him.

"If you need more time," I said softly, "I understand." I paused. "But I won't wait forever."

The next few months flew by. I kept my promise to myself and didn't bring up the topic of marriage again. I wouldn't broach the subject until after the New Year.

By the first week of December, the Ohio River was close to freezing over. Soon the steamboats would stop coming and going until spring. Abe was due back any day from his latest drumming trip.

After breakfast one morning, Miss Wright surprised me when she asked about Abe's whereabouts. When I told her, she responded with a harrumph.

"Why do you want to know?" I asked.

"He hasn't paid your room and board."

Abe had borrowed money from me several times, and each time he promised to pay my room and board in return, but apparently he had not kept up his end of the bargain. My stomach churned. "How much does he owe?"

"Seventy-five dollars."

I stifled a gasp. That was two months' board. I became nauseous. "I don't have that much right now. Abe has borrowed my money."

"Never you mind." Miss Wright's eyes held a steady glint. "I'll see Abe for it."

As I dressed for the evening, Abe stormed into my room.

"You can't go up there by yourself," Alice shouted from downstairs as Abe grabbed my arm.

"You told Miss Wright I took money from you?" he hissed. His breath reeked of whiskey. His eyes held a crazed glint.

"You're hurting me." I squirmed until I broke his grip. "I said you *borrowed* money."

"It's none of her business."

"It is when she's owed two months' board," I retorted. "When are you going to pay it?"

Abe's eyes darkened.

I smoothed my dress and said, "I have to work now."

Miss Wright appeared in my doorway. "What are you doing up here?"

"I'm leaving." Abe started to walk away but turned back to me. "We'll talk about this later."

*Yes, we will,* I thought, *and you're not going to like what I have to say.*

The house was quiet that night. I took some laudanum to calm my nerves but was still restless. Since I didn't have an overnight guest, I asked Miss Wright for permission to go out around eleven-thirty. I took a streetcar to Wielert's beer garden and pushed my way through the crowd, searching for Abe, but he wasn't there. Neither were any of his friends.

Discouraged, I left. It was too late to catch a streetcar, so I had to walk back to Miss Wright's. It was then I saw him, walking arm-in-arm with another woman. I quickened my pace to catch up to them and grabbed Abe's arm as I came alongside him. "What do you think you're doing?" I hissed through clenched teeth.

Abe stopped, startled by my presence.

"How dare you," I continued. "You come to my house and embarrass me and have the gall to consort with another woman."

The woman blanched and scurried off.

"Embarrass *you*?" Abe threw back at me. "You told Miss Wright I owed you money."

Abe continued onward. I followed close behind. He wasn't going to get away so easily from me. "When are you going to pay my board?"

Abe didn't answer.

"You're nothing but a liar," I said heatedly to his back.

Abe stopped short, turned toward me, and struck me, so hard that I fell to the ground.

"Stop! Leave her alone!" someone shouted. I peered up from the ground at the cigar boy from the Atlantic Garden.

As I struggled to stand, Abe pulled out his revolver.

"Don't you point that at me, Rothschild. I'll have you arrested." My rescuer couldn't have been more than twelve years old.

Abe withdrew his gun when he recognized the boy and yanked me up by my arm. We continued walking and arguing hotly, my cheek still smarting. The boy followed us to Miss Wright's, where he stood on the other side of the street, watching as Abe rang the bell. The second-floor window in the hall opened, and Miss Wright poked her head out.

"Go away," she shouted "You can't come inside. You've kept her out this long, you can keep her out 'til morning. I'll send a bill to make you pay for your fun." She slammed the window shut.

Abe stormed off, leaving me alone on the stoop. I glanced across the street. The boy had disappeared. Exhaustion crept over me as the opium took effect. I crouched down and leaned against the door, drifting off into the land of Morpheus. I dreamed my diamonds had fallen out of their prongs and I'd placed them in my jewelry box for safe keeping, but when I looked inside the box, they were all gone.

I jolted awake, freezing. I knew it was useless to try to gain entry to Miss Wright's, so I walked down the street to another parlor house where the madam took pity on me and woke one of her girls who didn't have an overnight caller. She gave me a nightgown and laid my clothes by the fire.

When I woke, it was nearly noon. As I dressed, I suddenly realized my hands were bare. I checked the nightstand, the small table next to the chaise, and the washbasin, but my rings weren't in the room. No one in the house had seen them. I rushed back to Miss Wright's with a sinking feeling.

"You know who took your diamonds," she said dryly when I told her what had happened. She peered at my face. "Did he hit you?"

I put a hand to my cheek. He must have left a mark.

Miss Wright insisted we summon a detective.

"Bessie, you mustn't let Abe take such advantage of you." Miss Wright was exasperated.

At first I refused, but in the end I gave in. I hesitated when the detective asked who had taken my rings.

"She knows who took them," Miss Wright said, "but she won't say. She's afraid he'll beat her."

"Miss Moore," the detective said, "I can't help you unless you tell me who stole your jewelry."

"But what if I can't prove he took them?" I cried.

"At least tell me who you think may have taken them, and I can talk to him and straighten this out," the detective cajoled.

I gave him Abe's address. The detective left for the Burnet House, and I sat at Miss Wright's, immobilized with fear. I still couldn't believe Abe had hit me. He had once protected me, but now he was treating me as if I were the enemy. It wasn't long before the detective returned. "He told me he had taken them for safekeeping," he said skeptically as he handed me my diamonds. "Do you wish to bring charges against Mr. Rothschild?"

I shook my head. I was thankful to have my jewels back but fearful over the potential consequences. Miss Wright didn't say anything, but I knew she wouldn't put up with Abe, or me, any longer.

I left the house and went to Weatherhead's drugstore. The pharmacist was waiting on a woman and a young girl at the soda fountain counter.

"What flavor syrup would you like with your medicine?" the pharmacist asked the girl.

"Raspberry," she said.

She was about ten years old, the age my Hannah would have been. I wondered what my little girl would have looked like now, how tall she might have been. She'd had my dark blue eyes, but as she grew older, would she have favored me or Leslie?

My sadness deepened. If only Leslie had married me, my daughter would be alive and not lying in an unmarked grave. Or if James had been willing to let me take her to Syracuse. I couldn't think of these things for too long or I'd go mad.

I browsed the shelves lining the store. I could have my pick of poisons—absinthe, belladonna, black cohosh, cannabis, morphine, opium. When the pharmacist was ready to assist me, I ordered a potassium bromide, a mild sedative, sat down at the soda counter, and stared out the window at the passersby. The initial bitterness of the medicine gave way to a sedated calm, but nothing could quench the growing bitterness I harbored toward Abe.

I considered my options. Staying at Miss Wright's wasn't one of them. If I went to another parlor house in Cincinnati, Abe could still easily find me. I needed to get as far away from him as possible. I would go back to Chicago.

Madeleine sat on my bed pouting as I packed. "You can't go," she whined. "Can't you stay and not see Abe?"

I sighed. Despite her time as a *demi-mondaine*, she was still quite naïve about the world.

"Will you come back?"

I stopped folding a dress. "I don't know." And I honestly didn't.

In Chicago I would collect myself and figure out what to do next.

After less than a year in Cincinnati, I left with only my clothes, the jewelry I had been able to hang onto, and my few remaining dollars.

# 23

I stared at the marble Clytie inside Mrs. Williams's home. I, too, had known the heartache of unrequited love. Clytie was lucky; she had become a flower. I had become a prostitute. An ineffable sadness filled me. I wanted to smash the statue to pieces.

"Bessie, you're here!"

A familiar voice shook me out of my reverie. Lottie bounded down the stairs and embraced me like a child who had missed her mother.

"We thought you were gone for good," she said.

I wanted to say I'd thought the same, but I didn't respond. Thankfully the door to Mrs. Williams's room opened, and I indicated to Lottie that we would talk later.

"My dear Bessie, how good to see you." Mrs. Williams surveyed me as if searching for the reason for my sudden appearance. I had sent her a letter from Cincinnati and gushed about my new life. I hadn't expected to be back in Chicago after a mere eight months.

"I'm sorry I didn't let you know beforehand about my arrival," I said.

"Not to worry," she assured me. "Let's go into the parlor where we can talk in private."

If anyone would understand my situation, it was Jennie Williams. She hailed from St. Louis, where she had married a man who had the prestigious job of mail agent with the Iron Mountain Railroad. When he was caught robbing the US mail and sent to the penitentiary, she moved to Chicago and became a successful madam.

"I'm glad you're here," she said after I told her about what had happened in Cincinnati. I was relieved when she welcomed me back into her home.

A week later, a letter from Abe arrived. I started to read his profuse apology, but it failed to move me, so I tucked the letter away in my vanity without bothering to finish it.

By ten o'clock that evening, the parlors were filled with the usual suspects: clerks, actors, and drummers. Some of the girls and their callers were singing a tune as the professor's fingers danced over the keys, and I was engaged in a boring conversation with a young clerk when the door to the parlor was flung open and in stepped two policemen.

"What is the meaning of this?" Mrs. Williams shouted. "I've paid my bribes."

The officers ignored her and proceeded to arrest everyone in the house. As the wagon pulled away, I could see that French Em's house was also being raided.

At the station, we were escorted past the strumpets of Little Cheyenne. They would be kept in cells while the rest of us *demi-mondaines* congregated upstairs, the only preferential treatment afforded to high-class prostitutes. As I started up the stairs, a familiar figure caught my eye. Mollie sat on a bench, her head lowered. I stood there for a moment hoping she would look my way, but an officer nudged me to keep walking.

After being charged with lewd behavior, I appeared before a judge and paid a fine of five dollars. Thankfully, I always kept money in my dress, and I was released immediately.

Two days later, I decided nothing would help put the humiliation of the raid behind me more than a shopping excursion to Field and Leiter. I could spend hours in the five-story marble palace at the corner of State and Washington. Dressed in my finest clothing, I mingled among the wealthiest of Chicago's high society, pretending—and almost convincing myself—that I was one of them.

It was a bright day and I lingered underneath the glass dome in the center of the store, basking in the warm light. I browsed the imported laces and embroideries, soft leather gloves, cashmere shawls, and exquisite delicate silks, and wandered through the upholstery department to see the latest French Gobelin tapestries, and to finger the silk satin damasks and cretonne fabrics.

I made my way to the hat section, where my favorite clerk was assisting another customer. He glanced at me but didn't acknowledge my presence. After the lady left, I approached to say hello, but he pretended to be occupied. Confused but undeterred, I said, "Good afternoon, Fred."

"Good afternoon, Miss Moore," he said rather curtly.

Puzzled, I hesitated for a moment. "What new hats have come in?"

Fred took off his glasses and set them on the counter. "Unfortunately, Miss Moore, I won't be able to assist you." A couple of women who had overheard him stared at me. I hoped they would walk away, but prurient curiosity kept them rooted to their spot.

"I… I beg your pardon?"

"I'm afraid no one here at Field and Leiter will be able to assist you anymore. Now please excuse me. Have a good day."

As Fred brushed past me, I couldn't resist the urge to stop him. "Have I done something wrong?"

He peered over his glasses with unmistakable contempt. "I suggest you read today's edition of the *Inter Ocean*," he said and turned on his heel.

I found the nearest newsstand, bought a copy of the paper, and rushed back to the house to read it. The news was dominated by the still-undecided and highly fought-over presidential election between New York Governor Samuel Tilden and Ohio Governor Rutherford B. Hayes. It seemed a lifetime ago that I had entertained delegates for the Republican National Convention. Then, on the last page, under "City Brevities," I saw my name listed with seven other girls "pulled from Jennie Williams's house of ill fame on Fourth Avenue." Of course, not a single gentleman caller's name had made the paper.

While it didn't matter to a madam whether her girls were exposed in such a manner—indeed, some viewed it as free advertising for their houses—and no one outside Mrs. Williams's sphere would know me on the street, it was still humiliating to see my name in print in this fashion.

As Christmas drew near, I still couldn't snap out of my dull mood, though the younger girls had bounced back quickly and were in good spirits, decorating the house with evergreen garlands and tinsel ornaments. Lillie tried to convince me to go with her to State Street to see the window displays at Field and Leiter, but I refused. I started a letter to Hannah but stopped. I couldn't lie and say things were going well, and I didn't want to tell her the truth.

The parlor houses were always closed on Christmas Day, so I decided to visit Mollie. I thought it would cheer us both up. When I rang the bell at her madam's house, no one answered. I rang again and waited. I was about to leave when the housekeeper, a disheveled woman with black circles under her eyes, finally opened the door.

"I'm here to see Mollie Stone," I told her.

She escorted me to the parlor, and a few minutes later, the madam presented herself. She didn't recognize me from my previous visit.

"You were a friend of Mollie's?"

"Yes," I said, alarmed by her use of the past tense. "Has something happened to her?"

"Mollie died early this morning."

I sank into a chair, in disbelief. The madam sat next to me and explained what had happened. One of the girls had found my friend in the bathtub, completely submerged, a bottle of laudanum on the bathroom floor. The girl's shrieks had brought the others out of their rooms and up from the parlor, along with the gentlemen they had been entertaining on Christmas Eve.

We went upstairs. Mollie had been placed on her bed, a blanket covering her body from the neck down. Her face was pale, her lips blue.

Still stunned, I couldn't cry. "Oh, Mollie," I murmured. "Why did you do this?" Guilt flooded me. I hadn't visited my friend as often as I should have. I hadn't done enough to prevent this from happening.

"It's not your fault," the madam said as if she'd read my conscience.

I looked at her beseechingly. "How did this happen?"

"She'd been drinking so heavily, she couldn't work. I told her if she didn't stop, she would have to leave. But after the raid she grew more and more despondent. Last night, after entertaining one guest, she came down to the parlor and asked if she could have some time before coming downstairs again. I didn't know why."

Every girl dreads being kicked out by a madam. Mollie had already been asked to leave Mrs. Williams's house. Being forced to leave another would have put her on the street, a place no girl wanted to be. How long would it be before I found myself in the same situation?

I suddenly remembered that when my da died, my brother William had opened a window to let out Da's spirit. He told me that even though we loved our da very much and didn't want him to go, it wouldn't be fair to keep his spirit here, that he needed to go to Heaven. I rushed to the window to do the same for Mollie. I hoped I wasn't too late.

"What are you doing?" the madam cried as cold air rushed in.

Gazing out the window at the snow-covered ground, I said, "Her spirit needs to be released." When I turned back to her, she regarded me as if I had gone completely mad, but I pressed on. "The window must remain open for two hours. Afterwards, it must be closed so her spirit won't try to come back."

My friend deserved to finally be free.

I, too, wanted freedom, but not through death. A chill came over me and I shuddered as if someone were walking over my grave.

# 24

I muddled through the next few days under a thick cloud of grief, Mollie never far from my mind. My mood further plummeted as New Year's Eve approached. Another year gone by and I was no closer to leaving this sordid life. I was becoming an old maid, a year older, a year closer to being out on the street.

A sudden desire to go to Mass overcame me. The other girls rolled their eyes whenever I went, which was not often, with my gold cross and chain untucked from beneath my collar and proudly displayed on my dress. There was an unwritten rule among fallen women that religion was taboo; not because they didn't believe in it, but because they considered it bad luck to mix religion with their profession. Superstition ran high among the *demi-mondaine*. In Watertown, Mollie and the other girls would spit on a man's back if he left the house without spending any money on them. I considered myself lucky if all I had to do was drink with a caller and not have to go to bed with him.

Whenever I attended Mass, I felt a sense of calm I didn't feel anywhere else. I was a world away from my life as a courtesan, though I never took communion, not being in a state of Grace. Inside the Cathedral of the Holy Name, I dipped a finger in the bowl of holy water, made the sign of the cross, and approached a pew in the back.

My knees had barely hit the kneeler when a bell rang twice, and everyone rose.

Afterwards, wanting to enjoy the beauty and stillness of the majestic cathedral, I remained seated as the other parishioners departed. When I rose to leave the pew, I saw a priest enter a confessional. I hadn't made a confession since Buffalo, and even then I'd done so only half-heartedly. The weight of my guilt over the life I lived had been pressing down on me for so long I didn't know how to get out from under it. Confession could be a first step. I approached the confessional with trepidation. Inside, I knelt on the hassock. A wooden panel with a grate at eye level was all that separated me from the priest on the other side.

"In the name of the Father, and of the Son, and of the Holy Ghost," I said, making the sign of the cross.

"The Lord be in thy heart, and upon thy lips, that thou mayest worthily and rightly confess thy sins," the priest responded.

I took a deep breath. "Forgive me, Father, for I have sinned. It's been ten years since my last confession."

"What sins have you committed, my child?"

"My sins are numerous, Father. I have sinned against the sixth commandment. I'm… an inmate at a parlor house."

When he didn't respond, I grew anxious.

"I see," he finally said. "Do you want to leave this life of sin?"

"Yes, Father."

"Why do you not leave?"

Heavy silence descended on the confessional like nightfall.

"I can't absolve you of your sins until you do what is required," the priest said.

Turmoil filled my mind as I left the cathedral. I needed to find a way out, but I also needed to make sure I could live on my own without ever having to resort to this line of work again. Every caller, instead of allowing me to dress well and live in luxurious surroundings, would bring me one step closer to my goal of rejoining respectable society. Once I had enough money, I would become a shop girl, wear plain clothes, and live in a proper boardinghouse. My upcoming sojourn to New Orleans suddenly took on a new purpose, and I immediately felt a weight begin to lift off my shoulders.

Two days before my departure, I was packing when the butler informed me I had a visitor.

"Who is it?" I said.

"He didn't want to say. I haven't seen him before."

*Could it be? Did I want it to be Abe?*

I went to my vanity, sat down, and brushed some stray wisps of my hair into place. When I was finished, I set the brush down and stared into the mirror. I had a few lines but hadn't lost my looks. I leaned closer to the mirror. Did my face bear any signs of the scarlet brand? The eyes peering back at me showed a sadness and weariness, but I didn't think my countenance exposed the sins of a soiled dove. I had never emblazoned my shame to the outside world. But time wasn't on my side. If it was Abe waiting for me downstairs, it wouldn't hurt to see him, I reasoned. If my feelings hadn't changed, I could send him away and never see him again.

Downstairs, I stood in front of the parlor door and braced myself. When I entered, I stopped, taken aback at Abe's appearance. He was more disheveled than I'd ever seen him: rumpled clothes, sallow complexion, dark circles beneath his eyes. My heart tugged ever so slightly.

He rushed over to me and took my hands in his. "I'm a sorry wretch. Can you forgive me?"

I remembered how valiant Abe had been when he rescued me from Pug, how he had protected me from George Ellis, how my life had seemed richer, more vibrant during the good times, and, just like that, my anger melted away. I fell into his arms, sobbing. He took me in his arms, and I laid my head on his chest. When my tears had subsided, he whispered, "Marry me."

I froze. I was expecting an apology, not a proposal. But hadn't I longed for this moment? I pulled away. The hard edge so frequently evident in Abe throughout my last few months in Cincinnati was gone, replaced by a disarming softness. Was he sincere? How could I know for sure?

"I have to go to Texas for business," Abe said. "Come with me. We'll get married."

His intense gaze made me feel lightheaded. I lowered my head. "I don't know. It's so… sudden."

He raised my chin so that I met his gaze. "I've missed you. I love you."

When I told Mrs. Williams, she tried to change my mind. "Are you sure? Men can't hide their faults forever."

"He can provide for me better than a hack driver or deckhand."

"Those other choices might be better than someone who mistreats you."

I recited an oft-repeated Irish saying: "Better the trouble that follows death than the trouble that follows shame." I'd never fully understood the phrase, until now. "Besides, Abe's promised me he will never act in such a manner again."

Mrs. Williams gave me a dubious look. "Your family would never accept you marrying a Jew."

"You don't know my family," I retorted. "Besides, wouldn't it be less shameful to be married to *someone*, no matter their religion, than to be a whore?"

"You could work in a factory."

"For small wages and a destitute existence," I shot back. "Or I could be some family's slave, if anyone would hire me. What kind of reference could I give to gain such employment? If I managed to obtain a position, if my past were revealed, I'd be out on the street quicker than I could pack my trunk."

Still, Mrs. Williams persisted. "I'm afraid you're headed for a Pyrrhic victory. You know why he keeps coming back for you. He doesn't love *you*, he loves your diamonds, and the value of your body to other men. When he gets your diamonds—and he will, mark my words—what will you have left to give? Only your body, paid for by strangers, so he can continue to live the lifestyle he wants."

I shook my head. Abe wanted to marry me. He might be the black sheep, but he came from a respectable family. He wouldn't want his wife to continue in the profession, and he need never tell his family about my past.

"If you insist on going, at least leave your jewels here," Mrs. Williams urged. "If he loves you, it won't matter whether you have them with you or not."

I appreciated her offer but refused it. "They're safest with me," I said.

# 25

The house was quiet the night before our departure. It was midweek and the bitter weather kept most Chicagoans indoors. The stores along State Street were deserted, except for those wealthy women conveyed door-to-door for their shopping excursions.

Some of the girls, jealous about my engagement, pouted and whispered among themselves. A few offered heartfelt congratulations. Mrs. Williams was polite. She opened a bottle of champagne in our honor.

The morning of our departure, I found myself alone downstairs. I walked over to the Clytie, kissed her marble cheek, and said giddily, "You silly girl."

When the train reached Danville midafternoon, my senses were heightened from the anticipation and excitement rushing through my veins. The frigid air only invigorated me more. I hooked my arm in Abe's as we left the depot.

A hack took us to the Aetna House, a stately two-story red brick hotel. At the registration desk, Abe asked the clerk to summon someone to marry us.

The clerk was flabbergasted. "How soon do you wish to be married?"

"As soon as possible. We're leaving on the early morning train." Abe smiled at me, and I beamed back at him.

While Abe tended to the arrangements and the hotel staff tidied the parlor, I readied myself in our room. I had worn my best traveling habit, a natural form brown and black silk dress with gold fringe and gold ribbons on the front, and elaborate braiding with tassels on the back. I had considered wearing my blue satin gown, but it was tainted with the memory of our argument over my visit to his brother's store.

A muffled voice from the other side of the door announced that everything was ready. I took one last look in the mirror and headed downstairs. In the parlor, Abe and I were introduced to the Justice of the Peace. My hands grew clammy inside my gloves, but Abe didn't appear nervous at all. He grinned and it calmed the butterflies flitting around my belly. As we said our vows, I pushed any doubts I had to the back of my mind. Our rocky past was behind us; the future gleamed with exciting possibility.

Afterwards, as I repacked for our trip, there was another knock at the door. This time it was a reporter with the *Danville News*.

"How did you know about our wedding?" I asked, surprised.

"I make it a habit to visit the clerk to find out if anyone interesting is in town, and he told me."

He asked where we hailed from and what our plans were and was disappointed that we weren't going to spend any more time in Danville. He offered his congratulations and bid us a fond farewell.

That night I slept more peacefully than I had in a long while.

The next afternoon our train rumbled through East St. Louis, Illinois, a flat expanse dotted with smoky factories and dusty stockyards, and crossed the new bridge connecting the railroads over the Mississippi to St. Louis, Missouri.

The Eads Bridge stood two stories high atop three graceful steel arches. Carriages, horses, and pedestrians traversed the top deck. The lower deck was reserved for trains. Below the bridge, dozens of steamboats lined the cobblestone levee. Past the levee, a sea of red brick rooftops extended toward the horizon. At the edge of the bridge, along the west bank of the Mississippi, the train dipped into a tunnel. We traveled in near darkness underneath the city, skimming the brick-lined walls before emerging into the waning daylight.

Inside the depot, a blur of travelers rushed here and there. A potpourri of cultures crossed paths at St. Louis—new immigrants from Europe, Asia, and Africa; traveling salesmen and other sharply-dressed businessmen; young men heading west for adventure and holding tightly to their gripsacks; country girls bewildered by the clamor and confusion. Nearly all of them were passing through, on their way south to Arkansas and Texas, or west to California, or to the newest state, Colorado.

My mind and heart felt as clear as the Midwestern sky. An omnibus took us to the Southern Hotel, St. Louis's finest, a six-story, block-long behemoth. Roaming between the potted plants in the white marble lobby were the high-class courtesans I'd heard about from girls who'd worked in St. Louis. They were what the "working girls" in the city aspired to, but you didn't dare try to enter their domain unless you had superb manners and handled yourself impeccably. You also needed protection from the city's highest officials. If I lived in St. Louis, I would have counted myself among these girls. Not anymore. I was a wife.

We dined next door, at the famed Tony Faust's Oyster House, stuffing ourselves with caviar, oysters, and quail over sauerkraut. The champagne and my new life made me giddy.

The next day we joined all the shoppers on the crowded downtown street. With all the hustle and bustle I didn't notice the three gilded metal balls hanging outside the store Abe took me to. But, catching a glance at the sundry clutter of goods in the window as we entered, I realized we were at a pawn shop. I didn't ask what we were doing there as we browsed the aisles of unredeemed goods: cloaks, gowns, books, pistols, a violin, an assortment of household items.

I stopped to admire a diamond and sapphire necklace at the jewelry counter, then found Abe toward the back of the store where a haggard-looking clerk was negotiating the price of a music box with its owner. I pitied this woman, most likely a domestic servant based on her attire, having to sell something obviously precious to her.

"Sir, I'm a widow. Without the money I need, my children won't be able to eat," the woman pleaded with the clerk.

The man, unmoved by her story as he no doubt heard similar ones dozens of times a day, responded flatly, "Madame, a dollar and fifty cents is all I can loan you for this piece."

The woman sighed heavily, relinquished the music box, and tucked the money into her dress.

The clerk turned to Abe. "How may I help you?"

Abe motioned to me. As I moved toward him, Abe turned back to the manager and said, "I would like to know how much you would loan for a couple of valuable diamond rings."

I stopped and stared at Abe. "I want to see what they would fetch," he said quietly. "Just curious."

I didn't take the last step to the counter. My husband's eyes flashed with impatience, but I didn't budge. He moved toward me. I took a step back.

"Bessie."

"If the lady doesn't—"

"She's my wife," Abe snapped to the clerk, his eyes still locked on mine. In one swift move, Abe stepped to me and grabbed my left hand. He pulled me to the counter and thrust my hand toward the man. "You can see the quality of the solitaire," Abe said.

The clerk nodded and jotted something down.

Abe let go of my hand and took the other one, pointed to the cluster of seven diamonds in my other ring. The man hastily scribbled a number on the paper and handed it to Abe. He read it and put it in his pocket without showing it to me.

"What do you think you're doing?" I demanded once we were outside. I didn't care who might hear us.

Abe's demeanor turned to one of amusement, which only infuriated me.

"Do you have a gambling debt you need to repay?" I hissed. Without waiting for him to respond, I said, "You can't have my diamonds!"

"Oh, yes, I can." He smirked. "We're married now. They're joint property."

My husband turned on his heel and, as he receded into the crowd, the full import of his words sank in. I was a possession, like my jewels. My independence, my control over my life had been taken from me the moment I said, "I do."

# 26

stood on the sidewalk, immobilized, as people rushed past me. Perhaps I had overreacted, perhaps Abe was only being pragmatic. He hadn't sold my diamonds, he'd merely expressed an interest in their worth. But a pawn shop would only give a tenth of their value. No one pawned jewelry unless they had no other choice.

I remembered how Abe had pried my rings off my hands when I fell asleep on Miss Wright's stoop. How quick I was to forget and forgive. My rationalization gave way to an unsettled wariness. A man thought he owned a woman the minute she became his wife. I had been on my own, in control of my life, more independent than most women, though it came with a price. Yet here I was. With trudging feet and heavy heart, I headed back to our hotel.

Abe didn't come back to our room until early the next morning. His breath reeked of whiskey. The headiness of getting married, of being a newlywed, and of everything a woman dreamed would come with marriage had melted away, leaving a coldness between us. The pawn shop visit cooled our ardor like a sudden, unexpected frost.

It would take two days to reach our destination in Texas. As we settled into the Pullman lounge car to read after dinner, I broached another subject. "I can't wait to finally meet your parents," I said tentatively.

Abe looked up, startled. "My parents? Absolutely not."

"Why wouldn't I meet your parents? We're married now."

"They'll ask too many questions."

"You needn't tell them about my past."

"It's not only that."

Anger welled, but I calmed down when I realized what his reason must be. "Is it because I'm a Gentile?"

Abe's reaction indicated he hadn't considered religion as a factor. "I'm not on the best of terms with my father. I've told you so."

After several moments of awkward silence Abe said, "I wanted to wait until after this trip, but I might as well tell you now." He paused. "You've made a name for yourself. We can capitalize on it."

He talked to me as if he were discussing a business deal, not a future with his wife.

"It will take a bit of time, but you can stay with me at the Burnet until we find a house to run. I—"

"A house to run?" I interrupted, my voice shrill, rising panic within me. "You mean a parlor house?" A passenger nearby glanced at us. My eyes narrowed as I lowered my voice. "Are you suggesting I… we… run our own brothel?"

Abe snapped his book shut. "Why not? You've shown you can make a good living."

"I married you so I could *leave* the business."

There were many madams who were married or pretended to have a husband to use as a "front." Miss Wright's longtime lover lived at the house with her, but I didn't want to follow in her footsteps.

"I don't know what all the fuss is about," Abe said, curling his bottom lip.

I folded my arms and stiffly leaned back in my chair. "I won't do it."

Abe remained unperturbed. "You're my wife now, you have to do as I say."

*Wife.* I thought being married would mean safety and security, protection and love, not being treated as a possession. I didn't want someone to lord over me. I saw now that I had more rights as a single woman than as a married one. Being forced to remain entrapped in a dishonorable life as a married woman was too high a price to pay.

I wrestled with my thoughts most of the night, until the rhythmic click-clacking and swaying of the train as it raced along the tracks lulled me to sleep near dawn.

When we arrived in Marshall, Texas, the weather was dark and gloomy, with near-freezing rain transforming the dirt streets into a carpet of mud. A hack took us to the Capitol Hotel on the town square.

"We're pleased to have you with us again, Mr. Rothschild." The proprietor acknowledged me. "And welcome to you as well, Mrs. Rothschild," he said as he handed Abe our room key and a newspaper. "I'll have your trunk brought up. Please let me know if there's anything we can do for you while you're here."

When we reached our room, Abe rushed right out. "I'm going to drum up some business," he announced. I didn't believe him, but I wanted to be alone. While he was gone, I lay in bed staring out the window at the courthouse across the square. I was a newlywed, married for only six days, and already I regretted my decision to accept Abe's proposal. But what could I do?

Restless, I picked up the *Tri-Weekly Herald* Abe had left in our room. The controversy over the presidential election was still ongoing, with the Democrats declaring New York Governor Samuel Tilden the winner, and the Republicans closing in on the electoral vote, with a few states still undecided. The popular actress Katie Putnam was starring in "Lena, the Madcap" at Mahone's Opera House. I briefly considered asking Abe if we might go but thought better of it.

In the next column on the same page, a man in Concord, New Hampshire had been hanged for poisoning his wife. The story included a heart-wrenching letter the man wrote to his two young children the night before his date with the noose. Mrs. Williams's parting words flashed through my mind. Abe was rash, but he wasn't a murderer.

Abe returned surprisingly cheerful. At supper in the hotel dining room, he acted as if nothing had happened between us in St. Louis or on the train.

"I've been thinking," he said as he ate his meal voraciously. "Cincinnati may not be the best place to open a house. My father owns a dozen homes in the city, but I couldn't rent one from him for our purposes." He wiped his mouth with his napkin. "I think we should settle in New Orleans."

I put down my knife and fork, my appetite gone. "I told you, I won't do it."

"You're being unreasonable."

"I'll tell your father of your intentions." I crossed my arms and held them close to my chest, a shield.

Abe's eyes darkened. "You will do no such thing."

I met his icy stare.

Back in our room, I said I had a headache and was going to bed. Abe grabbed his coat and left again. I hoped he would be gone all night.

# 27

At the train station the next morning, Abe announced his intention to stop in Jefferson on business before we headed back to Cincinnati. I kept my head down. I had cried all night and now shed more tears. We had barely spoken since dinner, and we didn't speak to each other the entire ride to Jefferson. By the time we arrived, I had devised a plan. When our train to Cincinnati reached Texarkana, I would disembark and find my way to the nearest steamboat landing. From there I would go to New Orleans. If that didn't work out, I would go home to Canton. Any humiliation I might suffer would be better than staying in a sham marriage.

A hack driver loaded my trunk onto his omnibus and took us to the Brooks House, a Victorian-style hotel with long galleries along the front and gables atop the roof. A Catholic church stood across the street. Perhaps I would go to Mass on Sunday. It always lifted my spirits.

We were assigned room number four on the second floor. The manager said he would have someone bring my trunk up to our room. When he added, "Welcome to Jefferson, Mr. and Mrs. Monroe," I wondered if Abe had yet another unpaid gambling debt.

The chambermaid brought towels and a pitcher of water. She kept asking questions, and although I didn't want to be alone with Abe, I didn't want anyone else in our room, either. When she left, it was all I could do to hold my tongue about his plans. I didn't want to eat, so Abe went to supper alone.

When he came back to the room, he acted tetchy. He'd obviously been drinking. I braced myself.

"I hope you've changed your mind about our plans," he said.

"*Our* plans?" I retorted. "I have not."

My answer brought a torrent of curses while Abe paced the floor. I burst into tears again at his hatefulness.

"I'll leave you," I managed through my sobs.

Abe waved a hand dismissively. "Go, damn you, go!"

"How could you do this to me?" I wailed. "I'll tell your father."

Scowling, Abe grabbed me and yanked me close to him. His eyes were filled with hate.

"You bitch, I thought I made myself clear," he said, then pushed me away and stormed out.

The next morning, Abe again acted as if nothing had happened. Puzzled, I brushed it off. We walked to the business district and browsed the stores. Everywhere we went the townspeople noticed us. I didn't want anyone to see my misery, so I played the part of the happy spouse. Abe obliged, and played the doting husband. We could both put on a convincing show when necessary.

While Abe went to a hardware store, I walked to the steamboat landing. A steep embankment led down to the bayou. I stood at the top, taking in the greyness of the bayou, the turbid sky, the soaked moss hanging from the cypress trees like heavy sacks of flour. Everywhere I looked, I saw shades of grey. My honeymoon had turned sour. It was just as well the world matched my mood.

My eyes were drawn to the bridge spanning the bayou at the edge of the turning basin. Abe was crossing it, walking away from town. He could keep going as far as I was concerned.

I left the landing and ventured to Forgotston and Ripinski's on Austin Street. "Purveyors of Fine Clothing and Shoes," the sign read. As I browsed, a young boy followed me. He couldn't have been more than five or six years old. I didn't want to embarrass him, so I pretended not to see him.

"May I help you?" The salesman's question made the young boy jump, and he ran out the door. When I left the store, the boy was lingering outside. He wouldn't approach me. I smiled. He cast his eyes downward and shuffled his feet.

Sunday, January 21 was a dreary day marked by a constant drizzle and a cold wind from the north. Abe said he was going to hire a buggy, why I didn't know. But, after a short time, he returned, agitated. When I asked him what was wrong, he only shook his head and grumbled something indecipherable as he paced the length of our room. His nervousness made me anxious. I wanted to go to Mass but decided against it.

We left the Brooks House around ten and walked to a restaurant next to the steamboat landing on Dallas Street. When Abe ordered two beers, I protested. "I don't want any," I said. He ignored me. I fidgeted with my rings.

A woman carrying a pitcher stopped at our table. "Goot morning," she said. She studied Abe for a moment and said something to him in German. He didn't acknowledge her.

The woman turned to me. "Vere are you from?"

"New Orleans," I said quietly. Abe glanced at me.

"Ah, vat a lovely city," the woman said. "I enjoyed my visit zere."

I didn't respond, and neither did Abe. After an uncomfortable silence, the woman said, "Vell, enjoy yourselves," and moved on.

The waiter brought our beers, and Abe opened his bottle. I didn't want anyone to see my hands shaking, so I asked the waiter to open mine. He regarded me curiously but opened the bottle.

After a few minutes of strained silence, Abe stood and said he would return soon. When he came back, he had a package wrapped in newspaper. "We're going on a picnic."

It was drizzling and we didn't have an oilcloth to sit on. But before I could protest, he hailed our waiter and ordered two more beers. "I don't want another," I said, but Abe continued to ignore me.

When the waiter brought the bottles, Abe headed toward the door. I grabbed my coat and rushed after him. Another customer left at the same time, walking close enough behind us to hear any conversation, so I remained quiet.

When we reached the bridge by the steamboat landing, I hesitated. "Where are we going?"

"There's a nice spot where we can eat our dinner."

About half a mile south of town we stepped into the woods near a pine tree felled by lightning. We walked up a small hill, my boots sticking in the muddy red clay. I couldn't fathom why on earth we were going on a picnic in such conditions.

"I thought you might like this view," Abe said when we reached the top.

I relaxed a bit. Through the bare trees, we could see the bayou. I had to admit it was lovely. We seated ourselves on a large flat rock by an oak tree to shield us from the light rain. I stretched out my legs and crossed them at the ankles. The tips of my mud-caked boots poked out from underneath the layers of my dress.

Abe pulled two chicken sandwiches and a jar of pickles from the package he'd brought and handed me a sandwich. A white-throated sparrow landed on a bare branch overhead and chirped as we ate in silence. I glanced at Abe, wanting to dispel the uneasiness between us, but he kept his eyes on his meal.

When we finished eating, Abe stood and walked to a nearby tree stump, where he set down his beer bottle and stared out at the landscape. He was far away, off somewhere in the brooding recesses of his troubled mind. He turned to me, brow furrowed, and started pacing, then stopped abruptly. "Why did you have to threaten to go to my father?"

I stared at him, not wanting another argument.

"I can't..." he trailed off. For a moment he seemed torn about something. His jaw set as if he'd come to a decision. "I can't take the risk."

I blinked back tears. "What do you mean?"

Abe strode over to me. His pant leg brushed my dress. I searched my husband's glowering face for clues as to what he meant. Church bells tolled in the distance. I wished I'd gone to Mass.

Above, a murder of crows cawed.

Abe raised his arm and a glint of metal flashed in the grey light. I screamed and threw up my hands. A dagger-like pain stabbed my left temple as my back hit the ground with a thud.

# 28

At first I couldn't feel anything, couldn't see anything. There was only darkness. Then a light appeared. It slowly brightened, dulled, intensified again. A figure moved toward me, a blurred shadow. As the figure drew closer, its edges became sharper. My da, young and healthy, stretched out a hand. But a movement below drew my eyes downward.

My body lay on the ground, blood trickling down my cheek. I saw Abe now running down the hill, though, before he did, he had taken care to place my black velvet hat over the bullet hole in my head. I looked at my da again. His hand was still outstretched, but I couldn't go to him. I had to stay to make sure Abe didn't get away with my murder. And so I willed myself to resist the forces beckoning me.

My body had to remain recognizable, no matter how long it took for someone to find it, and so I stayed to guard my corpse. He'd taken my life before I could redeem myself. Now I wanted his.

I hovered where the tall pines met the sky, on the lookout for anyone who would venture up the hill. The winter rain soon turned to snow again and then stopped; the quiet stillness was broken only by sounds of the natural world. In my new state, I sensed any predator long before it appeared. Whenever a buzzard, hog, or sparrow ventured too close, I swooped down and encircled the offender with a ferocity that stirred the wind, rustled the trees, and darkened the woods.

I waited fifteen days.

When melting snow dripped from the trees, the door to a cabin at the bottom of the hill opened. A woman stepped outside to gather kindling, singing as she foraged in the woods. She nearly stumbled over my body. I moved closer, near enough to hear her heart pound, each beat mingling with the sound of a nearby brook running fast after the thaw. Perhaps she thought I was taking a nap. Then she saw the maggots wriggle around my eyes and mouth and the tinder in her arms tumbled to the ground.

It wouldn't be long now.

Soon I heard the creaking wheels of a wagon come to a halt at the bottom of the hill. A party of five men approached the small clearing where my body lay.

One of the men knelt and removed my hat. "I'll be damned," he muttered.

I recognized the stocky, bearded man.

"What a shame," another man with a long face and walrus mustache said.

The bearded man's head jerked up. "You saw her too?"

The man with the long face nodded. "She was with a fellow who tried to rent a buggy from me."

"Is that so?"

"I didn't let him have it, John. Couldn't figure why a fellow would want to take a lady for a ride in the rain. He left in a huff. Later, I saw them walking toward the bridge."

An elderly man wearing eyeglasses knelt by my head and probed my wound. "She didn't kill herself. Bullet's angling downward." He leaned in closer. "She was shot at close range."

A gloved hand touched my corpse. I knew what the men were looking for, but my fingers, ears, and neck were all bare. The older man laid his hand across my stomach. My abdomen was bloated, like a balloon about to burst.

"Any idea how long she's been here?" John asked. His voice was authoritatively gruff.

"More than a few days." The doctor picked up my arm and jiggled it. "There's no sign of rigor mortis."

"Is it possible she's been here a couple of weeks?"

*Yes!* I screamed. But of course no one could hear me.

"Sure," the doctor said. "The ground's cold, her body's cold, we've had snow…"

The men gathered the remnants of my last meal that I had so carefully guarded from nature's predators: an empty, amber-colored beer bottle on a stump, another on the ground, chicken bones, pieces of pickle, breadcrumbs. They waded through the brook and the thick growth of northeast Texas timber, searching under rocks and between crevices, but they didn't find the gun Abe so callously used to snuff out my life.

As the winter sunlight waned, John covered my body with a wool blanket and carried me to the wagon. The woman who'd found me as she gathered kindling was long gone.

The horses started moving, and the wagon lurched forward. I hovered above as my corpse was taken back to town, not to a deadhouse next to a church, but to a cold storage room behind a dry goods store, where the men placed my body on a long wooden table.

Word spread that a woman's body had been found in the woods

across the bayou, and curious townspeople lined up to see me. They were kept waiting as a photographer set up his clunky accordion-like camera and took pictures of my body. After the photographer left, John ushered in the curious folk.

The room quickly filled. As an older gentleman crossed the room, he moved to avoid someone and bumped into me. I felt a sudden jolt, like the first spark when flint meets firesteel. Taken aback, I pulled away. But curiosity replaced my surprise. I followed the man and let my spirit touch him again. At first, I thought I was imagining things. But I could actually feel his thoughts, see his visions. He was remembering his recent journey from nearby Marshall to Jefferson. He had witnessed me crying in the waiting room at the train depot and wondered why I was so bereft.

I moved among the respectfully hushed crowd, touching each person, experiencing their sympathies, and speculations: "Poor child… can't believe she's dead… of course it was that man she was with… so beautiful… he's long gone, I'm sure." Some of them talked to John and shared their stories of seeing me in town.

"I was having breakfast at Kate's place and noticed them as soon as they came in," one man told John. "They hardly spoke to each other. The woman kept looking down at her hands and fidgeting with her rings."

"Did they order anything?" John asked.

"Two beers."

John's eyebrows shot up. "That early?"

"Yes, but the woman didn't want any. She seemed really nervous."

"Were they quarreling?"

"Couldn't tell. But she was upset. The man left and came back with a package wrapped in newspaper and ordered two more beers. I left when they did."

"You followed them?" John turned his head and spit a thin rivulet of tobacco into a nearby spittoon.

"To the bridge. They crossed it and entered the woods. It was raining that morning and I thought it odd to go for a walk."

This man, the last person to see me alive, had sensed something wasn't right. If only he had followed us farther.

When the room cleared, four women began the unenviable task of undressing me. They carefully removed my black woolen coat, Moroccan leather boots, black silk overskirt, grey silk dress, white chemise, and white flannel underskirt.

One of the women, clad in the plain homespun dress of a farmer's daughter, lingered over the rich fabric of my clothing, running a fingertip over the elaborate braided trim on my coat. To my surprise, it didn't bother me to watch them disrobe my body. It was only an empty vessel. My fury wasn't in my flesh, it was in my soul.

The woman who'd caressed my clothing leaned over my garter. As she started to remove it, she noticed a pin I had used to fix a broken hook and paused. She glanced at the others, oblivious to her hesitation, and continued to remove my garter.

One of the other women smoothed my dark auburn hair—still in a French twist—in a final gesture of compassion. After they'd completed their task, the women left, and the men who'd come to the woods to retrieve my body gathered around the table. They bowed their heads for a moment. I'd been intimate with many men, but not like this. Despite their show of respect, anger stirred within me at the last humiliation I would have to endure.

A tall, thin man with a long white beard and stovepipe hat entered the room carrying a doctor's bag. He set it down on a box alongside his hat. I observed from a corner as he walked slowly around the table with a pencil and tablet, pausing to record the small scar above my left nipple. The doctor measured my body and marked the height as five feet four inches. He opened my mouth. "Her teeth all appear to be natural," he announced.

He drew some tools from his bag: a small saw, scissors, a scalpel, and a few other items I didn't recognize. The preparation for an autopsy confused me. The bullet was lodged in my brain, so why cut me open? I moved to touch him. He was wondering whether my pale, bloated body had been with child.

I studied each man around me and felt their thoughts too. As the night air grew colder, so did the storage room. The men shivered, huddling closer around the table as the doctor opened my chest under the shifting light of a lantern. Handkerchiefs flew out of pockets to cover noses and mouths, except for the doctor, who worked quickly, time now the enemy.

I moved among the members of the coroner's party, learning the anguishes, the losses, the tragedies each had endured: the deaths of wives and children, the invisible wounds of war, misfortunes in business. I sought the man who had the strongest drive for truth and justice, the one who would find my killer and make him pay for what he'd done.

In John, I saw a young child, orphaned and bewildered; a young man sitting in a makeshift prison, his innocence ignored; and that same man, a few years later, burying an infant next to his beloved wife.

As the doctor removed my organs, a cauldron roiled in the depths of my soul. I would linger on Earth until I had avenged my murder, and I knew who would help with the task. While the others shivered in the cold room, the warmth of my spirit enveloped John.

# 29

By the time the doctor finished my autopsy, the gas streetlights on Jefferson's downtown streets had long since been lighted. I attached myself to John as he ambled in the darkness, his mind racing faster than his stride, making note of what he'd learned and what he needed to accomplish the next day.

A few blocks north he entered a small, one-story frame house. A slim black woman was seated on a worn sofa. I recognized her as one of the women who'd undressed me. She and John acknowledged each other, then she rose and walked to the back of the house. I heard a door open and close.

John peeked in on his two sleeping boys before he went to his bedchamber. He sat quietly, perched on the edge of the bed, his shoulders slumped, his hands clasped between his knees. He was praying. Feeling like an intruder, I moved away.

After a few moments, he reached for a picture on the nightstand. He stared into the face of the woman in the photo and brushed his forefinger lightly across the glass, as if only that separated them. I knew too well the devastation of losing someone who'd been the center of your world.

"Who are you?"

Startled, I spun around.

The woman from the picture stood before me in a blood-stained nightgown. Her straw-colored hair hung loose and disheveled. But she didn't appear to be a whole person. The human shape was there, but she was translucent, like when I stretched my silk stockings over my hand to check for runs.

I stepped farther away from John. "My... my name is Annie. But everyone calls me Bessie."

The woman's eyes bore into mine. I shifted uneasily, averting my eyes from the intensity of her stare. "What are your intentions with my husband?" she said.

I chose my words carefully. "I was murdered in the woods across the bayou. I want your husband to find my killer and make him pay for what he did to me."

Her features softened. "I can understand why you would choose John."

I nodded. "He has a strong sense of justice."

"He should. John's the sheriff." She noticed my surprise. "You didn't know?"

I shook my head.

She surveyed me again. "You're the one they're calling Diamond Bessie."

My eyebrows shot up. Someone must have overheard Abe say my name.

"You made quite an impression during your visit. I'm Edla Vines." She appeared close to my age. Like me, too young to die.

"Will you let me stay here?" I asked tentatively.

Edla regarded me and for a moment I feared she would say no. Finally, she assented: "Yes, you may."

She started to move away, but I couldn't help myself. "Why didn't you go to the Light?"

"I'll remain here until John finds a new wife to take care of our boys. They need a mother."

As if sensing what I wanted to know she added, "I died giving birth to our third son."

The infant in John's memories. They had wounds as deep as mine.

"Are you sure *you* want to stay?" she said.

"Of course," I blurted, surprised at her question. "Why wouldn't I want to remain until my killer has been hanged?"

"It's not easy."

I didn't answer, and Edla didn't elaborate. Instead she said, "I hope you're prepared."

A twinge of doubt tugged at my resolve, but I shrugged it off. I wouldn't have peace without justice.

Edla remained in her husband's room for the night. I imagined him reaching for her in his sleep, her essence a comfort as it wrapped around him. Sadness momentarily dampened my anger. I had no one to wrap my arms around.

I nestled into the sitting room at the front of the house to wait for dawn. Nourishment and rest weren't necessary in the afterworld. I only needed revenge. I listened to the breathing of the boys and their father deep in the land of Nod, and felt the house breathe too, like a man shifting his weight. Despite the sorrow, I was glad to be around the living again.

Sheriff Vines rose early. After dressing he hurried over to the Brooks House. He would waste no time investigating my murder.

"Took you long enough," the manager said when John entered the hotel.

John chuckled as the manager swung the register around and

pointed to an entry on the page dated Friday, January 19, 1877. "He signed right here."

John skimmed a finger along the pertinent line. "A. Monroe and wife, St. Louis," he read aloud. "Didn't you say their trunk's label showed another name?"

So the sheriff had inquired about me that weekend.

The manager nodded. "The trunk had the name A. Moore, and the initials N.O. I figured Moore was his real last name and New Orleans a former residence."

"Or perhaps it's the woman's last name and where *she* resides… resided?" John ventured.

The manager shrugged.

John's countenance turned thoughtful. I brushed against him and saw a memory of me walking toward him on the street. When I'd passed him, he had turned and kept watching me, his gaze one of appreciation mixed with curiosity. And… amusement? He had wondered if I might be a sporting woman. But his thought that I might have been a prostitute hadn't held judgment.

"I remember thinking she was a real Diamond Bessie," John said, lost in thought. It must have been him who had overheard Abe say my name, and he'd been interested enough to give me a sobriquet. John strummed his thick fingers on the registry desk. "When did the fellow leave?"

The manager thought for a moment. "He took the northbound train early Tuesday morning."

"When did you last see them together?"

"Sunday morning. They left around ten, and the gentleman came back alone around one. When I asked about his so-called wife, he said he'd left her with friends across the bayou."

The sheriff cringed as guilt crept in. Anger rose in me. That meant Abe had stayed in Jefferson for two whole days after killing me.

"You also mentioned some trouble between them."

"Several guests heard the couple arguing. Kept them up most of the night. Chambermaid heard them too."

The chambermaid lived in a small cottage behind the hotel. The manager knocked and announced his presence. "Jennie, it's Dr. Turner. I've got someone who needs to talk to you about the murder of that woman across the bayou."

A stout, middle-aged woman opened the door just enough to peep through the crack. "I done told you all I know."

"He needs to ask you a few questions. It's important."

The woman hesitated, then let them inside, though there was barely enough room for the three of them in her cramped quarters.

"Jennie, this is Sheriff Vines. He's investigating the woman's murder. Tell him what you told me."

The chambermaid pursed her lips but seemed to resign herself to telling her story again. "There was a whole lotta noise comin from their room. I could hear the woman screamin and cryin and the man yellin at her."

Jennie spoke slowly at first, but, noticing John's interest in the story, she became more confident and animated. "The next mornin they left, but when the man come back in the afternoon, the woman wasn't with 'im. I ask'd where his wife was, and he told me she was gonna meet 'im at the train. I noticed he was wearin a couple of the woman's diamonds."

"He was wearing her diamonds?" John asked skeptically. He couldn't imagine even the daftest of murderers being so brazen as to wear his victim's jewelry.

"Yes, Sir." Jennie paused. "The next mornin when I was cleanin the fireplace, I seen buried in the cracklins what look'd like papers he done burned." She shook her head. "I shoulda known somethin bad happened."

Two days after the discovery of my body, the women who'd undressed me returned to clothe me for my burial. They didn't wash my body as my mam had for my da. Nor did they wrap my hands with rosary beads or place a cross around my neck. They didn't know I was Irish Catholic. There was no special rosary for the dead, no candles placed at the head and foot of my coffin. No one watched over my body before the funeral or keened over my departure from this world.

The servant from John's house, Eliza, wanted to turn my body over to face the earth so I wouldn't "come back to haunt the town." But the other women opposed the idea. I had no interest in haunting their town, anyway. Only my murderer, if I could.

I had only been in Jefferson for a few days before my murder, but it seemed the whole town came to my graveside service. Merchants closed their stores and joined other townspeople as they followed the horse-drawn hearse to Oakwood Cemetery. The plush velvet curtains were pulled back to showcase the metal casket that several prominent residents had raised a hundred and twenty-five dollars to purchase so that my body would be preserved longer, in case my family came for me.

Among the crowd was the young boy who'd followed me into the clothing store the day before my murder. He said to his mother, loud enough for nearby ears, "When I grow up, I'm going to hunt down the man who killed Diamond Bessie."

"Ed, ya shouldn't say such things," his mother shushed in a thick brogue that reminded me of my mam.

I feared for my mother's sanity when news of my death reached Canton and regretted that I hadn't lived long enough to become the daughter and sister I should have been. The chance to redeem myself was gone. With each thud of dirt that hit my casket, the realization sank in deeper.

My desolation didn't escape Edla. She'd been hovering next to her husband and came over to me. "Do you want to go to the Light?"

My hopes and dreams may have been buried with my body, but the insatiable anger that remained burned bright. "No."

"Are you sure?"

How can one be sure of anything? I had been sure Leslie would marry me and that my killer would be my savior.

# 30

Before my funeral, Sheriff Vines sent a telegram with a description of my killer to nearby towns and cities across the country. He sent one to Cincinnati's police chief, but without mention of Abe's true identity, I knew it wouldn't lead to Abe's arrest—at least not yet. There was nothing I could do but wait for a break.

Two days after my burial, it came. A messenger from the telegraph office knocked on John's door as he was preparing to leave. Gasping for air after his apparent dead run from the telegraph office, he handed the message to John and said, panting, "It's from Marshall."

*Read Marshall paper today about murder of woman known as 'Diamond Bessie.' Recognized description of suspect as gentleman who stayed at the Capitol Hotel several months ago, and again January 18 of this year. Both times signed his name A. Rothschild, Cincinnati, Ohio. This is your man.*

*Charles Pepper*

"I'll be damned," John said.

I couldn't wait for John to go to Marshall, but he had to wait until the following day for the next train.

John waited patiently as a couple registered at the Capitol Hotel. Three short weeks earlier, I had stood there with my new husband. We'd been married a week and, as dismayed as I'd been over Abe's plans for us to own a brothel, I'd held out hope that I could salvage my marriage and my life.

"I realized as soon as I read the article that I could help you find the scoundrel," Pepper said as he handed the *Tri-Weekly Herald* to John.

### *The Jefferson Horror: A Beautiful Woman Found in the Woods, Murdered*

*The citizens of Jefferson have been intensely excited over the discovery of a terrible murder, the mere relation of which inspires a feeling of horror.*

*Those acquainted with the surroundings will remember that, on the old Marshall road this side of the ferry, there is a red hill on the first rising ground, and a pine tree blasted by lightning. West of this about fifty steps, a Negro woman hunting for wood Monday evening came upon the dead body of a woman.*

*She was richly dressed, had fine features, blue eyes, fair skin, full lips, and small hands and feet, and, although dead for several days, scarcely any signs of decomposition. The glittering diamonds she had been seen wearing, earning her the moniker Diamond Bessie, were gone from her earlobes and hands.*

*Who was she? What fate led her to such an end? With a great mystery over her life and her death, she has been consigned to her last resting place.*

*And the man she came to town with, who is he? He is about twenty-five years of age, five feet-eight inches in height, with black hair and dark brown eyes. Among his most noticeable features are an overhanging forehead and prominent eyebrows, heavy lips, broad nose, and large, stubby hands with remarkably wide thumbs.*

*All the facts show he stopped at Jefferson with no other purpose than to murder this woman. Why did he carry her to this distant point to perpetrate a crime so revolting? And what were all the motives that impelled him to commit this hellish deed?*

If only they knew. But I could no longer speak for myself. I had placed all my trust in strangers to do that for me. John set the paper down as the proprietor steadily thumbed through the pages of the hotel register until he found the entry for our recent visit.

"There it is." Pepper pointed to the pertinent line.

John pulled out a piece of translucent paper he had carried from Jefferson and carefully traced my husband's signature. When he finished, he nodded to Pepper. "Your telegram said this Rothschild fellow stayed here several months ago."

The proprietor flipped through more pages and swung the book around again. "He was traveling alone."

John leaned over to study the signature. "Did he say what kind of business he had here?"

"Said he worked for a firm in the notions line."

"He told the manager at the Brooks House he was a drummer for a millinery house, but I didn't see him carrying around any hats, or sewing accessories, for that matter."

"Sounds like an accomplished liar," Pepper said.

I wholeheartedly agreed.

John took aim at a spittoon. A rivulet arced over his boots into the brass cuspidor. "How long did they stay here last month?"

"Two nights, January 17 and 18."

"How did they appear to you?"

Pepper stroked his mustache. "Now that you ask, the woman seemed upset. Could tell she'd been crying. The gentleman wasn't bothered by her mood and didn't say much to her, except that they needed to hurry to catch the train."

Back in Jefferson, John went directly to the Brooks House. "The formation of the letter 'e' in both are almost identical, and so are both capital A's," he announced after studying the signatures. He moved his magnifying glass back and forth between the two lines. "The formation of the 'i' is also the same."

The sheriff handed the glass to Turner. The hotel manager peered at the signatures and agreed they were made by the same person.

"Why did he make such a simple mistake?" John wondered aloud.

At the time I hadn't thought it unusual that Abe had registered under different names in Jefferson than in Marshall; he had done that before when he wanted to avoid repaying a gambling debt. But now I realized that he had already decided to be rid of me when we left the Capitol Hotel.

"I reckon he thought he was safe using his real name in Marshall, but not here where he carried out the deed," Turner ventured. "Or maybe he used aliases both times."

"Perhaps," John said, "but I've a hunch we've got him."

"Your husband knows who killed me," I said to Edla when the sheriff returned home from the Brooks House. I bounced around giddily. If I were still alive, I would have danced a jig.

"Who is it?"

I stopped. "My husband, of course. I thought you knew that."

"You haven't told me anything about him."

"Abe Rothschild." My voice quavered as I said his name. I'd cursed him in my mind many times, but his name had not passed my lips since my death. Edla wrapped her arms around me. For the first time, I wept.

# 31

John had learned the name of my killer, yet he hadn't boarded the first train to Ohio. Instead, he sent a telegram to Cincinnati's police chief confirming Abe's identity, and now he was getting ready for an evening out. He grumbled to himself as he donned a long black frock coat over black trousers and a white high-collared shirt that sported a black silk puff tie. He left his gun and holster at home. I tried my best to hide my irritation as I asked Edla where he was going.

"The Queen Mab Ball. It's Mardi Gras."

"Ah, the mischievous fairies' midwife who sneaks into men's dreams."

"As small as the tip of my pinky." Edla held up a hand and wiggled her little finger. She laughed for the first time since we'd met—a light, lyrical sound that tickled my ears. I smiled, happy to hear and feel something other than misery.

We sat by the fireplace and I remembered how, as a child, I curled up in my da's lap while he read to me before bed. I'd loved the comforting strength of my da's arms, the sound his rough fingers made as they turned the page, his earthy smell from laboring on the farm.

"My da used to tease me when he'd tuck me into bed," I said. "He'd tell us, 'Dream sweet dreams lest Queen Mab visit you.'" Mab was queen of the Sid'he, Ireland's mystical fairies. "I was never afraid of her creeping into my dreams. I had my da to protect me." My voice cracked. "Until he died."

"How old were you?"

"Ten." My throat caught. I wanted to tell Edla more about the tragedies in my life, but I couldn't go on.

"I lost my father when I was young, too. I know how hard it is to lose a parent." Edla gazed at her sons, under Eliza's care, and said wistfully, "Now my own children live with that pain."

I placed a hand on Edla's. "They miss you, but I also sense that John and the boys—and Eliza—are comforted by your presence. You have a way of consoling others, whether they see you or not." I met her gaze. "Including me."

She gave me a warm smile. Edla was like a shaft of wheat, tall and willowy, delicate, pure, no chaff. How I wished we had met during our mortal lives. As earthbound souls we had different reasons for staying, but having someone to talk to eased the disquiet and helped pass the time that progressed on Earth without us.

"John understands the fear of being alone in the world," Edla said.

Beneath John's gruff exterior and commanding presence lay a softness and fragility, like the gossamer threads of a spider's web. A quick sweep of a broom was all it would take to expose the suffering John carried.

"He was orphaned as a child, wasn't he?"

"His parents died within days of each other. Yellow fever. John's uncle went to Alabama and brought him back here. He and his wife raised John along with their own children."

We sat in silence again, and my thoughts drifted back to my murder. "How do I appear to you?"

Edla was momentarily taken aback. "You're beautiful."

"You're kind, but…" I couldn't bring myself to ask.

"Yes, it's there." She meant the bullet hole. As long as I stayed on this Earth, I would appear as I had when I died. I had a sudden urge. "Let's go to the ball," I announced.

Green, gold, and purple banners festooned the walls of the ballroom at the Excelsior House. The costumes the women wore were as dazzling as the ones I'd seen on my visits to New Orleans. Dresses and veils trimmed with ivy, flowers, and glittering stars floated by. One woman had covered herself head to toe with the *East Texas Daily Ledger*.

We found John talking to one of the men who'd been with him when my body was found. "Who's that with your husband?" I said.

"Sol Spellings. He owns a livery stable."

"He seems sad."

"Sol lost his wife last year."

I looked around the room. We were the only earthbound souls there. "Where is she?"

"She didn't stay."

"Why not?" Why wouldn't a mother want to remain with her children, at least until her husband remarried, as Edla had committed to doing?

Edla shrugged. "It's not for me to judge."

I scanned the crowded room and couldn't help but notice one man who towered over the rest. Well over six feet, he resembled a lath—long and thin—and sported a profusion of wiry whiskers on his upper lip and chin. His closely cropped hair was plastered to his head.

When Edla realized who I was watching, she said, "That's George Todd. He's an attorney." She pointed to the shorter man George was speaking to. "And that's Edward Guthridge, the county attorney. He's the one who will be responsible for convicting your husband."

I moved closer and studied Guthridge. He looked Irish, and

temperamental, as Celts often are. His youthfulness was unsettling. "He doesn't look old enough to be the county attorney."

"He's young, but that's who you've got."

I tried to shake off my worry, but I knew it wouldn't be easy to prosecute my killer.

"Don't you think it would be a good idea for John to go to Cincinnati?"

Edla shook her head violently. "He has too many responsibilities here."

"But he *is* the sheriff."

Edla's eyes flashed with annoyance and she looked away. I pleaded with her. "I can't wait any longer, Edla. Please understand how agonizing this is."

Her head still turned from me, she said, "It would take several days for John to travel to Ohio and who knows how long he'd be there." She looked at me pointedly. "But that's not the only issue."

"What do you mean?"

"I assume you would want to go with John… and that could cause problems."

I was confused. "How?"

"Do you have more energy now that you're no longer in the woods?"

I did, but I thought it was due to my excitement over Abe's impending arrest.

"Spirits need energy like humans," Edla explained. "When you were in the woods you stayed in one place, so you didn't need as much. Now you need more to survive. Your energy comes from living things. After I died, I wanted to be close to John, so I attached myself to him, but before long he became ill. I thought his grief had made him sick, but when he didn't improve, I realized *I* might be the cause. I moved away from him to see what would happen, and he got well again. I still like to be close to John, but I'm careful."

"I see."

A thought occurred to me. I'd been so consumed with John learning the identity of my killer, I hadn't thought of visiting Abe. Was he remorseful at all for what he had done to me? Had he shed one tear? When Queen Mab sneaked into men's dreams, her excursions brought out the worst in the dreamers, their vices and transgressions. What torment could I wreak?

"I understand," I said to Edla. "But I must see my husband."

# 32

At Jefferson's depot, I attached my spirit to an older gentleman boarding the northbound train. He carried with him a valise filled with candies and catalogues for a confectionary wholesaler. He settled into his seat, his body aching from the pressures of being on the road for weeks at a time. The job of a drummer was a lonely one; salesmen often went long stretches without seeing their families. He slept most of the way to Little Rock where he ended his journey, and I found another salesman whose destination was St. Louis, and then another who brought me to Cincinnati.

I had never been inside the Burnet Hotel, which took up an entire block at the corner of Third and Vine, but its opulence was renowned. A London newspaper had proclaimed it "the finest hotel in the world," and when I entered the lobby and took in its marble columns, grand marble staircases, and the magnificent landscaped courtyard in the center, I could see why. Presidents and the well-to-do stayed there. And now also a murderer.

The luxuriousness extended to Abe's room. A massive mahogany bedstead occupied the outer wall next to a window adorned with lace curtains. To the right, a gilded French plate mirror hung above a marble fireplace, and next to that was a small writing desk. Along the wall closest to the door stood a rosewood wardrobe. And there, next to it, was my trunk.

One day while shopping along Baronne Street in New Orleans, a Saratoga in a show window had caught my eye. I'd been wanting to replace the small trunk I'd used since Watertown. The Saratoga boasted gleaming black cast-metal latches and hinges, and sturdy leather side handles. A light-colored canvas protected the hardwood slats. Inside were a myriad of compartments and a lift-out tray lined with silk. Next to my jewels, the trunk was my most prized possession.

I'd assumed Abe had gotten rid of it at one of his stops en route back to Cincinnati. Seeing it in his room brought on a new rush of bitterness. My ire grew when he stumbled in after a night of drinking with friends and threw his coat on top of my trunk. He didn't undress, just groped for the bed and fell into a deep sleep.

With each life-sustaining breath he took, I grew angrier. He wasn't troubled by my murder in the least. I moved toward his slumbering body and poured my rage into him. Slipping into his dream, we rode with Queen Mab in her chariot to the clearing in the woods where my body lay. My disfigured corpse rose and roared the disquieting howl of the banshee. Abe tried to run, but I held fast to his hand. As my wailing corpse let out another blood-curdling plaint, Abe cried out in his sleep and bolted upright. Satisfaction filled me.

It was noon before Abe roused, groggy from his fitful sleep. He grabbed a pitcher on the washbasin and splashed cold water on his face. As he reached for a towel, he winced. When the stabbing throe in his left temple subsided, he peered into the small mirror above the basin and froze. My face stared back at him. He shook his head, as if to make me disappear, and touched the mirror. I let out a sardonic laugh. Abe whipped around, but the room was empty. My dreams had become his nightmares, my thoughts his torture.

Abe walked over to the wardrobe to change clothes. I whispered, *Murderer*, and he scanned the room again. Clearly shaken, he grabbed his coat and rushed out the door, but went back for his gun before heading downstairs to the dining room. As he tried to compose himself, I murmured, *You know what you did.* His body went rigid, his face blanched.

When the mutton soup arrived, Abe pushed the bowl away. He ate only a few bites of his chicken and oysters and rice croquettes. His appetite had vanished. When the waiter offered a pastry, Abe declined.

"Is someone following me?" he said.

The waiter responded with a puzzled look. It was working. I was getting under Abe's skin.

Abe paid his bill, scooped up a handful of hickory nuts from a bowl, and shoved them into his coat pocket. Exiting the hotel, he headed north one block, then west along Fourth Avenue to his brother's store.

"How's business?" Charles asked when Abe entered.

"Slow. The beginning of the year is always that way." Abe rubbed his forehead. He couldn't focus.

"Are you all right?"

"Yes, yes, fine." Abe glanced around the store again. A lady at the other end of the counter was busy choosing a lace handkerchief. Abe lowered his voice. "I have a favor to ask you."

"What do you need?"

"Some money. I'll pay you back as soon as I'm back on the road again. I'm working a big order."

"How much?"

"Eighty dollars should keep me in good stead."

Charles's mouth dropped.

Of course Abe needed money. He didn't have me anymore. He ran a hand through his unkempt hair.

"Is everything all right?" Charles said. He searched his brother's face for an explanation.

"I'm fine, I'm fine." Abe pulled a few hickory nuts from his pocket and chomped nervously.

"I'll be right back," Charles said. He returned with an envelope and handed it to Abe. He regarded his brother with concern and said in parting, "Take care of yourself."

Abe ventured over to the Atlantic Garden on Vine Street. He thought he could escape my wrath among crowds, but I made sure he kept seeing me. After a dram of whiskey, he moved next door to Jake Aug's Clubhouse, where he drank some more. But he couldn't drink enough to escape me, and that night I again haunted his dreams.

Abe awoke late morning, more haggard and bleary-eyed than the day before. After dressing he grabbed his coat from the top of my trunk. But he did not instantly rush out the door. Instead, he stood and stared at my name, which I'd had engraved on my trunk. He pulled out a pocketknife, kneeled down, and started to scrape it away. I whispered, *Murderer.* He dropped the knife. I thought he would pick it up. Instead, he went to his writing desk to a sheet of manila paper and some sealing wax, covered the plaque bearing my name, put on his coat, and left.

In the lobby, Abe nearly ran headlong into a luggage cart. "Whoa there," the baggage man said.

Abe ignored the man but then stopped and turned back to him. "Say, would you be able to take my trunk to the train depot?"

"Sure, which one?"

"Doesn't matter, any of them will do. I'll pay you forty cents."

The baggage man scratched his head. "Okay."

After the man took my trunk, Abe left the hotel and walked north on Vine. He thought he could rid himself of me by getting rid of my last possession. At Jake Aug's he downed a grog. The rum and water braced him, and his fear of me faded. It was short lived. I siphoned his energy as I made his skin crawl, his head itch, his hands tremble. When I breathed, Abe took a breath. He was my shadow, not me his. He went from one bar to another and asked the same question of everyone he met: "Do you see someone following me?"

After nightfall, brimming with whiskey, Abe headed toward Cincinnati's German neighborhood, Over-the-Rhine. As we neared the construction site for a grand new music hall, I heard maniacal screams and wailing.

The land had once been home to a potter's field and lunatic and orphan asylums. Workers had exhumed the bodies to make way for the music hall, but the spirits didn't take too kindly to their burial ground being disturbed. Newspapers had reported sightings of ghostly apparitions. When medical students started coming in the dead of night to steal bones and skulls, a policeman was stationed there to prevent any more thefts, and to keep the crowds that came to witness the disinterring of the dead at bay. But the damage had been done.

These ragged, rage-filled spirits sensed my anger. "Why are you following this fellow?" The question came from an old man dressed in attire long out of style. He had no hair, few teeth, and was covered in excrement.

"He killed me."

"He did, did he? Most of us were murdered too."

More spirits, young and old, gathered. Dozens of them, hovering like a swarm of bees. Abe's pace slowed. He pulled his coat tighter.

"Our bodies were dumped into the ground here," the old bald man said. "Couldn't be bothered to put us in a plain wooden box. No, that would be too good for us crazies."

The spirits all spoke at once, following me as Abe kept walking. "Some of us died from cholera," another man said. "The treatment they gave us hurt so much, I *wanted* to die."

A woman nodded. "They poisoned me with hemlock."

These spirits weren't malevolent; they were angry at how they'd been mistreated.

"Why didn't you go to the Light?" I said, wondering why they didn't end their misery.

The old man with missing teeth rubbed his chin thoughtfully. "I dunno, guess I was too angry."

How well I understood that.

A young boy looked up. His eyes were hollow, his body emaciated. "I want to go," he said, shyly. Others followed suit, clamoring around me, talking excitedly.

"How do we get there?"

"I'm tired of being earthbound."

"There's nothing here for me but misery."

I hadn't helped anyone cross over, but it seemed simple enough. I guided the ones who wanted to go to express their desire to leave this Earth. A portal opened and, one by one, they ascended like celestial comets. For a moment I was tempted to join them. But one look at Abe reminded me why I wanted to stay. He had to pay for what he'd done.

Abe crossed the bridge over the Miami Canal into Over-the-Rhine and headed to a crowded beer hall. Some of the spirits sensed the vigor of the place and dispersed among the patrons, but a number of them remained attached to my husband. Ignored in life, in death they wanted the living to feel their anguish. They enjoyed draining Abe's energy and joined me in haunting him, whispering, *Murderer*. Abe shook his head, but he couldn't make the voices go away.

Near midnight, Abe stumbled back down Vine to Jake Aug's. He didn't want to go home. He rightly feared another disturbing night of hearing my voice, of my presence lurking in the shadows. He sat at the bar with his cousin David.

"How's Bessie?" David asked.

Abe threw his head back and laughed, more nervous than jovial. He slugged a gulp of whiskey. "She's doing fine."

Abe's flippant dismissal incited more rage within me. He'd stolen everything, including my life, and yet he showed no remorse. I swirled around him, making the hairs on his neck stand.

"Where is she?"

Abe rubbed the back of his neck. "New Orleans, and probably having a great time since it's Mardi Gras season." Abe scanned the room and whispered to his cousin, "Do you see someone following me?"

David darted his head around the bar, then knitted his brows quizzically. "I don't see anyone."

"Someone's following me," Abe mumbled. His hand shook as he set his glass on the counter.

"Who?"

"I don't know, but someone." Abe glanced around again.

David slapped Abe's back. "Don't worry about it."

The reassurance didn't ease Abe's anxiety, but it made me gleeful. When someone else remarked that Abe looked like he'd seen a spook, his face turned ashen, and he began to drink one dram of whiskey after another.

Around two thirty in the morning, Abe bid farewell to his friends. Outside, he hunkered down on the pavement, a dark, brooding figure against a backdrop of bright lights and merriment. He covered his face and moaned. "What have I done?" he howled. "What have I done?"

*You know what you did, you coward.* I spit my seething words into his ear like one of Queen Mab's curses. Abe reached into his coat and pulled out his revolver. I swirled around him, a tightly coiled snake ready to strike. Softly I whispered on the wind, *Murderer.*

Abe swung the gun up to his temple. "I'm a murderer," he cried, and fired.

# 33

ncredibly, as blood ran down the right side of his head, Abe's body remained upright. I had wanted his life, but watching him now, I also didn't want him to take the easy way out. I wanted him to suffer more, to be hauled back to Texas and hanged.

A night watchman ran up to Abe. "What happened?"

Abe groaned.

David came running outside. "Abe, what the devil!"

Onlookers spilled out of Jake Aug's, the Atlantic Garden, and the nearby *Cincinnati Enquirer* office.

The night watchman picked up the gun at Abe's side and opened the cylinder. One bullet was missing.

"Abe, who shot you?" David said.

"A man… a tall man, with long whiskers," Abe managed to say. He groaned again. Of course, no one had been seen running away.

Someone went to find a doctor while Abe's friends carried him next door to Weatherhead's Drugstore. They laid him down on the marble soda fountain counter. One of the men took off his coat, rolled it up, and placed it underneath Abe's head. Abe was barely conscious.

I had died almost instantly when Abe shot me. I saw now what happened to a person who survived a bullet to the brain. His breath, at times labored and shallow, grew rapid before subsiding again. He became dizzy and confused, his skin cold and clammy.

A doctor arrived and placed his fingers on Abe's wrist to take his pulse. "Too low," he muttered.

The door opened and David entered the drugstore with two others. I recognized one—Abe's brother, Charles—and knew immediately that the other was Abe's father, even though I'd never laid eyes on him before. Slight in stature, Maier Rothschild had a high forehead, full lips like Abe's, and the same round ruddy face.

"What's the prognosis?" Maier asked the doctor.

"Not good."

Maier stood stone-faced while the doctor tended to Abe. I wanted to know what Abe's father thought of this predicament his son found himself in, but I remained transfixed on the doctor. He pulled a long thin instrument from his bag. As he carefully inserted the tool into the wound, Abe's moans sounded like those of a dying animal. The doctor carefully extracted the bullet, flattened and covered in blood. He handed it to Maier. "It hit the frontal bone in his skull above his right eye, which he'll undoubtably lose. If he survives."

For the next few hours, Abe went in and out of consciousness. The doctor kept taking his pulse. "Forty-two," he said at one point. Then it was a hundred and fifty.

"It shouldn't be above sixty," the doctor said.

At dawn, stable enough to be moved, Abe's brother and cousin transferred him to a carriage, which was driven half a mile to a narrow two-story brick building on Fifth Street. Abe's mother awaited her son's arrival. A petite woman, Rosa appeared as fragile as a bone china teacup. Tired and distraught, she wrung her hands as Charles and Abe's other brother, Jacob, gingerly carried Abe upstairs. Rosa had prepared the bed and set a bowl of water and some towels on a nightstand. She and the doctor stayed with Abe. Periodically Rosa dipped a cloth into the water and tenderly pressed it on her son's face, murmuring soothing sounds. As glad as I was that Abe wouldn't get away with my murder, I felt sympathy for Rosa. No mother should have to bear the burden of a child who has lost his way.

Downstairs, Maier paced his store. I moved to touch him, my curiosity piqued, and felt the usual jolt. He seemed less concerned with Abe's condition and more worried over how his son's antics would affect the family in the eyes of their tight-knit German-Jewish community.

"I can stay," Charles said to his father.

Maier waved a hand. "Go to your store. Your business needn't suffer because of your brother's exploits."

Charles hesitated. "Do you think someone shot him, or that he tried to kill himself?" He recounted Abe's visit to his store. "Something was definitely amiss."

Maier's features darkened into a scowl. "I don't know what to believe when it comes to Abraham."

"His friends said he was acting strangely all night, and one of the papers reported this—" Charles handed a newspaper to his father. The headline read, "Was it Assassination or Attempted Suicide?" Even the reporter was skeptical about Abe's story that someone had shot him.

Maier set the paper down without reading it. From my attachment I knew he harbored doubt that his son had been shot, but he also didn't believe that Abe would try to kill himself.

That afternoon a curious-looking man entered Maier's store. Only five feet tall and squat, he sported a good-sized wart on his left cheek. He waited for the customers to leave before approaching Abe's father.

"Mr. Rothschild?"

"Yes."

"I'm Detective Charles Wappenstein. I'm here to place your son under arrest."

Maier's jaw tightened. "Why would he be under arrest?"

"Your son is charged with killing a woman in Texas."

It took a moment for the full import of the man's words to hit Maier. "That's preposterous. My son would do no such thing."

Detective Wappenstein handed Maier a letter. "We received this at headquarters today from Jefferson, Texas."

Maier's frown deepened as he read.

*February 14, 1877*
*Chief of Police, Cincinnati, Ohio*

*Dear Sir:*

*Since I sent you a circular and photograph of a woman murdered on the 21st of January, I have learned without a doubt the man who signed as "A. Monroe, St. Louis" is in fact A. Rothschild and is a resident of your city.*

*In Marshall, Texas, he registered at the Capitol Hotel as "A. Rothschild and wife, Cincinnati, Ohio," and about eight months ago at the same place in the same hand, registered under the same name. I have traced his signatures and am enclosing copies.*

*The Governor has offered a reward of $500 for his capture.*

*Respectfully,*
*John Vines, Marion Co. Sheriff*
*Jefferson, Texas*

Maier's hand shook slightly as he handed the letter back to the detective. "This is outrageous. My son is a salesman for one of New York's most prestigious houses. And he is not married."

Undeterred, the detective pressed on. "He travels a lot, doesn't he?"

"Yes, but—"

"Did he not travel to Texas recently?"

"I have no idea. He doesn't keep me abreast of his travel plans." Maier pursed his lips. The detective appeared unconvinced, but I sensed Maier was telling the truth.

Abe's mother entered the room. "Maier, who is this?" Her tone was guarded and shrill.

Maier turned to his wife. "Rosa, everything will be all right," he said and spoke to her in German.

"Mrs. Rothschild, I have a warrant for your son's arrest," Detective Wappenstein told her.

Rosa blanched and turned to her husband, mouth agape. Her look took me back to when I'd told Mam I was pregnant. She'd had the same confused expression.

Several clocks in the room chimed twice.

"Your son will be extradited to Texas to stand trial. I must speak to him now," the detective said.

Despite my empathy for Rosa, I was elated to hear those words.

I transferred my attachment to the detective as he and Maier headed upstairs.

"Abraham, are you awake?" Maier said.

He groaned.

"Is this necessary?" Maier pleaded. "Can't you see my son is suffering?"

"I'm under orders to arrest him."

Maier touched his son's shoulder lightly. "Abraham?"

Abe slowly opened his good eye.

Detective Wappenstein leaned over. "Mr. Rothschild, I'm here to place you under arrest for the murder of a woman in Jefferson, Texas."

Another groan from my husband.

"Do you understand?" The detective spoke a little louder.

Abe lay motionless.

"What is your opinion of this man's condition?" Wappenstein asked the doctor.

Without hesitation the physician said, "The wound will be fatal. I don't expect him to live many more days." The doctor glanced at Maier as if seeking his approval.

The detective had his suspicions that Abe would play possum as long as he could, but kept his thoughts to himself. "An officer will arrive soon to stand guard over your son."

"That isn't necessary," Maier protested.

"Captain's orders."

After the detective left, Maier found Rosa in their bedchamber and tried to comfort his wife. He put a hand on her shoulder, but she brushed it off. "You were always too strict," she exclaimed bitterly.

Maier bristled. "And you coddled him too much." He moved away from Rosa and sat on the edge of the bed, his fingers gripping the mattress. They were both aware of the kind of people Abe ran around with, of his gambling and drinking, but they didn't know about me. They had no idea Abe had killed his *wife*.

The tense silence lingered as Maier left the room and went back downstairs. I remained attached to him as he paced the hallway, fury creeping into his step, his mind racing. Abe had always been a hell-bender, but Maier couldn't believe his son would do something as reprehensible as committing murder. He went back upstairs and told the doctor he needed a minute alone with his son. He waited until he no longer heard footsteps before speaking.

"Abraham, you need to tell me what happened. The truth."

"I told you," Abe said weakly, "a man… following me… shot me."

Maier frowned. "Why was this man following you?"

"I don't know."

"You don't know who he was or why he followed you?"

"No."

Maier tried not to sound exasperated. "Abraham, you've been arrested for murder. You know what the Torah says about taking someone's life; it is a sin against all of society. Killing another Jew is one of the most heinous sins you can commit."

Abe was silent for a moment. "She was a Gentile, Father."

"A Gentile?" Maier raised a hand to his forehead, trying to smooth the wrinkles that had seemed to deepen overnight. Suspicion rose inside him. "Was your cousin involved in this?"

Abe was surprised at the question. "No," he said sharply, wincing from a sudden spasm.

Maier didn't know whether to believe his son. He frowned at Abe. "I have tried to give you every opportunity you desire," he said. "You are educated, you have a good job. You have everything you could want, and yet you continually try to destroy everything we hold dear." His body shook. "I promise you, *mein sohn*, you will not bring this family down."

And I promised myself, no matter how long it took, no matter the cost to his family, I would see justice done.

# 34

As Abe teetered between life and death, I anxiously awaited Sheriff Vines's arrival. Detective Wappenstein had sent a telegram to Jefferson. John was on his way, and he wasn't coming alone. The manager of the Brooks House, Dr. Turner, had accompanied him, as had the county attorney, Ed Guthridge.

After the men shook hands, Wappenstein said, "The papers here printed an article about Mr. Rothschild's suicide attempt. Your second letter arrived the morning after the suspect shot himself. Colonel Wood—our chief—handed it to me, pointed to the story, and said, 'Doesn't this solve the mystery of the shooting?' I said, 'It sure does. The murder apparently weighed heavy on his mind, and remorse made him attempt suicide.'"

"Murder will out itself," John replied. "A criminal will eventually be exposed."

"How is the prisoner doing?" Guthridge inquired.

"Barely hanging on, or so I'm told." Wappenstein's words held more than a hint of skepticism. "It will be good to have another expert opinion on Abe's chances for survival."

As the detective led the men toward a streetcar stop, I transferred my attachment to John. Despite the long journey from Texas, the sheriff had newfound energy, and he was concerned they might be too late.

Wappenstein wanted to know about Abe's visit to Jefferson.

"Several others and I went to the hotel," John explained. "We inquired about the fellow going around with the fancy woman wearing diamonds. They registered as man and wife, but we thought she might be a sporting woman. Jefferson is a small place. Everybody notices a stranger in town, especially an attractive young woman with flashy jewelry, which is rather uncommon in our part of the country. And they both dressed fancily."

"You were right about the woman." Wappenstein motioned for the men to board the streetcar and he followed behind. Once they had settled into the car, he continued. "The information from your first letter gave us enough to learn she resided at one of our city's most popular brothels." To John he said, "Did you inquire about the business that brought the fellow to Jefferson?"

The streetcar jerked and John grabbed onto the railing. "We inquired more particularly about the woman. She interested us more than the chap. I guess, in hindsight, we should have paid more attention to him." Another pang of regret in John. "We don't take kindly to our town being used as a dumping ground."

When the party arrived at police headquarters, Abe's doctor had already been summoned to explain his patient's condition.

"When I tended the wounded man, it was my opinion the wound would be fatal," Dr. Davis reported. "I remained with him all through the night and administered stimulants. He experienced frequent spasms and his pulse vacillated wildly. It is my opinion, gentlemen, he will never leave his bed. He may die from the effects of inflammation. The right eye is completely gone."

"What is his pulse now?" Dr. Turner said.

"It's still vacillating, though not as much as it was the first night."

"So perhaps the wound isn't as serious as you may believe?"

Dr. Davis shrugged. "I can only tell you what I have experienced with the patient to this point."

"I would like to examine him myself," Dr. Turner said.

Abe's doctor squared his shoulders. "Now would not be a good time."

"With all due respect," John interjected, trying to hide his agitation. "Time is of the utmost importance. Your patient is also our prisoner. We need to see him."

"We need to identify him, to make sure we have the right man," Guthridge added.

When the party entered Maier's shop, he glared at the men. "I don't want all of you up there at once," he snapped.

The men obliged. Guthridge and Wappenstein waited downstairs while John followed the doctors up the narrow stairs to Abe's room. The only light came from an overcast sky through half-closed shutters, the only sound, Abe's labored breathing.

I read John's thoughts. When his parents were on their death beds, he'd been too young to understand what death meant. But he had never forgotten what the house had felt like. He had known with a certainty he couldn't explain that his parents wouldn't live much longer. John didn't sense imminent death in this room. Abe was fighting to live, despite what his doctor said.

Dr. Turner walked the few steps to the bed. "That's him. I could pick him out from among a thousand."

"Are you sure?" Abe's doctor said. "Maybe I should turn him a little so you can—"

Dr. Turner held up a hand. "I am sure this is the man." He leaned over and started to remove Abe's bandage.

"Please don't hurt me," Abe whimpered.

"My prognosis is still that this wound will be fatal," Dr. Davis said.

"Not with proper treatment," Dr. Turner countered as he examined Abe.

"I do hope you're not suggesting that I would not give my patient the best care," Dr. Davis huffed.

"I'm not suggesting anything. I believe he can recover from this wound."

Downstairs, Wappenstein thanked Maier for his cooperation. Abe's father stood silent and stone-faced. John rapped his knuckles on the glass counter and added, "Much obliged." He started to follow the other men out the door, but turned back to Maier.

"I do have one question," John said. "Did your son have a trunk with him when he returned home? A Saratoga?"

"No," Maier responded, surprised. "My son doesn't own such a trunk as far as I know."

As the men headed back to police headquarters, Guthridge brought up something that seemed to be on all their minds. "Do you think his family will do everything they can to keep him from appearing well enough to be extradited?"

John nodded. "The shame would be hard for any family to bear."

"We should transfer the suspect to a hospital where we can keep a closer eye on him," Guthridge proposed.

John looked to Dr. Turner. "Is it safe to move him?"

The doctor nodded. "In my opinion, his condition is good enough for transport."

The next evening, as the northern winter sun waned, an ambulance pulled into the alley behind Maier Rothschild's store on Fifth Street. Two officers stationed themselves at the back entrance. A crowd formed behind the homes on the other side of the alley. Abe emerged from the back of his father's store, his arms slung over the shoulders of two officers. Maier followed close behind as the officers led Abe the short distance to the horse-drawn ambulance.

As the ambulance began to move, so did the crowd. The spectators formed a line behind the wagon as it made its way up Central Avenue. By the time the party reached the hospital, the number of onlookers had grown to several hundred. Abe was given a private room.

Myriad souls roamed the hospital's halls. Some of them were dis-oriented, not understanding they had died and needed to cross over, while others, wailing over their departures, hovered around loved ones, not wanting to leave them. I didn't expect some of them to be so young. A little girl wearing a nightgown carried a rag doll with her as she walked the halls. I briefly thought about helping her cross over, but I didn't want to take my attention away from Abe.

John lingered outside the door to Abe's room. Abe was already vexing the police officer assigned to guard him.

"Here they come. Here they come. Oh, take them away!" he screamed.

"What's the matter?" the guard said.

"Something's touching my head!"

"Nothing is touching your head."

I delighted in Abe's angst. He didn't aim his gun true, and now he had to live with the wound he'd inflicted on himself.

"Yes, it is!" Abe clawed at his bandages. The officer grabbed hold of Abe's flailing arms and pinned them down.

"I want some brandy," Abe demanded.

"We haven't got any."

"Yes, you have. The doctor told me so and I want it right away." Abe pouted like a petulant child.

"We haven't got any brandy, I tell you," the officer hissed. "Lie still and keep quiet and don't make such a fuss. What will people say about you?"

"What do I care?" Abe whimpered. "I don't care for the whole world. Give me some brandy, I tell you!"

Abe's antics didn't impress the officer. "You don't care what anyone would say, do you? What about the people who call you a murderer?"

John and I listened closely as Abe quieted.

"I'd like to see anyone who saw the crime committed," Abe said with a smirk and shouted for brandy again.

# 35

John's fatigue returned. At first he blamed the long journey from Texas to Ohio. Then, inexplicably to him, he started dreaming of my trunk, and of trains. In the dream, a railway baggage man pushed a cart full of luggage, my trunk on the bottom with valises piled on top.

John didn't believe Abe would have been careless enough to take evidence that could be used against him all the way home. And Detective Wappenstein had already checked Abe's room at the Burnet House. But I persisted.

"I'd be glad to show you Mr. Rothschild's room," the bellhop at the Burnet said when John explained the reason for his visit.

Abe's room appeared as he had left it. The bed was unmade, the knife he'd used to try to scrape my name off my trunk still lay on the floor. John opened the armoire and searched through Abe's clothing. His hand lingered on the rich fabrics. John had never been able to afford such finery. "How long has Mr. Rothschild lived here?" he inquired of the bellhop.

The young man stood in the doorway watching John. "About two years."

"What do you know about him?"

"Not much. But he's friendly and a good tipper."

John opened one of the compartments in the armoire then glanced at the bellhop. "Did he ever bring women to his room?"

The bellhop's eyes bulged. "Oh, no, sir, the hotel would never allow that."

John walked over to Abe's desk and rummaged through the drawers. Not so much as a five-cent piece. "When did you last see him?"

"About a week ago. He comes and goes a lot. Mr. Rothschild's a salesman, but I'm sure you already knew that."

"Did you notice anything unusual?"

The bellhop shook his head. "I don't remember anything peculiar. Couldn't believe it when I heard Mr. Rothschild shot himself."

John moved to the center of the room and took another look around for anything he might have missed. Finally came the question I'd been waiting for him to ask.

"When Mr. Rothschild came back from his last trip, did he have a trunk with him?"

The bellhop thought for a moment. "Why, yes, he did. Hadn't seen it before."

John's pulse quickened. "Do you know where it might be?"

"No, sir, I don't. I don't remember him leaving with it, but I'm not here every day."

I saw the dream about my trunk flash through John's mind. He pulled a few coins from his pocket and gave them to the bellhop. "Thank you for your help," he said and rushed out of the room. He didn't wait for the elevator, but instead bounded down the stairs.

Cincinnati had some twenty train depots, and it took the better part of two days for John and Detective Wappenstein to search their lost luggage departments. They were down to the last few depots when they arrived at the baggage room of the Cincinnati, Hamilton, and Dayton

Railroad, which, like the others, was bursting with trunks and valises of all shapes and sizes: barrel tops; flat tops; trunks made of oak slats, walnut slats, embossed metal; Jenny Linds; stagecoach trunks; small, square-shaped hat trunks; and leather and carpet valises.

It was John who spotted a Saratoga that matched Dr. Turner's description under a pile of odd-shaped leather and cloth suitcases. The claim ticket showed it had originated in Jefferson, Texas, and had passed through Little Rock, Memphis, and St. Louis before arriving in Cincinnati. John ripped off the brown manila paper that Abe had pasted to the side of the trunk, and there, in black letters, was my name, the "A" partially scraped off.

A baggage handler entered the room with a cart full of suitcases. "Did you find what you came for?"

"Sure did," John said. "This trunk, right here."

The baggage handler stopped his cart. "I remember that one."

"How so?" Wappenstein jumped in.

"A man paid me forty cents to bring it here."

"How long ago?" John said.

"I don't remember exactly, but it was several days ago. You're lucky you found it when you did. Another couple of days and it would have gone to the 'old horse' department and been sold as unclaimed baggage."

John and Wappenstein exchanged satisfied grins.


Back at the police station my trunk became an object of curiosity among the deputies. Wappenstein suggested summoning my madam to identify it, to make sure they had the right one. Guthridge, who had returned from the prosecutor's office, didn't see the harm in having someone else identify it.

"All right," John concurred.

Wherever she went, Frances Wright created a sensation. Men flew out of their seats, tripping over each other's feet to welcome her. "My dear Wappy, how nice to see you again," Miss Wright purred when she entered the station, her full-length mink nearly trailing on the floor.

Colonel Wood ordered his deputies to clear out of his office. They all left, except for one gentleman, a short odd-looking man with a fisheye. He held a pad of paper and pen.

"Gentlemen," Colonel Wood said to his visitors, "this is Lafcadio Hearn, one of Cincinnati's finest reporters."

Hearn stood at an angle, to shield his clouded eye, but he couldn't completely hide it.

Miss Wright brushed a hand across my trunk and murmured, "My poor girl."

John made the first inquiry. "What does the A stand for?"

"Her real name was Annie. Most of the girls in our line of work use a stage name. Have you looked inside?"

"Not yet."

"We were waiting for you to arrive," Wappenstein explained.

John shook his head. "I don't think it's a good idea to open the trunk."

"Why not?" Guthridge said.

John regarded the county attorney incredulously. "It could be considered tampering with evidence."

"But what if the jewels are inside?"

Miss Wright snorted. "Honey, there ain't gonna be any diamonds in there. That's what Abe wanted."

"I think we should at least take a look. His lawyers could argue this isn't her trunk. The only way to make sure is to open it and see what's inside," Guthridge argued.

"He's got a point," Wappenstein acknowledged. I didn't see either how opening my trunk could be a problem. I wanted to see what Abe may have left, whether he pawned my clothing, as I was sure he had with my diamonds.

With everyone in agreement, Guthridge lifted the heavy top. He pulled out two light-colored silk dresses, my black silk dress trimmed with merino wool, and a pair of slippers. He stepped back to let Miss Wright retrieve my unmentionables: silk stockings, chemises embroidered with the initials B.M., and an assortment of other undergarments.

John glanced at Miss Wright. "I assume these are Bessie's clothes?" Miss Wright gave a solemn nod.

My toiletries were also inside the trunk, along with a silk pincushion and a small tin jewel box. Guthridge picked it up. It was empty. I knew it would be, yet I was still disappointed. Why, I didn't know; I wasn't alive to enjoy my jewels.

John shook his head. "First he signs his real name at the Capitol Hotel, then he brings the trunk back to Cincinnati instead of disposing of it elsewhere. I'd say the fellow is a saphead."

"Abe never thinks before he does anything," Miss Wright said. "He's impetuous."

"Did he ever threaten to kill her?" Guthridge asked.

Miss Wright shook her head. "Not that I heard. But they were always fighting. He said Bessie owed him money and he'd have it, one way or another."

During the discussion the reporter had remained silent. He kept glancing around, as if he was looking for something. Perhaps he sensed my presence. Some people had that gift—or curse, as it may be. "She took all this abuse?" he said to Miss Wright.

"I don't know why, but yes, she did. We told Bessie she should give Abe the mitten. She did at least once, but they didn't separate for long. They had a strong attraction to each other, why I'll never understand. He was perpetually finding fault with her for not making more money."

A sudden sadness overcame John, so strong it startled him. And me. I began to weep, so hard I feared my tears would spill over into the real world or that the living would hear my cries. Why *hadn't* I listened to Miss Wright, or to the others who had warned me about Abe?

John fought to control his emotion. "How long did she board with you?"

"Less than a year. Bessie kept to herself most of the time. But she was smart and knew how to charm a man." Miss Wright's tone turned sorrowful. "She's… she *was*… one of my most popular girls."

"Are you sure the murdered woman is the same one who lived here in Cincinnati?" The reporter spoke with an Irish brogue mixed with a slight French accent. All heads turned toward him.

"We have no doubt," John replied.

"You heard Miss Wright confirm it," Guthridge chimed in. "Why do you ask?"

"My paper received a story from Baltimore regarding a family that claims the victim was actually a woman named Alice Kirby. Seems Mrs. Kirby eloped with her husband's brother and they left Baltimore. The family says the description of the woman you found matches their missing relative, down to the clothes."

Miss Wright's petite frame straightened under the heavy weight of her fur. "I can assure you the woman was my girl, and Abe Rothschild killed her. I'm as sure of it as I am the sun shines."

Hearn yielded to Miss Wright with a slight nod of his head.

Guthridge turned to her. "Will you come to Jefferson and testify against Abe?"

Without hesitation Miss Wright, with a grim expression, said, "It would be my pleasure."

Vengeance would be mine.

# 36

Sheriff Vines wanted to go home. He had grown weary of Cincinnati and I didn't blame him. Dr. Turner had returned to Jefferson, his task of identifying and examining Abe complete. John and Ed Guthridge were tired, homesick, and low-spirited over the delays forced by Abe's lawyer. They took no interest in anything other than my case, for which I would be forever grateful. They were determined not to fail, but after two weeks, they were no closer to gaining custody of Abe than when they'd first arrived. It frustrated me too.

Abe's father had hired the most well-known defense attorney in Ohio, who had yet to have a client sent to the gallows during his twenty years before the bar. But this was only an extradition hearing. While Charles Blackburn kept Abe from appearing at the hearing, the papers reported his client's every move. Even though he was resting easy, sitting up, and reading with his one good eye, Abe stayed out of court. John was convinced Abe would live, and the longer his prisoner stayed out of court, the more anxious John became.

John and Guthridge read the papers daily. The reporters seemed to know more about the case than they did, a constant source of irritation. One day an article caught John's eye. "I'll be damned." They were eating their midday meal. Guthridge sipped his soup as John read aloud the first line. "The following from Danville, Illinois may be accepted as conclusive evidence of the marriage of Abe Rothschild to Bessie Moore."

Guthridge set down his spoon.

"She was as pretty as a picture," John continued. "Her auburn hair contrasted handsomely with her large blue eyes, and her lovely complexion and graceful form would have tired the heart of an Italian sculptor. He hailed from the sunny South and registered as Abe Rothschild, New Orleans.

"They arrived yesterday and drove to the Aetna House, where matters were arranged, and the date, day, and hour settled. All that was needed now was a dollar's worth of parchment with the county clerk's autograph, and some obliging person with authority to marry them. These were at hand, and before the couple had strolled through our parks, visited our skating rink, or viewed our much talked about monument in the public square, they were married. Justice McMahan officiated.

"A reporter offered the congratulations of *The News* to the happy pair last night, and found them in room fifty-two at the Aetna, preparing to catch a car early in the morning. They plan to go south to Texas via the Evansville, Terre Haute, and Chicago Railway. Bon voyage, Mr. and Mrs. A. Rothschild."

Bon voyage, indeed. How well I remembered standing in that parlor, gazing into Abe's eyes, looking forward to our future together. How quickly things change.

The afternoon of Abe's hearing, the judge had to order a deputy sheriff to keep the aisles clear of the crowds gathered to get a glimpse of my murderer. Abe's attorney entered carrying a brown leather case, followed by another man. I recoiled. It was Tom Snelbaker, Cincinnati's former police chief, and a frequent visitor at Miss Wright's house.

Snelbaker was a Punchinello of the worst sort and I despised him. His presence with Blackburn made me more than uneasy.

A few minutes after two o'clock, Abe entered the courtroom draped over the arm of the policeman who'd been guarding him at the hospital.

Once seated next to his attorney, Abe glanced around the room before staring up at the ceiling, where I hovered above the judge's bench. He sported a black cashmere Prince Albert coat and trousers, and a silk handkerchief that matched the ashy hue of his face covered his right eye. Occasionally, he shifted his gaze but it always returned to the same spot. He sensed my presence, and I wasn't going to give him a moment's rest.

After the first day of the hearing ended with no ruling from the judge, I attached myself to Snelbaker. I didn't trust him. When he took a street-car to Sixth and Vine, I knew where he was headed. The house hadn't opened yet for the evening, but the preparations were well under way. I heard chatter upstairs as doors opened and closed and a girl ran into another bedchamber needing to borrow a hair comb or stockings, or seeking help buttoning a dress. I heard Madeleine's sweet voice. It felt strange not to be able to talk to her, to be inside Miss Wright's house at all, invisible and unheard.

As Snelbaker waited in a parlor for Miss Wright, he ran his hands through his pomaded hair and straightened his necktie before the parlor mirror. Miss Wright entered, with her beloved terrier as usual.

"It's always a delight to see you, Tom." Miss Wright motioned for her butler to close the door. She took Snelbaker's hands and pecked his cheeks. "How is the private detective business?"

"Very well indeed, thank you."

Miss Wright sat down and motioned for Snelbaker to do the same. She placed Jewel on her lap. "To what do I owe this pleasure?"

"I've been working with Charles Blackburn. You may have heard he's defending Abe Rothschild at the extradition hearing."

"Yes, I've been reading the papers." Miss Wright's gold bracelets jangled as she stroked Jewel. "So that's why you're here?"

Snelbaker nodded. "A gentleman from St. Louis is trying to blackmail Abe's family."

My ears perked up. So did Miss Wright's. She leaned forward.

"He sent a representative here to work Abe's father. The old man referred him to Blackburn, and he asked me to keep an eye on the fellow, to find out exactly what incriminating evidence he might have against Abe."

"Who is this gentleman from St. Louis?"

"George Ellis."

Miss Wright shook her head. She'd never heard of him. I was dumbfounded. George Ellis was Abe's gambling partner. "He sent a letter to Abe," Snelbaker went on. "Said he had information that would clear him, and that he wasn't humbugging."

That scoundrel couldn't possibly know anything that would "clear" my husband. "I highly doubt it," Miss Wright said. "Abe killed Bessie, I'm sure of it."

Snelbaker continued. "When Mr. Ellis didn't get the reaction he wanted—"

"You mean money?" Miss Wright didn't mince words.

"Yes. When the family didn't bite, Mr. Ellis changed tactics. Now he's threatening to go to the prosecution in the hopes that Abe's father will pay up."

"What would he say now?"

"Mr. Ellis is willing to testify that he saw Bessie in Jefferson the weekend she was killed and that she told him she feared for her life."

Despite George's willingness to tell a false story on my behalf, I didn't want that cretin's help.

"I see," Miss Wright said. "This is certainly interesting, but why are you telling me?"

"Since Bessie was one of your girls, and I assume you know Abe quite well, I wanted to find out what kind of evidence you have against him."

"He abused Bessie, but why would I tell you more?"

"I'm thinking of future possibilities," Snelbaker said.

"You mean future propositions?"

Snelbaker nodded.

"I love propositions," Miss Wright admitted. "They have served me well."

Nervous, I moved closer to my former madam. She sighed and said, "But I have already accepted one. I'm going to Texas to testify against Abe."

Relief flowed through me.


That night, heavy rains fell over Cincinnati. By morning, the Ohio River had risen more than five feet. The dismal weather continued as the extradition hearing reconvened. The judge ruled Abe could be taken back to Texas, but Blackburn wouldn't concede. He asked for an hour to draw up a bill of exceptions.

"You are free to file anything you wish," the judge replied, "but this court has no further control over the prisoner." A rap of his gavel ended the hearing.

While Blackburn rushed out of the courtroom to prepare yet another motion, John and Ed slipped out with Cincinnati's prosecutor. They hurried through an underground passage connecting the courthouse with the jail. The jailer went to Abe's cell. I accompanied him.

"You're wanted downstairs."

"Who wants me?" Abe asked suspiciously.

The jailer unlocked Abe's cell and swung open the door. "Make haste, you're wanted quickly."

Reluctantly, Abe followed the jailer downstairs. Seeing John, he blanched. I wished I could share my elation with someone—anyone.

"I won't shackle you if you promise not to give me any trouble," John said calmly, but his tone was clear. He wouldn't put up with any shenanigans.

The men took Abe to a carriage awaiting them. An hour later they reached the Indiana border and the tension inside the carriage eased. John allowed the driver to stop so Abe could write a letter to his brother, which Cincinnati's prosecutor offered to deliver.

*April 5, 1877*

*Dear Charles:*

*I was greatly surprised at my sudden departure and felt badly at being unable to bid you all goodbye. Send my clothes as soon as possible and have the Commercial and Enquirer send me the papers daily. You will have to send them the money in advance. Let me hear from you full particulars.*

*Regards to all, your brother,*

*Abe*

Once again, it was all about him. No apology for the shame and disgrace he had caused his family, only concern with what *he* wanted.

At Lawrenceburg, Indiana, the three men boarded the Ohio and Mississippi Railway, but there would be no luxurious Pullman sleeper for Abe. Instead, they shared a wooden bench.

John and Guthridge's minds were focused on what lay before them. If the fight over Abe's extradition held any indication, they had a long road ahead of them. Edla's prediction that pursuing justice would be painful was proving true. I was beginning to wonder whether it would have been better if Abe had died outside Jake Aug's. What if the effort to see him hanged failed?

I pushed those thoughts out of mind and stared out the window, watching the scenery pass by as the train click-clacked through the rolling hills of Kentucky and Tennessee, across the murky Mississippi, through Arkansas, and back to the place I now called home. My roots had been sown in Ireland, spread to Canton, New York, and they were now eternally embedded in Jefferson, Texas.

# 37

None of the passengers on the train suspected a murderer sat among them. Abe acted more like a man traveling for pleasure than a prisoner awaiting trial. He talked John up as if they were old friends, but John kept a vigilant eye on Abe at all times.

When we crossed Black Cypress Bayou, north of Jefferson, I grew nervous with anticipation. I could see a crowd forming as we approached the depot. Edla was there too. Abe squirmed a little, wondering if a mob would take him to the nearest tree.

As Abe stepped onto the platform, whispers rippled through the crowd. The mayor stepped forward and shook Abe's hand. "Welcome back to Jefferson," he said awkwardly. A few other townspeople also shook hands with Abe. I was overjoyed at Abe's return, but I couldn't believe the welcome reception the town was giving him. Abe was a prisoner, not a dignitary.

John motioned for Abe to board a carriage. He and Guthridge followed. The crowd parted as the carriage slowly left the depot. John and Ed paraded Abe through town to show everyone they had caught their man. Shopkeepers and their patrons stepped outside, staring at Abe with expressions of disgust or plain curiosity.

The jailer greeted Abe and took him to a cell on the upper floor of the two-story brick jail on the outskirts of town. No visitors were allowed Saturday, but the throngs of people lingering outside kept their eyes trained at Abe's window, hoping for a peek at the prisoner. Periodically he waved to the crowd, which continued to grow throughout the night.

Sunday morning, folks set out picnics amid the soon-to-be flowering dogwoods around the common area outside the jail. Around eleven o'clock, the jailer came outside and announced that the prisoner could receive visitors. A steady stream of onlookers walked past Abe's cell, stopping to gaze at him like a caged animal. He sat on a sturdy bedstead he'd already had delivered to his cell, along with quilts and a down pillow, and a table and chairs.

I went to the cell window. Below, John milled through the crowd. A woman seated on a blanket packed the remnants of a picnic while her children played nearby. Several men stood around, chatting. There was another woman, alone, her back to me. *Odd*, I thought, *for a woman to come by herself to a jail.*

One of Abe's visitors caught my attention. I recognized his tinny voice. Lafcadio Hearn, the reporter from Cincinnati, had heard about Abe's departure and caught the next train to Texas. The jailer opened Abe's cell door for Hearn.

"How kind of you to come all the way down here," Abe said as he offered a cigar.

Hearn waved it off. "Mr. Blackburn believes you were kidnapped."

Abe laughed jovially. "That couldn't be further from the truth. I was sorely disappointed I didn't have the chance to say goodbye to my friends and family, but I am being treated well here, as you can see."

Too well, in my opinion.

Abe clipped off one end of the cigar he had offered to Hearn.

"I came to see for myself," Hearn said. "Mr. Blackburn threatened to have the sheriff's head for letting the jailer hand you over to the Texas authorities."

"Is that so?" Abe said, amused. He lit a match and slowly rolled his cigar on the flame.

"What will be your line of defense?" Hearn inquired.

Abe took a puff and exhaled. "I can't say. It belongs entirely to my counsel."

"But you were here this past January, were you not?"

"Yes, I was."

Hearn untucked a newspaper from under his arm and turned to a page that showed Abe's signatures at the Capitol and Brooks hotels.

"Are these your signatures?"

Abe leaned over and studied them. "By George, those are mine," he said nonchalantly. "I hope you'll come to my trial," he added.

"I would have planned on doing so, but I may be moving to New Orleans soon."

The mention of the Crescent City reminded me of the last time I was there, how I'd brushed off the feeling that I would never see it again. Had I already harbored doubt?

After Hearn left, people continued filing by. The line seemed endless. A woman holding an infant approached.

"You must be tired from holding your child," Abe said to her. "Why don't you sit down for a minute?" He motioned to a chair next to him. "May I?" Abe asked the woman as he reached for her child.

The woman hesitated, then handed Abe her babe. As he dandled the baby on his knee, I grew infuriated at how easily he played with the child. How dare he act like a gentle fatherly figure! I consoled myself, though. Abe would never be a father. He would swing from the end of a rope soon.

# 38

Edla was thankful to have John home. "I told you I would take care of your husband," I said, and we laughed over the absurdity. Then she grew serious. "After you left," Edla said, "a woman named Belle Gouldy told someone she saw you alive the week after you were killed, and the rumor spread around town."

"But that's impossible!"

"I know. The problem is…" Edla paused, her concern evident. "She told a lawyer, whose business partner, a criminal defense attorney, is also a congressman."

The law office of David Culberson and William Armistead was located in the same building where my body had been taken after it was recovered from the hilltop. I had never seen so many books in one place, other than in a library. They filled several bookcases from floor to ceiling.

A man of medium height and slender build arrived first. From Edla's description, I surmised he must be William Armistead. While Armistead was impeccably dressed, Culberson entered the office looking more like an absent-minded professor than a powerful member of Congress, his attire rumpled, his coat jacket draped slightly askew.

The two men greeted each other warmly, like father and son.

"How was the journey home?" Armistead said, taking a seat by the congressman's desk.

"Tiring, especially after the events of these past months."

"How is Ruther-fraud?"

Culberson chuckled as he settled into his chair. "Now, now, Hayes is our president. There's nothing we can do about it." The congressman took a cigar from a drawer.

"Is it true about a compromise to elect him?"

"So I've heard." Culberson lit his cigar and leaned back as he took a puff.

Armistead nodded. "Have you heard about the murder of the woman known as Diamond Bessie?"

Though I had been listening to people talk about me for some time now, it was still strange not to be able to shout my presence, to tell them I was there listening to every word.

"I read about it in the *Jimplecute* and in Washington's paper. Her body was brought here, as you probably know." Culberson motioned toward the part of the building used as the makeshift morgue.

Armistead nodded. "She and her companion caused quite a stir when they came to town. Everyone noticed them, including a woman who came to see me recently."

"Who?"

"Belle Gouldy."

Culberson arched his eyebrows.

"She said the gentleman the murdered woman came to town with couldn't be the one who killed her."

"Why not?"

"Belle claims she saw the woman the week after she was said to have been killed."

"Did anyone else see the woman alive?"

"Belle is the only one."

Culberson rubbed his chin.

Armistead continued. "The suspect is a gentleman from Cincinnati by the name of Abe Rothschild."

The last name caught the congressman's attention.

"Rothschild?"

Armistead nodded. "A Cincinnati judge ruled in favor of extradition, and Mr. Rothschild arrived here recently. You may want to hear Belle's story. If it's true, Rothschild may well be innocent."

"And if her story isn't true?"

"I believe, as you do, that every man is entitled to a defense."

Culberson smiled. "I've taught you well."

"Yes, you have." Armistead added, "I've already invited Miss Gouldy to come see us today."

I didn't have to wait long. Late morning, a woman entered. I recognized her as the same one I'd seen alone at the jail. She had also helped undress me. She was striking, with glossy black hair, green eyes, and an olive complexion.

I moved closer. I didn't have any hesitation about attaching myself to her. If she wanted to interfere with my pursuit for justice, I didn't care how much energy I sucked from her. I stepped into her body as if I were slipping on a dress. I sensed her nervousness immediately. And something else that Edla hadn't told me about this woman. She, too, had been a prostitute.

Belle smoothed the front of her skirt and clasped her hands together in the most ladylike manner. Armistead took a seat next to her.

"Thank you for coming to see us," the congressman began. "William says you have information about the man suspected of killing his companion across the bayou."

"Yes, sir." Belle's voice quavered.

"Was her body found near your father's farm?" Culberson spoke in a frank but warm tone. He wanted to make Belle feel at ease. I preferred her to be as uncomfortable—and unbelievable—as possible.

"No, on the other side of the road leading to Marshall." Belle's eyelids fluttered. She was already fatigued from my presence within her.

"Miss Gouldy," Armistead said, "why don't you tell Mr. Culberson what you told me?"

Belle straightened as she tried to shrug off the drowsiness. "I was visiting a friend at her boardinghouse and I happened to look out the window and see the couple walk toward the building. Her clothes were so beautiful... and her diamonds. The gentleman was also dressed handsomely. I knew they wasn't from around here.

"A few weeks later, my friend came to the house at my father's farm. Said a woman had been killed 'cross the bayou and the coroner needed help undressing the body. When we got to where the gal had been laid out, I recognized her right away. A couple other women were there, too. We took off her coat and dress. When I leaned over to remove her garter, there was a broken hook and a pin stuck in it to keep the garter together. I remember being surprised, with everything else so fancy and perfect."

"The pin reminded me of something," she continued. "A week later, I passed a man and woman crossing the bridge going the other direction. The woman looked familiar, and I turned around. They had stopped. The woman leaned over and fiddled with her garter. The man moved to block her," Belle lowered her eyes, "so no one would see her limb exposed."

"Are you sure it wasn't another woman?" Culberson said.

"It was the same woman." Belle blinked. "I'm certain." But she wasn't. Deep within herself, Belle had doubts. She wanted people to believe her, but she wasn't completely certain about what she'd seen. She was trying her hardest to convince herself she was telling the truth, but why? What did she have to gain by telling this story?

And then I saw the answer.

When Belle glanced at Armistead, her heart raced. Visions passed through her mind—of the two of them in bed.

The congressman kept probing. "What about the man… was it the same gentleman she came to town with?"

Belle shook her head, almost too forcefully. "I didn't recognize him, but it wasn't the same man."

"How do you know for sure?"

"The man crossing the bridge with her had lighter skin than the man accused of killing Diamond Bessie."

After Belle left, William turned to his partner. "What do you think?"

"She seems sure about what she saw." Culberson leaned back in his chair. "But her reputation concerns me."

"Yes," William said. "There is that."

Culberson thought for a moment. "Regardless, I suppose it wouldn't hurt to reach out to the family and offer our services. They're going to need counsel here. Jefferson's citizens won't take kindly to a Yankee coming down to defend him."

I left the law office worried but hopeful that Belle's past would prevent her from ruining my chance to see Abe hang. The irony wasn't lost on me.

# 39

Edla wouldn't let me see the newspaper. John had tossed it aside in disgust and left the house, and I wanted to know why. I pleaded, but Edla blocked my way. No matter how quickly I moved I couldn't get past her, and despite us both being ethereal spirits, I couldn't see through her. Finally, Edla gave in. "Oh, all right, if you insist," she said and stepped out of the way.

A letter Abe had written to friends at Cincinnati's jail after his arrival in Texas stared up at me from the front pages of the *Jefferson Jimplecute*.

*Dear Friends,*

*I arrived safely one week ago and am getting along well here, much more pleasantly than I did at Cincinnati. I have a nice, large well-ventilated room with every comfort I could ask for. I am allowed to promenade the streets twice a day, an hour in the morning and one in the evening. Everybody is kind and courteous to me and all seem bent to make me feel like anything but a prisoner.*

*My visitors number between fifty and three hundred daily. Some even present me with bouquets, and I am permitted to have the society of ladies whenever I please.*

*I'm sorry I didn't have the opportunity to say goodbye to you, dear friends. As far as my case is concerned, it scarcely troubles my mind, or rather I never think of it unless my attention is drawn to it.*

*Would be pleased to receive a long letter from you.*

*With affection,*

*~Abe Rothschild*


By the time I made it to the end of the letter, I was seething. How dare he gloat.

"'Promenading around the streets of Jefferson?'" I screamed. "'The society of ladies whenever he pleases?'"

The newspaper noted that the "society of ladies" were not the exact words used by Rothschild, though giving the same sense. In other words, Abe enjoyed the company of prostitutes.

"And his case hardly troubles his mind?" I whirled around the room. "Murdering his wife doesn't bother him?"

"You know it's not true," Edla said, soothing me. "It's all lies."

And it was. There wasn't a shred of truth in his letter. I followed John every day. He visited the jailer regularly. Not once had I seen anything remotely like what Abe had described.

Regardless, I had bigger worries now. Abe's father had hired Congressman Culberson and William Armistead. They were assembling a formidable defense team and had asked for a habeus corpus hearing to have Abe released from jail until his trial. Belle Gouldy would testify. As preposterous as her story was, if Culberson and Armistead were successful, Abe might leave Jefferson and never be seen again. But John couldn't do anything. The law allowed such a hearing.

The attorney prosecuting Abe was the wet-behind-the-ears Ed Guthridge. I instilled my reservations in John—inserting them into his dreams, with Edla's permission—until he decided to do something. Not long after Abe's letter was published in Jefferson, John went to a building on Austin Street and ascended the stairs to the second floor, to the law office of George Todd, the tall, thin man John had spoken to at the Queen Mab Ball.

"Have you heard Rothschild's family hired Dave Culberson?" John said once he was settled into a chair across from Todd.

"Yes, I have."

"I'm worried."

Todd leaned back in his chair, steepled his long fingers. "You don't think Guthridge is up to the task?"

"No, I don't. I don't want to say anything disparaging about him, but Ed's too inexperienced to go up against the likes of Culberson and his team. He'll be eaten alive."

The sheriff fiddled with his hat in his lap. "There's already been a problem."

"Oh?"

"Ed insisted on going into the grand jury room. I told him he couldn't be inside while the jury deliberated on the indictment. He went in anyway."

Todd leaned forward, picked up a briar root pipe. "Was anyone else there?"

"No. Only me, Ed, and the members of the grand jury."

Todd lit his pipe, took a puff, and leaned back again. "To secure a fair and impartial trial, the accused should be as vigorously and ably prosecuted as he is defended."

"That's why I came to you. I know Dave is a close friend of yours and you've never been on opposite sides of the bar, but you're the only lawyer here—hell, you're the only one for miles—who can match him."

Todd acknowledged the compliment with a slight nod. "Do you believe Rothschild murdered her?"

"I have no doubt." There was no hesitation in John's voice.

Todd grew thoughtful. "The difficulty, as you know, is that the State makes no provision for employing anyone to assist the county attorney."

"Yes, but I'm sure something can be arranged," Vines ventured.

"I'm sure something can," Todd said. "*Si vis, potes.* If you desire, you are able. That's been my motto since my days at the Hampton Academy in Virginia."

John and I breathed a collective sigh of relief.

# 40

On the first day of the habeus corpus hearing, a long line of townspeople stood outside the county jail across the street from the courthouse, withering under a burning sun to get a glimpse of my husband. He emerged, squinting when the glare hit his one good eye. A patch covered the other. He was dressed immaculately as usual, down to his shirt with gold studs. His swagger as he was escorted across the road to the courthouse exuded indifference and cockiness, not the demeanor of a man whose life was at stake.

Belle, the star witness, reveled in her role. From the time I'd spent attached to her, she never once thought what she was doing was wrong. Even my excursions into her dreams didn't deter her. When Culberson finished questioning her for the defense, George Todd stood and took a few steps towards the witness box.

"Miss Gouldy, when you saw the deceased woman's body, did you tell anyone you'd seen this same woman the week after her husband left town?"

"At the undressing I told my brother and another man standing near me."

"Who was that other gentleman?"

"Charles Campbell."

Todd moved closer to the witness box. "Miss Gouldy, are you not still a prostitute working at the Greenlight in Marshall?"

"Objection," Culberson cried as he shot out of his chair.

Judge B.T. Estes banged his gavel to quiet the outburst from the crowd. He turned to Belle. "You're not bound to answer any questions that would tend to your disgrace."

Belle nodded and tilted her chin upward as she answered Todd. "Two years ago, when my mother died, I promised her I would lead a different life and help raise my brothers and sisters. And that's what I have done."

As the hearing wore on, I realized why Culberson had wanted it in the first place. The defense got to meet every witness the prosecution would introduce at trial, at least the ones in Texas. Todd didn't believe it necessary to bring Miss Wright all the way from Cincinnati for the hearing, only for the actual trial. He was confident bail would be denied, despite Belle's story.

Todd and Guthridge also learned Abe's defense. Abe's father had hired five additional attorneys to work with Culberson and Armistead, at the congressman's urging, John presumed. Maier was spending a small fortune to try to keep his son from the noose.

When it was announced that Judge Estes had reached a decision, everyone took their seats. The judge surveyed the crowded courtroom before he spoke. "The fact that this case has received unusual attention is undisputed. All I'm concerned with is this: Is there enough evidence to show the defendant may indeed be guilty of this crime, and if so, should he be held without bail or should he be allowed to await his trial a free man. After hearing all the testimony, I have determined there is sufficient evidence to suggest that the defendant may indeed be guilty. Therefore, bail is denied." Judge Estes rapped his gavel one final time. "The prisoner will be taken back immediately to the jail to await his trial."

At the defense table no one seemed surprised, though a moment of disappointment crossed Abe's face. I was gleeful.

Soon after the habeus corpus hearing, Culberson asked the court to delay Abe's trial. It had been eight months since my death, and I was no closer to seeing justice. I was beside myself. To get my mind off Abe and the delay, Edla wanted me to go with her to Oakwood Cemetery. She always followed John for his weekly visit to her grave.

I hadn't been to the cemetery since my burial and hadn't paid attention to the surroundings. The softly sloping landscape was dotted with marble angels and crosses resting atop headstones nestled under majestic oaks and fragrant magnolias. Once again, I was grateful to the town for giving me a proper burial in such a peaceful place. If only my soul could find peace, too.

John stopped at a tall marble slab. I read the inscription: "My Wife," with Edla's name underneath, along with her birthdate, February 7, 1847, and date of death, February 3, 1873. I remembered watching John walk over to Edla's grave after my burial. I hadn't followed him and Edla, wanting to give them privacy. A smaller marker stood next to Edla's for their infant son, William Connor Vines.

John stood still, the hypnotic symphony of cicadas drumming loudly around us. He kneeled and placed flowers on both graves. Edla swirled around her husband, moving her diaphanous hands as if trying to wipe the tears spilling from him.

When he stood, I put an arm around my friend. "John loved you deeply."

Edla leaned her head against my shoulder. "I'd just had our second son when I became pregnant again. William came too early. He was so tiny, I feared he wouldn't live. Soon after, I started having agonizing seizures… I didn't make it through the night. William left John a few months later."

I stroked her hair and softly said, "Why isn't William here with you?"

Edla sighed. "He's better off in Heaven."

"But you haven't been to Heaven yet. How do you know?"

"I waited for William when he passed. There were other souls around us. I felt their warmth and pure love." Edla lifted her head. "When you die, you are made whole as God promised. Why deny my child that pleasure?"

I didn't know what to say.

"I believe," she said. Her tone seemed to question whether I did too.

"When I died," I said, "I didn't make it to the Light. I was too angry." I looked away, wistful. "No one will be there for me."

"Someone will." Edla sounded certain. She peered into my eyes with kindness. "It's not a sin to doubt."

As we stood there, invisible to the living world, William Armistead walked past us. He tipped his hat to John as he strolled by. Toward the back of the cemetery, Armistead opened a low wrought-iron gate and entered a family plot. He stood before a tall monument topped with an angel, her white marble hand poised mid-air, a robe flowing around her ankles. William took off his hat and fiddled with it while he said a prayer.

I glanced around, expecting to see other souls. "Why aren't there any other spirits here?"

"Ghosts don't like to stay around graveyards," Edla explained. "There's no energy here. Souls like us prefer to be around the living."

Indeed, the cemetery was serenely quiet.

Curious, I moved toward Armistead. He placed a hand on the angel's feet, bowed his head, and wept. He couldn't see me, but I didn't want to move any closer, so I waited until after he left to approach the gravesite. The name on the tombstone was Anna Culberson.

Edla joined me. "William was in love with the congressman's daughter. They were to marry after she finished her schooling. He was trying a case in Linden when Anna took sick and died."

"When?"

"The year after I passed. She was only nineteen. William has never gotten over it."

Not long after our visit to the cemetery, the county attorney brought an indictment against Belle Gouldy for perjury. John served as foreman on the grand jury and made sure Guthridge stayed as far away as possible when the jury met.

In the indictment John wrote that Belle "willfully, wickedly, completely, feloniously, and deliberately made a verbal false statement, under the sanctions of an oath."

When one of the jurors noted that I had also been a sporting woman, John put him in his place. "She may have once been a lady of the night, but it was her *husband* who killed her."

On a late fall day, I followed Armistead to the Gouldy farm. The bottom of the attorney's coat flapped lightly as his horse trotted across the Polk Street Bridge, his face sober despite the brightness of the late fall sun. Past the bridge, Armistead headed east. Soon a farmhouse came into view. For a moment I was transported back to my father's farm, before Hannah and her husband took possession of it, though the Gouldy farmhouse wasn't as well-maintained as my family's. A low picket fence hadn't been whitewashed in a long time and some shingles on the roof were missing, but otherwise the one-and-a-half-story log cabin, with its sloped roof, could have been the same house.

Belle was outside washing clothes. She smoothed her skirt as William dismounted his horse. "Good afternoon, Mr. Armistead. What brings you out this way?"

"Forgive me for stopping by unannounced, but something's happened." His voice was tentative.

"Yes?"

"The grand jury finished meeting."

"Oh?" Belle brushed away a wet strand of hair clinging to her cheek.

I had been at the grand jury hearing where Belle's brother and Charles Campbell told the same stories they had given at the habeus corpus hearing. Other witnesses had also come forward. Belle apparently had told a number of variations of her story about me.

"You've been indicted for perjury."

Belle's face went blank. "I... I don't understand."

"It means the attorneys prosecuting Abe Rothschild believe you lied about when and where you saw the woman he was with."

Clasping her hands together, Belle protested. "But I didn't... lie."

"The grand jury couldn't find anyone to confirm your story."

Belle's face bloomed, unable to hide her embarrassment. "But what I said about seeing Bessie is the truth." A trembling hand went up again to tuck that nagging strand of hair back into place.

"Unfortunately, we can no longer call you as a witness."

The news visibly stung. "Am I going to jail?"

Armistead fiddled with his hat. "There's a chance, yes."

Belle clenched her lips. "It's because I'm a fallen woman, isn't it?"

Armistead shifted his feet, cleared his throat, and avoided the question. "Your indictment doesn't necessarily mean you're going to jail. The sheriff will have to arrest you, but we'll do everything we can to keep you from seeing the inside of a cell."

Belle folded her arms. "I can't stay here. I have to leave."

"I can't advise you to go, but I also won't stop you."

As they stood there in awkward silence, Belle wished William would cross that invisible wall standing between so many of us. But all he could see was Anna Culberson's face.

Despite my relief that Belle wouldn't be able to tell her story at Abe's trial, knowing the agony of unrequited love myself, I empathized with her. She was a farm girl who wanted a better life but had made wrong choices. I understood her plight all too well, but I was still glad she wouldn't endanger my chance of seeing justice done.

Late that night, a sudden insistent rapping at the door roused John from his bed.

"A mob came and took one of the prisoners," a man at the door said. "They got the jailer out of bed—scared his wife half to death— and made him hand over the keys to the jail."

"Did they take Rothschild?" John asked.

"No. Jim Johnson, the fellow who killed that mail boy on his delivery route."

"I'll ready my horse."

About a dozen men from the town had gathered at the jail. "There were about thirty of them. All wearing masks," the jailer told the group.

"Were any of the other prisoners harmed?" one man asked.

"No, thank goodness. The mob's leader told Rothschild they were going to let the law take its course, but if they thought there was any chance he wouldn't be convicted, they would come back for him and hang him like a dog. Scared Abe out of his wits. He thought for sure they were going to drag him out of there, but they left him unharmed."

The men mounted their horses, their side arms and long guns at the ready. I joined them as they headed due west into the brisk October night. As the sapphire sky gradually faded to twilight pink, the posse came up a hill to a stand of oak trees. The sheriff waved his hand to signal everyone to stop. They were too late. There, silhouetted in the predawn light, a man hung from a rope.

Solemnly, the posse dismounted.

I stared at the body as it swayed. The man's head was tilted to one side, his hands bound behind his back. His eyes and tongue bulged from his swollen face.

I thought of Abe. Would his neck break instantly with a quick and mostly painless death, or would he dangle for hours, his legs kicking and twisting as he struggled for air?

A shadowy figure interrupted my reverie.

Jim Johnson moved around, disoriented. He hadn't realized he'd died. Or maybe he was afraid he would go to Hell. When he saw me, I stood resolute. He didn't try to come closer.

"Who are you?" he said.

I didn't speak.

"Are you alive?"

"No," I replied curtly.

One of the men in the posse cut the body loose from the tree. It hit the ground with a hard thud. His spirit didn't flinch.

"Why are you here?" he asked.

"Why are *you* here?" I shot back. This spirit was different from the ones I'd encountered in Cincinnati. I sensed malevolence in this man.

He didn't answer.

"Did you kill the delivery boy?"

Again, no answer.

A light appeared, even though the sun had not yet risen. A young boy stood in the radiance. At first, I was curious as to why the victim didn't cry out at the man who had killed him, then I realized he didn't need to. His murder had been avenged. I felt badly for the boy, but I envied him. After a moment the boy disappeared.

The man seemed frightened by what had happened, as if the light might come back and whisk him away to a place he didn't want to go.

A few members of the posse wrapped a blanket around the man's body and tied it onto one of the horses. As John and I started the journey to Jefferson, I didn't look back.

# 41

I hadn't anticipated that the anniversary of my death would be so difficult, but I awoke on the morning of January 21 overwhelmed by sorrow.

"The first one is the hardest," Edla said.

At first, I didn't understand what she meant. But the memories of that day rushed back, and I relived every moment of my murder frame by frame, a series of tintypes frozen in time. If I were still alive, I would be halfway into my twenty-seventh year. With many more years still ahead of me, I would have had time enough to redeem myself, to find a better husband, a better life. Anger eclipsed my grief—anger over my death, over the endless delays with Abe's trial. I had been so sure he would have hanged by now.

In their latest successful attempt to delay the trial, Abe's attorneys had claimed that some critical witnesses couldn't be found. Two would say that they knew both me and Alice Kirby, the woman from Baltimore whose family thought my body was hers. A third witness would say that I had been a "lewd and dissolute woman for six or eight years," and that I'd had an abortion in New Orleans. That incensed me the most.

Abe's attorneys had subpoenas sent to the counties where these witnesses supposedly resided, yet not one of them showed up for the hearing. "Do these witnesses really exist?" Todd had challenged in court. "They are not to be driven from their right to testify by any hue and cry," Culberson had rebuked.

Despite Todd and Guthridge's best efforts, the judge granted yet another continuance.

By March the snow had succumbed to the changing of the seasons, leaving the ground bare and brown, though nature hadn't completely released her wintry grip so spring could begin. With Mardi Gras, the city exploded in color. Purple, green, and gold banners hung from the wrought-iron balconies, welcoming revelers who arrived all the way as far west as Dallas, as far east as Shreveport, and as far south as Nacogdoches. Throughout the day maskers roamed the streets, and when dusk landed, merrymakers dressed as Punchinellos, harlequins, and jesters carried lit torches, accompanying the floats that paraded the gaslit Austin and Dallas Streets.

Edla was stoic as John dressed for the Queen Mab Ball, but her placid poise couldn't hide the storm stirring beneath the surface. She had always eagerly anticipated the occasion with her husband. But this year he was going with someone else. John had taken an interest in a young woman whose father had introduced them at church one Sunday.

"I remember when you were this high," John had said, holding his hand down below his waist. Fourteen years younger than John, Louella had barely been a young woman when Edla died.

Edla had committed to staying earthbound until John remarried, but she couldn't mask her anguish when her husband turned his attentions toward the pretty, vivacious brunette. Edla didn't have to say a word as John readied for the ball, whistling a snappy tune. Her eyes conveyed everything.

That night, braced against the crisp late winter chill, Kate Wood stood at the entrance to the Excelsior House under a waxing crescent moon. She had recently bought the hotel and proudly welcomed her guests into the ballroom. Edla wanted to stay home, so I went alone. I was admiring the costumes when I noticed John and Louella, along with George Todd and his wife, talking with Mr. and Mrs. Culberson in a corner. Todd towered over everyone else, standing ramrod straight as usual. Both John and the congressman looked ill at ease in their formal attire. Culberson tugged at his cravat, as if it was all he could do to keep from untying it. I moved closer, wondering why John and Todd were acting so friendly with the man defending my murderer.

"Are you concerned about the criticism you've been receiving for defending Rothschild?" John said to the congressman. Rumors had been circulating that Culberson's defense had damaged his reputation and would keep him from running for reelection.

"Not at all," Culberson retorted. "Every man, no matter how guilty he may look, deserves his day in court. Rothschild deserves a fair trial like any other. You, of all people, should understand that."

John responded with a sheepish nod, but I was confused. What did Culberson mean?

The congressman raised his whiskey glass. "We all make our own choices. The important thing is going to bed at night satisfied with what you've done."

When the group dispersed and Culberson was alone with his wife, Eugenia said, "I'll be glad when the trial is over so you can concentrate on your campaign."

"The trial won't happen at the spring term."

Eugenia's mouth dropped. So did mine. "Why in heavens not?"

"We're going to move for a change of venue. Rothschild can't get a fair trial here. You know that."

*Move the trial? To where?* I panicked at first, but it subsided as I realized it didn't matter where Abe's trial was held. He had killed me; there was no way around it.

"But everyone knows he's guilty," Mrs. Culberson said with exasperation.

Culberson raised his glass, took another swig. "My point exactly."

Eugenia remained undeterred. "You were able to convince Sam Houston not to allow Lincoln to bring federal troops here and instead let Texas secede from the Union. Your powers of persuasion are far better than most, but I agree with the rest of the town. Abe Rothschild killed that poor woman."

"I agree murder is a serious crime, and it should be severely punished. But all of the evidence against Rothschild is circumstantial. I would hate to see an innocent man hung more than I'd hate for a guilty one to get away with murder."

As far as I was concerned, all the evidence pointed to my husband. If not Abe, who else would have wanted to kill me? I willed myself to remain calm. I had to trust that Guthridge and Todd would be successful.

Back at the house, I avoided any mention of Louella, but I was curious about Culberson's comment to John. What should he, of all people, understand?

"I suppose you should know," Edla said, to which I gave her a puzzled look.

"After the war, there was so much tension between our men and the Yankees who came down south. One night a group of Union loyalists and some former slaves held a meeting at a cabin outside of town.

One of the Yankees, a Mr. George Webster Smith, registered voters in Marion County. He refused to register any man who wouldn't take the Oath."

"Oath?" I had only been a child when the war ended and didn't know what Edla was talking about.

"Every Southern man had to swear that he'd never pledged his allegiance to the Confederacy, or he couldn't vote. Hardly any of our men could truthfully take such an oath. They resented that the Negroes could vote but they couldn't. You know men don't like to be told what they can and can't do," she added with a soft chortle.

"Neither do women," I retorted.

"Yes, but it's accepted in society that a woman must follow a man."

*How well I know that*, I thought bitterly.

"A group of our men—John was not among them—confronted Mr. Smith. There was a gunfight. Mr. Smith survived and was taken to the jail. The next night, the men who had gone to the cabin went around town riling up anyone they could find. They got about seventy men, including John and his uncle, to follow them to the jail."

Edla stopped. I let her take her time. "Apparently the mob wanted to take matters into their own hands and hang Mr. Smith. When the jailer wouldn't let them inside, someone broke the window to his cell and shot and killed him. John regretted being there. He didn't shoot anyone, but he ended up getting arrested. The Union soldiers had to build a makeshift prison because there were too many accused to fit in the county jail. John was held in the stockade for almost a year. It took a toll on us. I'd had our first child. I would go visit John at the prison, take him food. It was filthy. The prisoners suffered greatly. Thankfully he was acquitted."

Edla grew quiet again. How well I knew the consequences of making bad choices. But I still didn't understand what this had to do with the exchange between John and Culberson. Edla realized that.

"Dave Culberson was John's attorney."

"Oh."

I had sensed a bond between John and the congressman but hadn't realized how strong it was. John felt beholden to the congressman for saving his life, though this feeling hadn't affected his pursuit of justice for me. He had convinced George Todd to offer to assist the county attorney and John had made sure he was the foreman of the grand jury that indicted Belle Gouldy. There wasn't anything else for John to do at this point. It was all up to Todd and Ed Guthridge.

But if the congressman could persuade a jury to acquit John, it could also happen with Abe. The thought was most unsettling. I squirmed. Edla knew what I was thinking. She tried to reassure me. "Don't worry," she said, "it will be all right."

For the first time, I wasn't so sure.

# 42

As Culberson predicted, he easily obtained a change of venue, to nearby Marshall. He argued that his client shouldn't be tried "in a community so fatally prejudiced against him." I wanted to shout that they were prejudiced with good reason.

Abe's long confinement had begun to show around the edges. The papers in Jefferson reported that ill feelings between him and Jefferson's jailer had been festering for a while. I didn't care how much he disliked being in prison. He was alive and I wasn't.

When John arrived at the jail to transport Abe to Marshall, he was in irons. The jailer, fearing Abe might start a fight with him, had sent another prisoner into Abe's cell to shackle him. Abe had somehow obtained a knife and cut the other inmate. He was finally restrained, and John took Abe by train to Marshall's jail atop a hill at the edge of the town square across from the courthouse. On the other side stood the Capitol Hotel, where Abe and I had stayed when we'd first arrived in Texas.

Fall came, and with it, finally, a court date. Abe would stand trial in December.

My husband emerged from the Marshall jail, his face pale and his once-trim midriff paunchy from nearly two years of confinement. But he wore a defiant smirk. There was a time when I found his cool rashness exhilarating. But now I saw it for what it was—arrogance and contempt.

Inside the courtroom Abe smoked a meerschaum pipe while he chatted with his attorneys. He seemed so unconcerned about the proceedings, if I didn't know better, I would have thought he was one of the spectators rather than the defendant.

Reporters from all over the country, recognizable by their notepads and pencils, had come to Marshall for the trial. I looked for the fish-eyed journalist from Cincinnati, Lafcadio Hearn, but didn't see him.

Abe's parents also weren't among the crowd. I couldn't fathom why they hadn't come. I also searched for Miss Wright but didn't see her. I hoped she wouldn't let me down. George Todd had written to Detective Snelbaker, and the detective had responded he would come but didn't say anything about Miss Wright or George Ellis. John had gone to all the hotels and shops in Jefferson, but no one had heard of Ellis. Something wasn't right.

At nine o'clock Judge Augustus Booty, a slender middle-aged man with a receding hairline and large ears, took his seat and rapped his gavel. "I understand," he began, "that the defense has filed a motion for continuance."

I groaned and braced myself for another delay.

Instead of the congressman, who I also hadn't seen, William Armistead rose. As he stood, the judge raised an ear trumpet to his right ear and leaned toward the attorney.

"Your Honor," Armistead said in a raised voice, "we request a delay due to the absence of some important witnesses as well as our colleague, the Honorable David Culberson, who is detained in Washington due to his congressional duties."

The backlash against Culberson for defending Abe hadn't kept him from running for Congress again. He'd been reelected in November. Now those duties might keep him from leading Abe's defense. It seemed luck was on my side.

Armistead continued. "We also have information about some of the prosecution's proposed witnesses who are reported to be of bad character, who conspired to blackmail the defendant's family, and to convict him unjustly."

Murmurs rippled through the crowded courtroom. They quieted with a stern glance from the judge.

"We don't believe the prosecution is aware of these witnesses' less than desirable reputations," Armistead said. "But we wanted to make the court aware, to protect the right of our defendant to a fair and impartial trial."

"Quiet," Judge Booty said to the muttering spectators.

He turned his attention back to Armistead. "Which witnesses are you referring to?"

"One of them is Detective Thomas Snelbaker, who we believe is being promised a monetary reward and is being influenced by an improper motive."

Todd's head jerked toward Armistead. I glanced around the court-room. My attention had been so focused on Abe, I hadn't seen the detective enter. He sat a few rows behind the defense's table, looking snide as usual.

"Mr. Snelbaker went to Abe's father," Armistead explained to the judge, "and said he and a few others would not come to Texas to testify against his son if Mr. Rothschild gave them a rather significant sum of money."

More murmuring among the spectators. I was stunned. Surely Miss Wright hadn't tried to blackmail Abe's family with Ellis and Snelbaker.

John was sitting in the front row behind the prosecution's table,

Edla unseen by his side. Her husband's face reddened. Todd gripped the arms of his chair.

"From what I understand," Armistead continued, "an indictment against Mr. Snelbaker is being considered in Cincinnati as we speak."

At this, Snelbaker rose. "Your Honor, I am the person of whom Mr. Rothschild's attorney speaks. I would appreciate him consigning himself to facts and not to supposition." The detective sat back down.

"It is not my desire to attack Mr. Snelbaker," Armistead said. "But there are important issues to be discussed before this trial moves forward. May I continue?"

*What*, I wondered with indignation, *could be more important than a murdered woman?*

The judge nodded his assent.

"We have knowledge that Mr. Snelbaker worked for the defendant's father—"

The detective shot out of his seat. "Your honor, I must insist—"

The judge held up a hand. "Mister... what is your name again, sir?"

"Thomas Snelbaker."

"Please approach the bench. And you too, counselors," he said, motioning to both tables.

Abe appeared unmoved by the scene, his hands folded in his lap, face impassive, his body immobile. But I detected it. That smirk. He'd been waiting for this.

"What allegations are you making against this potential witness?" Judge Booty asked Armistead. Despite not being able to hear well, he handled his courtroom authoritatively.

"I am trying to show Mr. Snelbaker was working for the defendant's father during the defendant's incarceration in Cincinnati."

"I most certainly was not working for Mr. Rothschild," Snelbaker said indignantly.

"But you were employed by his attorney, Mr. Charles Blackburn, were you not?"

The detective hesitated. "Yes, earlier this year, but—"

"That's enough," Judge Booty said. "Who are the other witnesses you alluded to, Mr. Armistead?"

"The dead woman's landlady, Frances Wright." Armistead held up papers Maier had given him. "I request permission to introduce into evidence several letters and telegrams proving these people were attempting to bribe the defendant and his father."

I wanted to shout that Miss Wright had not accepted Snelbaker's offer. I had been there when she said she would testify on my behalf.

With clenched jaw, Todd said, "We haven't had a chance to see this evidence."

I glanced at Snelbaker. A smirk played at the corners of his mouth. He was enjoying the commotion he had caused. I wanted to smack him.

Culberson's partner handed Todd the documents. "The first one is a handwritten note from George Ellis in St. Louis, delivered to Maier Rothschild's home in Cincinnati."

Guthridge read the note and handed it to Todd. Once he'd read it, Todd said, "This isn't signed or dated. It could have been written by anyone at any time. It's useless as evidence."

"There's more." Armistead nodded toward the stack of papers Guthridge now held.

The men continued reading. Todd took special exception to a telegram he had sent to Snelbaker requesting Miss Wright's and Mr. Ellis's presence and offering to pay for travel expenses.

"We took unusual pains to bring witnesses here from Cincinnati," Todd explained to the judge. "The legislature provides no means to bring witnesses from a distance and, as we are determined to bring the guilty to justice, we offered fifty dollars for the witnesses' expenses."

The judge frowned. "I've heard enough. The trial will proceed." I admired this judge's no-nonsense attitude and his desire to move my case forward.

When Todd sat down, his hands gripped the chair so hard his knuckles whitened. Detective Snelbaker had been playing both sides of the fence and had only come to Texas after his attempts to blackmail Abe's family had failed.

"Your Honor," William said, "there is one more item that must be addressed."

Judge Booty was familiar with the history of the case and lacked the patience of his counterpart in Jefferson. "What is it?" he said with more than a hint of annoyance.

"We wish to file a motion to quash the indictment based on evidence that Marion County's attorney, Edward Guthridge, was present when the grand jury in Jefferson discussed the indictment, and when the jurors voted."

I listened more closely, uncertain why that mattered.

"If Mr. Guthridge was present while the grand jury deliberated, the indictment is not valid."

"Motion is denied," Judge Booty said without hesitation. "We will begin with jury selection."

Despite my keen disappointment over Miss Wright's betrayal, the trial would go on without the congressman, the one person I thought could destroy my chances of seeing Abe hang. I couldn't believe my luck that Culberson couldn't leave his duties in Washington.

# 43

By the end of the first day of the trial, eight jurors had been selected, but not without a fight. Armistead questioned everyone so thoroughly I feared there wouldn't be enough men in the county to seat twelve jurors. Everyone had heard of the case. One man, when asked if he had an opinion, said, "I do. I would hang the son of a bitch." Laughter had erupted, but not for long once Judge Booty reached for his gavel.

Two days later, when only one more juror was needed, the bailiff examined his list and called William Sanders to the stand. Like most of the potential jurors, he was a farmer. Evidence of his labor covered his denim overalls.

Todd stood. "Mr. Sanders, do you have any knowledge of this case involving the defendant, Abe Rothschild?"

"Yes, sir."

"What do you know?"

"Only what I seen in the papers and what I done heard 'round town."

"Have you formed an opinion as to his guilt or innocence?"

"Sure have. I think he's guilty as hell."

A rumble started through the courtroom but stopped with a glare from Judge Booty.

"If you heard testimony convincing you otherwise," Todd continued, "would it change your mind?"

"I guess I could, but it would take a lot to do that."

William Armistead rose from his chair. "Your Honor, it's obvious this gentleman has made up his mind about the defendant—"

Judge Booty held up a hand. "Mr. Armistead, I'm sure you are aware you have used all of your challenges."

"Yes, your Honor."

"Sit down. It's not your turn to question Mr. Sanders." The judge motioned for Todd to continue.

"You say it would take some evidence to alter your opinion?"

"Yes."

"But you *could* do so if the evidence you hear differs from what you previously heard?"

Sanders thought for a moment. "If the evidence presented shows he's innocent, sure, I could change my mind. That would be the fair thing to do."

Todd handed off to Armistead, who approached the witness box.

"Mr. Sanders, when did you form your opinion about the guilt of the defendant?"

"The first time I heard about it."

"Have you heard anything since then to change that opinion?"

"Not yet."

"What if we were to introduce testimony to show this man is not guilty?"

"Sure, that would do it."

"If we didn't, then your opinion is formed conclusively?"

"If the evidence is the same as I have heard it."

"No further questions."

As Armistead walked back to his seat, Todd rose. "Your Honor, the prosecution accepts Mr. Sanders as the twelfth and final juror."

Mid-stride, Armistead spun around to face the judge. "Your Honor, I am still of the opinion that Mr. Sanders should not be seated as a juror. He is clearly prejudiced against the defendant."

Judge Booty frowned. "To the contrary. Mr. Sanders said he could alter his opinion if presented with evidence showing your client is not guilty of the crime he is accused of committing." He addressed the farmer. "This court holds you qualified. You may take a seat in the jury box."

As Mr. Sanders took his seat, I surveyed the twelve men who would hear the damning testimony that would lead to Abe's conviction. I was certain they wouldn't let me down.

Opening arguments and examination of the first few witnesses consumed the rest of the day. The proprietors of the Capitol Hotel and the Brooks House testified first. Guthridge showed the jury the hotel registries with Abe's signatures. A few jurors nodded to acknowledge the handwriting was identical.

The next morning spectators craned for a look at my trunk, which sat in front of the judge's bench. It was covered in dust except for the damaged nameplate, which someone had cleaned to make sure the etching was clearly visible. The trunk had been in storage for almost two years but looked the same as when I'd last seen it in Cincinnati.

"Who is your first witness this morning?" Judge Booty asked the prosecution once he'd settled into his chair.

"The State calls Edward Guthridge," Todd said.

As the county attorney made his way to the stand, Todd moved toward my luggage.

"Mr. Guthridge, when did you first see Mrs. Rothschild's trunk?" Todd planned to use my married name as often as he could to drive home the point that Abe had killed his *wife*, not a lover. He had introduced my marriage license as evidence. The reporter who had visited us at the Aetna House in Danville, Illinois had unwittingly done the prosecution a huge favor by making our nuptials public.

"In Cincinnati, at police headquarters," Guthridge answered.

"Who was with you at the time?"

"John Vines," he said with a nod toward the sheriff. "Also Detective Wappenstein, who's a member of Cincinnati's police force, and lastly, Mrs. Rothschild's landlady."

John glanced at Abe who gave no reaction.

"Who was the landlady?" Todd asked.

"Frances Wright."

"Why was she present?"

"To identify the trunk. Mrs. Rothschild boarded at the woman's home." Guthridge was careful not to mention Miss Wright ran a brothel.

"What did she say about the trunk?"

"That it definitely belonged to Mrs. Rothschild. We wanted to make sure, so we opened the trunk and—"

"Your Honor," Armistead interjected, "there is no way to know for sure who handled this trunk while it was in Cincinnati and when it was transported back here. Some enemy of the defendant may have filled it with letters, photographs, clothing, and such to endeavor to ruin the accused. Your Honor knows what transpired with Detective Snelbaker before this trial began. Some scoundrel filled with malice would certainly seize an opportunity like this to manufacture damaging testimony. It would be unjust and an outrage, under these circumstances, to permit the trunk to be opened."

Judge Booty considered the objection. "Sustained."

The curious crowd murmured its disappointment. Abe straightened in his chair and grinned at his attorneys. John's jaw tightened. I didn't have to attach to him to know he was recalling what he'd said to Guthridge at Cincinnati's police headquarters.

When Armistead cross-examined the country attorney, he moved close to the witness stand. His typical gentle demeanor had disappeared. He was more aggressive, a tiger ready to pounce. "Mr. Guthridge, when you opened the trunk at police headquarters in Cincinnati, was the defendant present?"

"No, he was not."

"Did you have an order from the court to open the trunk?"

Guthridge shifted in the witness box. "No, we did not."

"Why not?"

"We didn't believe it was necessary."

"Even if it meant damaging the integrity of your evidence?"

"That was not our intention—"

"Thank you, that is all."

John tried to make eye contact with the county attorney as he left the witness stand, but Guthridge studiously avoided him. John had been right about not wanting to open the trunk without a court order. Opened or not, he and I couldn't help thinking of the impact my trunk, looming large in the courtroom, had on the jury.

When court adjourned for the afternoon recess, John took a carriage with Todd and Guthridge to the restaurant at the Texas and Pacific Railway depot. The men found a table tucked in a back corner. Unfortunately, some courtroom spectators had also made it to the same restaurant and, amid the clatter of utensils, I overheard customers discussing the trial as if they were theater critics. This production wasn't a *tableau vivant* with its static scenes of actors in costume, carefully posed and motionless, but rather a dramatic performance with the courtroom center stage, the judge and counsel in leading roles, and the witnesses with their bit parts. The plot couldn't be more tantalizing: a dead prostitute murdered at the hands of her dashing husband. But would the end of act three satisfy the audience, and me?

Guthridge leaned forward and lowered his voice. "Isn't it a blessing Culberson isn't here?"

Todd straightened his slender frame. "I submit to you William Armistead is every bit as able as Dave Culberson. It's going to be difficult to win this case, whether Dave is here or not."

"I've known William a long time and wholeheartedly agree with George," John said.

"Actually," Guthridge said, "I looked forward to going up against the congressman. I haven't had that pleasure yet."

The men chuckled at the young attorney's naïveté.

"In due time," John said, "in due time."

"What about the chambermaid, Jennie Simpson? Are we going to call her?"

I studied Todd as he contemplated the question.

"It's too risky."

"She's one of our strongest witnesses," Guthridge countered.

"She is, but I doubt an all-white jury would give a Negro's story any credence. I think we can win without her."

Todd's answer disappointed me. Jennie would testify she'd seen Abe wearing my diamonds at the Brooks House after he'd left me in the woods, offering a motive for Abe's actions. I hoped Todd would prove correct in his strategy.

# 44

On the evening of Friday, December 20, 1878, George Todd stood solemnly before the jury box, ready to give the final summation for the State. I hovered near the prosecution table, optimistic but also anxious. Edla was next to John.

"Gentlemen," Todd began in a somber tone, "all of you are God-fearing men, and judging a fellow man is no easy task, even less so when that man is staring death in the eye. But that is what you have been called to do. It is your duty, and I trust you will make the right decision."

As he spoke, I scanned the jurors' faces. I'd paid close attention to each of them during the trial. Not once did I feel any of them waver in their opinion of Abe's guilt. Today was no different, but they still had to hear from Armistead.

"Our laws against murder were drawn from the Jewish code," Todd intoned, "delivered by our Almighty God himself to the leader of the children of Israel. When Moses climbed that mountaintop and proclaimed the Commandments, Christianity wasn't born yet, but today people of many religions follow these edicts." He paused. "Did Abe Rothschild kill his wife? Yes, without a doubt, he did. Why did he come to Marshall and Jefferson? What kind of business did he have there?" Holding up a forefinger, Todd said, "Only one: to kill his wife."

He let that statement sink in. I tore my eyes away from the jury to look at Abe. He stared straight ahead, immobile, eyes locked on the wall behind the judge.

"When the defendant and his wife traveled by train from Marshall to Jefferson, other passengers observed Mrs. Rothschild's diamond rings. One was a large solitaire, the other a cluster of diamonds. Both valuable. She was richly and fashionably dressed and attracted universal attention wherever they went. But Mrs. Rothschild was not happy." Todd moved closer to the jury box. "Something was troubling her. Her tears were already flowing. She was visibly distressed."

I remembered the older gentleman I'd accidentally brushed up against when he came to see my body, who had first made me aware that I could read the thoughts of those still alive, how he had seen me crying at the depot and wondered why I was so sad.

"When the couple arrived at Jefferson, they acknowledged themselves as husband and wife. Why did the defendant register at the Brooks House under a false name if he didn't have anything to hide? And what about their behavior that weekend? You've heard accounts of tension between the defendant and his wife, loud arguments overheard by guests at the hotel."

Several witnesses, including one woman whose room had adjoined ours at the Brooks House, had testified that they heard us yelling.

Todd leaned in toward the jury. "That Sunday morning the defendant tried to rent a buggy, to take a lady for a ride around town, as he put it, despite the miserable conditions. When he was turned down, the defendant remarked that they would walk." Todd spoke his next words slowly. "In the rain." He paused again. "But first, he took her to a public house and plied her with drinks. He went across the street to another restaurant and brought back sandwiches for a picnic. *In the rain.*" Now his voice rose slightly.

"Why didn't they eat in the comfortable, dry confines of a restaurant, or the Brooks House? The defendant wanted a reason to get his wife away from anyone who might see or hear the deed he was about to commit. As they walked around town that morning, they must have seen the church spires pointing to the sky and heard the church bells ringing. It was God's day. Instead of listening to a sermon or a chorus of voices singing a simple hymn, Mr. Rothschild held a gun to his wife's head. The last thing she heard was the sound of a bullet ripping through her brain."

It had been difficult listening to the testimony during the trial, and now hearing Todd recount my last moments on earth, the pain sharpened. Edla squeezed my hand. Her presence calmed me.

Todd turned toward Abe and let his eyes rest on my husband. "He left her body on the cold, wet ground, placed her hat over the fatal wound, and returned to the hotel. When asked about his wife's whereabouts, he stated that he'd left her with friends across the bayou. But no friend has ever come forward." Todd faced the jury again. "Because there were none. Bessie Rothschild was a stranger to our town. She didn't know anyone here but her husband." Another pause.

"When asked again about the whereabouts of his wife, the defendant said he'd left her at Kate Wood's restaurant. Then he said she would meet him at the train. Two days later when Mr. Rothschild left Jefferson, he took all the baggage they had with them. If his wife was still alive, why wouldn't he have left her with some clothes? He knew full well she would never return to claim her baggage because he had killed her.

"What was the motive for this murder?" Todd was nearing the end of his closing argument. "There were rumors that Mrs. Rothschild was with child and that it was unwanted by her husband, but the doctor who performed her autopsy confirmed she was not. She was, however, wearing a great deal of diamonds—and her husband wanted possession of them. So he killed his wife… of only eleven days."

Todd scanned the jury box, making eye contact with some of the jurors. "The prisoner was seen wearing his wife's jewelry, openly… brazenly… coldly, after he left her body on the hilltop. Then, back at the hotel, he made no inquiries when his wife failed to return. He did not go looking for her. Had she been left across the bayou, wouldn't she have been seen by someone? Where did she stay? Who gave her food and shelter? Who saw her alive during all those dark and wintry days between January 21 and February 5?" Todd paused. "All that's needed now is your verdict. One word: Guilty. May God be with you."

Todd stood for another moment before taking his seat. A heavy air filled the silent courtroom.

As William Armistead started his closing argument, my mind drifted. I caught snippets of his words… "Have we heard anything that proves this man committed murder?… It's all circumstantial…" It didn't matter what he said. After Todd's performance I was confident, buoyant. My husband would pay for his crime.

The next morning, Christmas Eve, brought a cold, damp wind from the north. While reporters, spectators, and counsel awaited the verdict, I slipped into the jury room.

The members had chosen their foreman, who picked up a pencil and drew a picture of a noose on a wall. He stepped back and said, "That's my verdict," and wrote his name, Dick Weathersby, below the noose.

The next juror stood up, walked to the wall and signed his name underneath the foreman's. The next juror did the same. One by one, each of them added their names.

When they were finished, Weathersby wrote their verdict on a piece of paper and signaled to the bailiff that they had reached a decision. I was elated. I couldn't wait to see Abe's face when he heard the words that would send him to the gallows.

The jury walked in slowly, in "measured tread," reporters later wrote. I locked my gaze on my husband. He stared straight ahead, impassive as always, as the foreman handed the clerk the verdict.

In a clear voice the clerk announced, "We, the jury, find the prisoner guilty of murder in the first degree."

Abe paled but otherwise appeared indifferent.

*Guilty.* I said the word over and over again, savoring its sweet ring. Edla and I hugged, shedding tears of joy.

One of the jurors who had been a deputy during Abe's stay in Marshall helped escort Abe back to the jail. Outside the courthouse, a crowd gathered to see the convicted murderer. As Abe walked alongside the former deputy, I heard him say to the juror, "You're a hell of a fellow. Smoke a man's cigars, drink his whiskey, and hang him."

# 45

As quickly as winter came and went, so too did interest in Abe. Culberson immediately filed an appeal, but the townsfolk stopped talking, and the papers stopped writing about the case. No one doubted he would hang. There were other, more serious matters to tend to, like the town's dying steamboat trade, its lifeblood. I'd thought it odd for a riverport to be so far from a major river. To reach Jefferson, stern-wheelers had to travel from the Red River through Caddo Lake and navigate the narrow bayous to the inland riverport.

By July, water was the only thing moving. For days, the sun didn't blink. It held its steady, unrelenting gaze, scorching anything its rays touched. Only the cotton fields embraced the blazing heat. Acre after acre of flower buds blossomed into oval bolls that, upon opening, thrust out a mass of slender white fibers, smaller versions of the puffy white clouds lolling in the sky overhead. There was so much cotton, the fields resembled snow-covered ground.

The heat kept everyone indoors, including John and Louella. Their courtship had progressed throughout the trial, until, finally, John asked Louella's father for her hand in marriage. Edla had resigned herself to this inevitability, but she couldn't hide her sadness. I could see how much it hurt her to watch Louella take over what had once been her role, her purpose in life. Fortunately, Louella was kind to Edla's children, John Junior and little Phillip, now ten and six. Edla was grateful, but she also dreaded the day when they would call another woman Mother.

John and Louella's wedding was a small affair. Her hands trembled at the lifelong commitment, but her face glowed. *Louella didn't have any doubts as I'd had*, I thought wistfully. She knew she was marrying a good man.

Edla stayed for the nuptials but planned to cross over before the wedding night. Seeing her husband intimate with another woman would be too much to bear. She tried to convince me to go to the Light with her.

"Do you really want to stay here? Is it worth it?"

"Of course, it is. Besides, it won't be that much longer."

When it was time for her to go, Edla caressed my face. "My dear Bessie, you don't know how much I'll miss you."

Tears flowed, and for a moment I felt human again. More alive than when I was living. Here we were, a Yankee and a Southerner, a courtesan and a lady. She was a jewel of virtue and I wasn't, but she had never held that over me. Not once had Edla ever asked about my life as a *demi-mondaine*. She always treated me like a lady. She knew about Leslie and my little girl, all the troubles and tragedies I had endured and, yes, brought on myself, but she never judged. She was a far better person than I, but she never held that over me either. I didn't know what I would miss more: my life on Earth or my friendship with Edla.

She touched my face again and I closed my eyes. When I opened them, she was gone.

Abe sat in Marshall's jail eleven months before the Court of Appeals took up his case. I wasn't worried. The only thoughts I entertained were those of seeing him hang from the end of a rope.

Two months after the appeals court met, in late January of 1880, John received an urgent message from Guthridge. John and Todd arrived at the county attorney's office at the same time. On the desk in front of the county attorney lay a thick, sealed envelope.

"Gentlemen, inside this package is the majority opinion of the Court of Appeals. It arrived today. I wanted you both here as I read the decision."

John took a seat closest to the spittoon. Todd lowered his long frame into a chair. Despite my confidence, I grew anxious as Guthridge removed a sheath of papers from the envelope. He read the first part.

"The court ruled in favor of Judge Booty, that he was not prejudiced in denying the request for a change of venue out of Harrison County," he informed the attorneys.

John nodded, pleased with the outcome on the defense's first challenge.

As Guthridge read the next part to himself, he shifted in his chair. I wanted to know what had made him uncomfortable, so I moved behind him and peered over his shoulder.

*In prescribing the duties, privileges, and powers of the grand jury, almost the first mandate of the law is that the deliberations of the grand jury shall be secret. The district attorney may go before the grand jury at any time, except when they are discussing the propriety of finding a bill of indictment or voting upon one. Indeed, it is one of the grounds for setting aside an indictment and holding it for naught when some person, not authorized by law, was present when the grand jury was considering the accusation against the defendant.*

I recalled Guthridge going into the grand jury room and coming out, jubilant over the jury's indictment of Abe.

Todd grew impatient. "What is it, Ed? What does the opinion say?"

The attorney rubbed his forehead. "It says that Judge Booty committed an error when he denied the defense's motion to prove the allegation that I was in the grand jury room while they were voting."

Guthridge struggled to continue reading aloud the opinion: "It may be there was no truth to the allegation. If so, that was the time and place to determine it. The law gave to the prisoner the right, upon a proper allegation, to have the matter inquired into, and this right he was deprived of by the action of the court. The State was demanding his life, and in such a case no right, however unimportant, is to be denied him."

"That doesn't sound good," John said.

Guthridge didn't respond. As he kept reading his face grew more somber.

"What is it? What does it say?" Todd demanded.

Guthridge sped through a few more pages, shook his head, went back to a previous page, muttered to himself the name William Sanders. I remembered Mr. Sanders was one of the jurors.

"That principle of the law," the attorney slowly read, "which regards every man charged with a crime as innocent until proved guilty and declares that jurors shall be free from prejudice and preconceived opinions, is a vital one."

Guthridge stopped. His face blanched.

"What does it say?" Todd snapped.

The attorney stared at the document, as did I. He didn't want to read the next part.

"Read it," John pressed impatiently.

Guthridge hesitated but obliged. "The appellant, stranger though he is and guilty though he may be, has not had a fair and impartial trial, in that he was deprived of the right of inquiry as to the mode and manner of his presentment, and was tried by a juror who had already prejudged his case. Let the judgment be reversed, and the cause remanded for further proceedings in accordance with the forms of the law."

"Reversed?" John said incredulously. "That bastard's been acquitted?"

Todd jumped in: "No. The opinion states another trial must be held."

Guthridge's face was crimson with anger, or perhaps it was humiliation or embarrassment, or all three. I didn't care. A jury of Abe's peers had convicted him. *Everyone* knew what he'd done. There were no other suspects. Abe was the only person who had a motive to kill me. He had taken my trunk with him to Cincinnati. He was seen with my rings. Oh, why hadn't Todd let Jennie Simpson testify?

That thought further enraged me. I swirled around Todd, wrapping my diaphanous spirit tightly around him. I wanted to strangle him. He loosened his tie, wiped his brow. Despite the cold, I made him feel the heat of my wrath. I sensed his deep disappointment in himself. He had wanted justice for me. How could I fault him for that? This setback only made his conviction stronger.

Newspapers across the state and around the country roundly condemned the decision. But surprisingly, the papers in Marshall actually supported the appeals court. "Give the devil his due, lay all prejudice aside," the *Marshall Tri-Weekly Herald*'s editorial said. "Will anyone pretend to say that it looks like a fair and impartial trial to place such a prejudiced man on the jury? Would the editor himself, if on trial for his life, not regard it as a great wrong to be forced to accept such a juror?"

The Marshall paper noted the "great many unmerited reflections upon the Court of Appeals for this decision" and that "in every instance the facts have been misrepresented. The Rothschild case was not reversed on a technicality or a 'trifling quibble,' as another paper asserted, but on the very principle of the law which guarantees to every man charged with crime a fair and impartial trial."

My only consolation was that Abe had to stand trial again.

# 46

The second trial was set for June. When the first day of the summer court term began, Culberson and his team once again introduced a slew of motions. It angered but didn't surprise me when Judge Booty announced the first case to be taken up that term would not be Abe's, but that of a cellmate who'd only been in jail a year. I had been waiting three years for justice to be carried out, but Judge Booty was hesitant to revisit Abe's case.

Finally, as summer gave way into fall, the trial was rescheduled for the end of November. The first week of the month, despite the criticisms against Culberson for defending Abe, he was reelected to Congress for a fourth term.

I hadn't visited Abe since his conviction had been overturned. I didn't want to see his smug face. But with the second trial looming, I went to the Marshall jail. Abe had been there for more than two years. He wore a casual knit jacket of the finest make and the latest style, and the eye patch was gone. He now sported a glass eye. Surrounding him was all manner of reading material. In one corner, a pile of newspapers almost touched the ceiling. Books and magazines were scattered about. It looked more like a library reading room than a jail cell. Abe had wanted for nothing during his imprisonment, except his freedom. His carefree demeanor irked me.

"Hey, Colonel," one of the other inmates shouted to Abe, "got anything I can read?"

"How about the latest by Wilkie Collins? Or..." Abe fumbled through his collection. "Mrs. Oliphant has a new novel, *A Beleaguered City*. It's a ghost story."

The other inmate stretched an arm through the bars of his cell. "Give me that one."

The jailer came upstairs and told Abe he had a visitor. Reporters were already arriving for the impending trial, so I assumed it was another journalist there to let Abe once again proclaim his innocence.

"Bring him up," Abe said.

The man had brought a phonograph to record Abe's voice. I had heard of this invention. It was a strange-looking contraption: a metal cylinder wrapped in tin foil set on a base with a hand crank.

"Would you care for a cigar?" Abe asked his visitor, holding out a box he kept in his cell.

The man took one but didn't light it. He set it down while he placed a horn shaped like a witch's hat into a tube on one side of the cylinder.

"Place your mouth close to the horn and speak loudly into it," he instructed Abe.

"What should I say?"

One of the other inmates yelled out, "Say, I'm Colonel Rothschild."

I resented watching Abe being treated like a celebrity. No one could visit me, no one could record my voice. He had wronged me and yet here he sat, jovially enjoying his imprisonment. He was a murderer, but he may as well have been allowed to roam the country free as the air.

The visitor turned the crank and the cylinder started to move. Abe leaned into the horn. "Hello, my name is Colonel Abe Rothschild." The man motioned for Abe to repeat the sentence. As Abe said his name again, I whispered "murderer" to him, just as I had in Cincinnati so long ago.

The man stopped turning the crank and rewound the cylinder. Abe's voice sounded scratchy and distorted, but his words were clear enough. And then I heard it. I was as stunned as the others. The cell fell quiet, each man unsure whether he had actually heard a woman's voice on the recording. Abe's face paled. He started to perspire.

The effect my voice had on Abe invigorated me. I attached myself to him and entered his thoughts as I had years before, calling him a murderer over and over. I left Abe when the visitor and the jailer had gone. He lay on his bed, groaning from the sudden onset of a fierce headache.

The following day, Abe's parents and his brother Charles arrived. Distance and time hadn't made it any easier for Rosa. When she saw Abe she broke down. "*Mein sohn*," she wailed.

Abe told them about the visitor with the phonograph. "It's a marvelous invention," he exclaimed, trying to act cheerful. But having her son confined to a jail cell for so long proved heartbreaking for Rosa. After her brief visit with Abe she kept to her hotel bed. Finally, Charles took her back to Cincinnati. Only Maier stayed for the trial.

Judge Booty first had to hold a hearing to determine whether Ed Guthridge had been in Marion County's grand jury room. If so, the indictment was no good and they had to start all over again. Two of the original grand jurymen summoned to court swore Guthridge was not present, but two other witnesses swore that he *was*. George Todd tried to argue that the county attorney's presence was not "at a time or in a manner as to come outside the meaning of the law." But the testimony was damning, and Guthridge wasn't there to defend himself. He had been appointed US attorney for the eastern district of Texas and wasn't involved in my case anymore. Todd had written to Guthridge, but he had declined to appear on account of his new duties. But both Todd and I knew the former county attorney didn't come because he didn't want to be embarrassed again.

The indictment was declared invalid and Abe's case was sent back to Jefferson. It was as if there had never been a trial. Another indictment would need to be brought against Abe before the second trial could begin. Word spread that Dave Culberson would step away from his duties in Washington to take the lead for the defense. I didn't know how much more I could endure. My spirits were as low as when I'd been murdered.

# 47

The grand jury in Jefferson swiftly handed down an indictment against Abe. George Todd's brother had been elected as Marion County's attorney, but he was ill and couldn't attend the trial. It would be up to George to obtain another conviction. He sat at the prosecution table by himself, while Abe's team crowded around the defense table.

Jury selection got underway mid-December. The same judge who had overseen Abe's habeus corpus hearing sat behind the bench. Everyone wanted to see Dave Culberson, and the courtroom was filled beyond capacity each day. After four days, a jury was seated and the first witness took the stand. The new trial began much the same as the first, with many of the same witnesses testifying for the State again, but this time my trunk did not appear in the courtroom.

When it was Culberson's turn to present his case, the congressman focused more attention on the weather during the time my body lay in the woods, and introduced more doctors than Armistead had at the first trial. I cringed when Culberson asked the doctor who'd performed my autopsy, "Isn't it strange the body had not been disturbed by any animals?" I realized it might have been a mistake to have guarded my body. Being recognized perhaps wasn't as important as making sure a jury would believe I had lain in the woods such a long time with hardly any decay.

Facing Culberson's formidable presence, Todd decided he had no choice but to put Jennie Simpson on the stand on the eighth day of the trial. He needed strong, damning testimony. And with two black men allowed to serve on the jury, I thought maybe, just maybe, her account would be given the credence it deserved.

Jennie was the last witness for the prosecution. Head high, shoulders back, she strode into the courtroom with the air of an actress about to give a stirring performance.

"Miss Simpson," Todd began, "would you please tell the court about your first encounter with the defendant?"

Jennie took a deep breath and moved to the edge of her seat in the witness box. "I was told to go to room number four and take some towels and a pitcher of water for the new guests. Everybody was already talkin about 'em. A young woman opened the door and I could see right away she been cryin. Her eyes was puffed up like big balls of cotton and they was all red and swollen."

"What happened when you entered the room?"

"When I walked in, the tension was somethin fierce. It was so thick, I could see somethin was wrong." Jennie's eyes shifted toward Abe and back to Todd.

"Mister Rothschild was sittin in a chair by the window, readin a newspaper. Didn't turn aroun, just kept readin. I walked over to the table and set down the pitcher and towels. I'm also suppose to make sure the room's all tidy, so I was doing that and seen Miss Bessie had set down by the fireplace. Her head was tilted down." Jennie bowed her head as if to mimic me. She looked up and with a tear rolling down her cheek, said, "It upsets me when I think about what he done to—"

"Objection!" Culberson roared as he shot out of his seat.

"Miss Simpson," Judge Estes admonished, "you need to keep to the facts now, you understand?"

"Yes, Sir," Jennie said.

The judge motioned for Todd to continue.

"Did you say anything to the woman while you were in their room?"

"Yes. I ask'd Miss Bessie how long they been married. But she didn't say nothin, just kept her head down. Mister Rothschild spoke up and said they been married two years. I ask'd Miss Bessie how long they been travelin. She said three weeks, that it was for her health. Mister Rothschild said she had a spleen in her side."

"Did you ask any other questions?"

"I ask'd where they from, and he said Boston and New York."

"What transpired Saturday night at the Brooks House?"

Jennie's eyes widened. "The whole night he kept yellin at her and I could hear him beatin her and she was cryin so loud. She said, 'Please don't hit me no more.'" Jennie put her hands in front of her face to show how I must have tried to ward off Abe. Todd glanced at Culberson, anticipating an objection, but none was offered.

"Did you see the defendant and his wife the next day, Sunday, January 21 of 1877?"

"I seen them in the mornin when they was leavin the Brooks House. In the evenin I seen Mister Rothschild. I ask'd where his wife was."

"What did he say?"

"He told me he left her at Mrs. Wood's restaurant and she would be back later."

"Did you see Bessie again?"

"No, Sir. Never saw her again."

"Did anything happen Sunday night?"

"He was pacin his room most of the night. He liked to have never stopped walkin the floor. I figured somethin must have been on his mind."

"Objection," Culberson said without leaving his seat this time. "Miss Simpson could not read the defendant's mind."

"Sustained."

Judge Estes said to the jury, "You will disregard Miss Simpson's last statement."

He turned to Todd. "Proceed."

"Did you see the defendant again?"

"Monday mornin I seen him in the dinin room. I ask'd him if he wanted anything to eat and he said just coffee. Said he'd took sick the night before."

Todd walked to the jury box and placed a hand on the rail. "Was the defendant wearing anything unusual?"

Jennie leaned forward. "Yes, he was. He was wearin Miss Bessie's rings. I said to myself, 'Oh my goodness, those are Miss Bessie's diamonds.' I didn't dare say nothin though."

"Are you sure the rings belonged to Mrs. Rothschild?"

"Yes," Jennie said emphatically.

"Was that the last time you saw the defendant before he left town?"

Jennie shook her head. "I seen him one more time. Monday night when I was gettin ready to go to my room, I ask'd Mister Rothschild again bout his wife. He said she was gonna meet him at the train in the mornin."

When Judge Estes called for a recess, one of the spectators remarked, "Looks like Abe's finally gonna hang."

"Culberson's still got his turn," another man remarked, "so I wouldn't be so sure."

The first man snorted. "Ain't no way no one, not even the honorable congressman, can keep Abe from the noose now."

"He's going to hang, Sir. He's got to." The statement came from a young boy about nine or ten years old. It was the boy I'd seen in a store in Jefferson, the same one who'd told his mother at my funeral that he was going to hunt down Abe when he got older. The boy was taller but had the same inquisitive eyes and a solemnity about him that seemed older than his years. I was touched at his insistence.

"Aren't you McDonald's boy?" the first man asked.

"Yes, Sir. I'm Edward Bergin McDonald," he said with pride.

"That's a big name for such a little boy," the other man said.

Another man jumped in. "He's not a little boy, he's almost a man. Aren't you son?"

Edward grinned.

"Tell me, why are you so interested in this trial?"

The boy grew shy. "I dunno. It's such a famous case and all."

"And she was mighty pretty, wasn't she?"

Ed blushed. "Yes, Sir."

"Well, I guess it's okay for you to stay," the first man said, "though some things being said aren't meant for such young ears."

"Aw, let the boy watch the trial," another man said. "Ain't gonna hurt him none."

# 48

When court resumed, the bailiff escorted Jennie back to the stand. She enjoyed the gawking from the spectators who came to see the woman who would send my killer to the gallows. Silence fell over the room as Culberson approached the witness box.

"Miss Simpson, you said the defendant was wearing Bessie's rings. Was he wearing jewelry when they arrived in Jefferson?"

"Yes, Sir."

"So the rings could have instead belonged to Mr. Rothschild." Without waiting for Jennie to respond, Culberson continued, "They both possessed jewelry, and I doubt you knew them long enough to know which pieces belonged to whom."

The chambermaid straightened. "I know what I seen."

"On which fingers was he wearing the diamonds that allegedly belonged to Bessie?"

"I don't remember which fingers. But I know they was there."

"What time do you usually go to bed?"

"Most nights aroun ten o'clock. I has to get up early and start my chores before the guests wake up."

"What time on the second night did you hear the defendant and the woman in their room?"

Jennie eyed the congressman warily. "I don't remember exactly, but it went on for some time."

"And you heard all this commotion?"

"Yes, it kept most everyone on the floor up most of the night."

"Are you sure you heard the noise yourself, or did you hear others talking about something they may or may not have heard?"

"I heard it myself," Jennie said indignantly.

"How can you be so sure when your sleeping quarters are in a separate building several yards from the house?"

Jennie shifted in her seat. "Sometimes I'm in the house late at night, if I got things to take care of."

"But you wouldn't have been in the main house most of the night, would you?"

"I didn't have to be there long to know what I heard," Jennie stammered.

"Yes, but you told the court earlier the noise kept you up most of the night. Now you're saying it didn't."

Jennie leaned forward. "No, that's not what I'm sayin."

"What are you saying?"

Jennie paused before answering. "I heard Abe hittin Bessie and yellin at her."

"But you weren't inside the Brooks House all night. And you didn't actually *see* any abuse, did you?"

When she didn't answer, Culberson eyed the judge, who turned to the chambermaid. "Miss Simpson, you need to answer the question."

"No," Jennie said sulkily.

The congressman placed his hands behind his back and slowly moved toward the jury, stopped, and turned to face Jennie.

"Now, the next night you say you heard Abe pacing his room even though your quarters are away from the Brooks House, and Monday morning, when you saw Abe in the dining room, he was wearing some of Bessie's rings. Correct?"

"Yes, Sir."

"Are you a jeweler, Miss Simpson?"

Jennie was dumbstruck at the question. "I'm no jew'ler."

"So you're not an expert on diamonds or diamond rings?"

"No." Jennie eyed Culberson with distrust.

"Do you own any jewels yourself?"

Jennie frowned. "I don't have no money to buy me any diamonds."

"So you've never examined a diamond ring under a jeweler's glass?"

"Course not."

"How many times did you see the couple when they visited Jefferson?"

"Several."

"For how long each time?"

"A few minutes."

"How can you be so sure the rings you say were on the defendant's hands actually belonged to Bessie?"

"Cuz I seen them. I know they was hers."

"Can you describe Abe's hands?"

"They're big. Bigger than I'd expect on a man his size."

"What about Bessie's hands? How would you describe them?"

"They was small and dainty, like a woman's hands suppose to be."

Culberson waited a moment before asking his next question. "If Abe's hands are bigger than Bessie's, how could he have been wearing her rings? They wouldn't fit his fingers."

Jennie had obviously never thought of that, but she wasn't ready to accept the theory. "I don't know," she said petulantly. "All I know is he was wearin her rings."

# 49

The end of December 1880 brought the coldest weather since I'd come to Jefferson. A hard snow covered the ground, and a damp wind from the north whipped around the courthouse, rattling windows and seeping under doors. But it didn't keep the spectators away. When word spread that closing arguments would begin, the courtroom was so full, people spilled into the hallway, down the staircase to the first floor and out the door.

George Todd made the same eloquent argument as he had at the first trial. As David Culberson stood to deliver his address, I hovered close to the jury box. The congressman buttoned his jacket and walked toward the men sitting solemnly in two rows, the weight of their responsibility evident on their faces. "Gentlemen, we have listened to numerous witnesses, but have we heard anything showing that the defendant committed murder? I submit to you we have not. Mr. Rothschild and Bessie were quarreling. What couple doesn't argue? Is that any proof? Of course not."

How I wished Edla was here with me.

"Sunday morning they were seen at Kate Wood's restaurant, and again as they crossed the Polk Street Bridge. Later at the Brooks House, when Abe was asked about Bessie's whereabouts, he replied that she was with friends. It's been argued she didn't have any friends in or around Jefferson. Perhaps she did, perhaps not. I needn't remind you of her questionable character. Who's to say she didn't make friends easily?"

This brought a few chuckles from the spectators and jury, but ire from me.

"In fact, how do we know the woman didn't con the defendant into marrying her? Many a man has been duped into marrying a woman for nefarious reasons."

Several members of the jury nodded. I became enraged. How dare Culberson say this. I wasn't there to defend myself!

"There's also the question of whether Bessie's body could have lain in the woods for fifteen—*fifteen*—days with such little decomposition. We heard from several doctors, most of whom said it was impossible for the body to lie there so long and remain recognizable.

"And, as we all know, Abe didn't leave town until *two* days after the alleged date of the murder. If Abe did kill her, why didn't he leave Jefferson immediately? A guilty man would have fled right away, by any means possible. This is a case of guilt by association and nothing more. The fact that Mr. Rothschild was the person traveling with Bessie does not mean he killed her.

"This case has received considerable attention. Some papers have already declared Abe guilty. But we must remember that a man is innocent until proven otherwise. I say to you, nothing has been shown to prove he committed murder. I ask you to remember that when you decide the fate of this man's life."

The room remained silent. The congressman's final words hung in the charged air.

Judge Estes cleared his throat and read his charge to the jury. "Gentlemen of the jury, the defendant, Abe Rothschild, is on trial before you, charged with the crime of murder. The law holds and presumes him to be innocent until his guilt is affirmatively established by legal evidence beyond a reasonable doubt. The burden is upon the State to establish by evidence the charge made against the defendant, and if the State has failed to do so beyond reasonable doubt, the defendant is entitled to an acquittal.

"The Court instructs that if you believe from the evidence which has been submitted to you, beyond a reasonable doubt, that the defendant, Abe Rothschild, did with express malice shoot with a pistol and kill the deceased, you will find the defendant guilty in the first degree, and assess his punishment at death or imprisonment at the state penitentiary for life.

"It is your privilege exclusively to weigh the testimony and to judge as to the credibility of the witnesses. You are further instructed that this is a case of circumstantial evidence. All the facts proven must be consistent with each other and with the fact of the guilt of the defendant. You will now carefully consider the case and return your verdict."

While the jury deliberated, the spectators milled about. Some speculated Abe might walk away a free man. I wished Edla was with me to reassure me that he would be convicted again. I was too anxious to listen in on the jury—I didn't think I could bear to hear anything other than a guilty vote, so I waited inside the courtroom.

A man took out his pocket watch. It was nearly eight o'clock. The jury had been deliberating close to four hours when a knock came on the inside of the jury room door. The bailiff opened it, conferred with one of the jurors, then walked over to the judge's chambers. A few minutes later, the judge entered the room and took his seat at the bench.

"In a few moments the members of the jury will come back into the courtroom and render their verdict. I caution each and every one of you to refrain from any sort of outcry once the verdict is announced. There will be no outbursts, or you will be charged with contempt of court."

Judge Estes turned to the sheriff. "Please clear the aisle."

The sheriff and his deputies escorted spectators blocking the center aisle into the hallway, pushing some of them farther down the hall and stairs. When the sheriff reported that the order had been complied with, Judge Estes instructed the bailiff to bring the jury back.

I studied the twelve men as they walked into the courtroom. They were stone-faced, giving away no hint of their decision. The foreman handed a piece of paper to the county clerk, Frank Malloy, the man who had watched me walk across the bridge that fateful Sunday.

The judge instructed the clerk to read the verdict.

Malloy carefully unfolded the paper. I detected a flicker of shock. In a loud, clear voice, he said, "We the jury find the defendant, Abe Rothschild, not guilty."

For a moment there was stunned silence. A grinning Abe and his attorneys stood and shook hands. His father embraced him and sank into a chair, overcome with relief. Todd and Guthridge stared straight ahead, in disbelief. Behind them, in the spectator gallery, John Vines sat immobilized.

The judge began polling the jury. As each one said, "not guilty," a fury rose within me. I moved toward my husband like a tempest. My enraged spirit knocked The Bible to the floor, but there was so much pandemonium in the courtroom no one noticed. The judge pounded his gavel, but the commotion only grew louder.

I swirled around my husband, again hissing *murderer* into his ear. Abe whipped his head around but there was nothing to reflect my visage. I coiled my spirit around my husband's neck, whirling closer and tighter with each revolution. The veins in his neck swelled. He couldn't breathe. Abe staggered from the table where he'd sat during the trial, clutching at his neck, and collapsed on the floor by the spectators' railing.

The thud silenced the courtroom, and Abe's fall broke my grip. Maier rushed to his son.

Armistead yelled for a doctor. "Give him some room," the attorney commanded as he removed his coat and placed it underneath Abe's head.

One of the doctors who'd testified on Abe's behalf pushed through the crowd and leaned over Abe. "Probably too much excitement, coupled with the release of the stress he's been under," he said.

Abe opened his eyes and I peered straight into them. This time, instead of me lying on the ground and my husband standing over me making sure I was dead, I was the one glaring down at him. But I wasn't a murderer like my husband. Until that moment I'd never realized the power I had as an earthbound soul; but even if I could get vengeance, I would be no better than him. I moved away.

Abe looked frantically around the room, mumbled, "Where is she?"

"Don't move," the doctor instructed Abe.

Maier took Abe's face in his hands. "Who are you talking about?"

Abe glanced around again. "No one," he said and grinned at the worried faces around him. "No one. No one at all."

# 50

John slipped out of the courtroom while Abe lay on the floor. The jailer, who'd been prepared to escort Abe back to his cell to await a date with the hangman, instead took the sheriff home in his wagon. I eddied around John as I had at my autopsy, wishing I could comfort him, but I couldn't even console myself.

He moped around the next day, still logy and stupefied by the verdict. Louella couldn't shake him out of his doldrums. I ached to tell John that he and George Todd, and even Ed Guthridge, had done the best they could.

I had vowed to remain earthbound until Abe hung from the end of a rope, but all prospects for that had been exhausted. Maier had spent a fortune to keep his son from the noose and it had paid off.

My thoughts drifted to Mollie. I had often looked for her in the afterlife, wondering if she had stayed. But I'd learned from Edla that my friend had most likely gone to another realm, where suicides must wait until they would have met their natural death before being allowed to go to the Light. It had given me pleasure to think about Abe being in that state. Those who had cut another person's life short also were relegated to their own realm until the person they killed would have reached their age of natural death. But now, Abe could go wherever he wanted, live whatever life he desired.

One day not long after Abe left Jefferson, John visited the county clerk's office. My trunk, a reminder of their defeat, still sat in Frank Malloy's office. I'd been so desolate over the outcome of the trial I'd forgotten about it. Seeing my trunk again only worsened my profound gloom.

"It's a fine trunk, isn't it," Frank said when John inquired how long he planned to keep it. "It's a shame for it not to get any use."

"I suppose it can't sit here forever," John said.

Frank threw his hands up. "I don't know what to do with it."

"What about Rudolph Ballouf? I'm sure he wouldn't mind taking it. Someone's bound to buy it."

I couldn't believe what I'd heard. That was my last remaining possession.

Frank agreed, and Rudolph Ballouf, a kindly gentleman with large, droopy eyes, readily agreed to display it in his store.

As word spread, visitors who came to Jefferson stopped at the store to see the trunk once owned by Diamond Bessie. Its history kept anyone from buying it. No one wanted something that had belonged to a young woman murdered by her husband. After a while, curiosity faded, and the trunk got lost in a pile of hardware—until, one day, Ballouf removed the nameplate and moved my trunk to the front of the store again.

Soon after, a gentleman passing through town bought it. He considered the dresses inside a bonus. As the salesman completed the transaction, my anger swirled with the dust the new owner wiped off the trunk. The poor gentleman who had the misfortune of buying my trunk hardly slept that night at the Excelsior Hotel as I once again became Queen Mab, sneaking into his dreams. By the time he made it to his destination, New Orleans, he was hagridden from constantly seeing an image of a young, murdered woman.

Being back in New Orleans reminded me how much I had enjoyed my time there. Now the magical side of the Crescent City was revealed. The spirit world blended into the real one so seamlessly I had difficulty telling where one ended and the other began. If only the living knew how many spirits moved among them. The intersection of Canal and City Park Avenue, where every direction pointed to a cemetery, served as a portal to the underworld such as I had never seen.

The ghosts of Confederate soldiers and riverboat captains buried in the cemeteries walked around aimlessly in their uniforms. And there were too many victims of yellow fever and other vicious diseases to count. I encountered the spirits of pirates who'd been executed at Jackson Square, and an old monk sporting a long hoary beard and the traditional dark robe of the Capuchins sang Kyrie as he walked by St. Louis Cathedral. A sense of peace and comfort came over me. I had forgotten what it was like to feel something other than turmoil and the bitter root of resentment.

"What's wrong, my child?" The old monk asked me.

I wondered why he still lingered.

"I consider it my duty to help the good people of this city, especially the ones who can't take care of themselves."

I wanted to ask him how he did that as an earthbound spirit but he silenced me by asking if I wanted to go to the Light.

I shifted uncomfortably, too embarrassed to tell him why I had come to New Orleans.

"I'm not ready," I said. But, behind him, in the far-off distance, a faint glow beckoned me.

The man who'd bought my trunk reluctantly gave it to his wife, hoping the images that had plagued him didn't have anything to do with the luggage.

She emptied its contents, admiring each dress and undergarment as she ran her hands over the rich fabric. She had nice dresses, but none as exquisite as mine. The woman wanted to wear them, but she hesitated, wondering what had happened to the owner of these beautiful pieces.

At my behest, she too began dreaming of a woman lying on the ground in the frozen woods, eyes staring blankly into the bare sky as maggots crawled over her face and in and out of a bullet hole in her skull. She kept quiet as she didn't want her husband to question her sanity. But the strain of seeing my disfigured face took its toll, and her physician suggested she take the waters at Hot Springs.

The man's wife loathed packing her trunk, for she had convinced herself of a connection between it and her awful visions. She had stopped wearing the dresses she'd found inside but the nightmares I so carefully planned persisted.

At Hot Springs, the wife, pale and frail after the travel, collapsed into bed.

"Edith," her husband said, "you must take the waters."

"I can't," she protested. "I don't have the strength." She wouldn't allow the curtains to be drawn open and stayed in the darkened room, unable to eat or sleep.

It had been five years since my first visit to Hot Springs, and the town had grown since I was last there. The new, grander hotels and bathhouses, built after a fire had destroyed much of Bathhouse Row, catered to a wealthier clientele, and I didn't see as many veterans hobbling about. It grieved me to think of my first visit to the Springs, the small window of happiness in my brief life, when my desire to leave my life as a *demi-mondaine* seemed possible. My memories of traveling to see Abe, wondering if that first spark of attraction would last and what it might lead to, came sharply into focus.

I'd been consumed with rage and revenge for so long, I hadn't stopped to reflect on the choices I'd made. I could blame Abe or Leslie for what had happened to me, but if I were being truly honest with myself, I also had to admit my own culpability. When Leslie lifted my skirts, he wasn't thinking past that moment, and neither was I. It had been entirely my choice to submit to him, though I still didn't believe I should have been the only one punished for the deed. And, with Abe, if I had been willing to see the depth of his deceptive behavior, if I hadn't willfully ignored the warning signs, I could have spared myself.

My bitterness toward the Sisters also waned. They had dedicated their lives to the Church, taken new names, broken ties to their own families. They had done so willingly, where I had been forced to do so, but as much as I hadn't cared for the nuns, I understood now why they looked down on me and the other girls. They were Brides of Christ, not as exalted as priests, but above parishioners, and certainly above penitents. No wonder they considered us eternal sinners.

I recalled when I'd collapsed on the street in Watertown. Was it mere coincidence I woke in Mrs. Harding's brothel? Would anyone else have rescued me? I didn't know whether fate had anything to do with our decisions, but I did know this: My fate was now in my hands.

As I regarded the woman I had followed to Hot Springs, suffering because of me, I thought of my mam and how she must have been tormented over my death. I'd been her flesh and blood and I'd made her bear the anguish of a wayward daughter. I'd become intimate enough with pain to know how you absorb it until you can no longer remember living without it.

The woman I now haunted had nothing to do with my murder, yet I was making her bear the brunt of my anger. She had become so weak from my attachment, her husband, in desperation, forced her to drink a can of hot mineral water.

I detached myself, and the nightmares and visions of me ceased. Soon the paleness in her face and limbs was gone. She dressed and went to the dining room with her husband, took the waters at a bathhouse. I'd given her life back, though Edith and her husband would always believe it was the miracle mineral waters of the Springs that had cured her.

# 51

A sugary haze draped the North Country like a bride's veil. Wooden buckets hung below taps on the maple trees, while fires crackled underneath large kettles set up in yards to boil the sap. I remembered the times as a young child when my da let me place the first spile into a tree near our log house, how much I savored the first taste of the season's maple syrup. For weeks my clothes would smell of sugar as the honey-sweet aroma wafted through the woods.

Mam had stopped making maple syrup long ago, and Hannah had taken over that duty at the farm. When I last saw my mam, I'd been shocked and dismayed at her appearance. She had only worsened since then. Partially paralyzed, her body trembled, and she had difficulty walking.

Hannah visited our mam every day. My sister's family had grown to eight children, five girls and three boys. The eldest, Maggie, was now a gangly fourteen-year-old, and the youngest, Kittie, eighteen months. Hannah brought the three youngest to Mam's. She held Kittie in her lap while the other children played quietly on the floor. For a moment I was overcome with envy that I'd never had the chance to have a family like my sister.

◇

"Are you thinking about Annie again?" Hannah said when our mother seemed more melancholy than usual.

They were in the sunroom, drinking tea. Mam sat in her rocking chair as usual. She set down her teacup. "I don't understand why your sister doesn't write or come home."

"Mam," Hannah said softly, leaning forward and placing a hand over Mam's, "Annie is gone. Remember the letter her friend sent?"

Someone had sent a letter? It must have been Madeleine, or maybe Lottie.

Our mother's voice grew shrill. "But the newspapers said that murdered girl was named Annie Stone."

That's why Mam hadn't come to Jefferson. She had always held out hope I might still be alive.

Hannah stroked our mam's shoulder. "We've talked about this many times. Annie Stone's brother cleared up the confusion. Remember?"

Either Mam's mind had deteriorated beyond comprehension, or she chose not to believe Hannah. I was thankful I hadn't tried to appear to Mam. The bullet wound in my temple would have been too much of a shock. But I had to do something. I wrapped my spirit around her. Mam closed her eyes and leaned back in her rocking chair as my warmth soothed her.

"I know it's hard to accept," Hannah said.

When Mam opened her eyes, they brimmed with tears. "I wasn't there for her, or you, when your father died." She gulped back a sob. "I shouldn't have let her go to Buffalo. I've regretted that for many a year."

I wished so much I could say, "It's not your fault. I was too young to understand your grief, and I was too selfish."

"You did the best you could." Hannah stood and kissed Mam's forehead. "Let's be hearing no more of it."

Before Hannah could straighten herself, Mam said, "I want to talk to Annie."

"But that's impossible."

"No, it isn't." Mam paused. "I want to have a séance."

I was as stunned as Hannah. Had she felt my presence enough to ask for this?

"A séance? We can't do that," my sister protested.

Mam's lips pressed into a thin line.

I remembered as a child hearing stories of the Fox sisters, who claimed to communicate with a spirit in their Hydesville, New York home. They started giving public performances and traveled as far away as England to show off their abilities. My parents had ridiculed the sisters and scoffed at those who took part in séances. Now my mother wanted to conduct one in her own home.

"It's against our religion," Hannah said. But no amount of reasoning could persuade Mam to give up the notion.

"I don't care. I want to talk to my daughter," she insisted.

"I don't know anyone who can do such a thing." My practical sister was exasperated.

"I'm sure you can find someone." Mam stood and left the room, ending the matter.

I didn't know Canton had a spiritualist until Hannah discreetly inquired. She didn't want anyone to find out. The date was set and the closer it came, the more Mam's humour improved. It gave her something to look forward to, some hope.

Mrs. Wolcott arrived on the appointed afternoon. She, my mother, and my sister sat around the kitchen table, which had been prepared with three candles surrounding a plate of bread. Mrs. Wolcott instructed Mam and Hannah to join hands with her.

"Beloved Annie Moore," the medium began, her eyes closed, her head tilted toward the ceiling, "we bring you gifts of life unto death. Commune with us, Annie, and move among us."

As Mrs. Wolcott repeated the chant, I enveloped my mam with my essence. She broke free of the medium's hand and hugged her arms close to her body.

Alarmed, Mrs. Wolcott said, "Mary, you can't break the circle. We have to hold hands."

"She's here," Mam said.

Hannah observed our mother with a mixture of skepticism and astonishment. "Who?"

"Our Annie," Mam said faintly, then raised her voice. "Oh, my darling daughter, how I have missed you so." She started to weep. I swirled around her more tightly. The candles flickered. Mrs. Wolcott's eyes widened when one blew out.

Hannah frantically cast her head about the room. I moved my spirit so it touched her, too. She grew still, her eyes tearing up.

"Mammy," Hannah cried out, "I feel her too."

My sister leaned over and hugged Mam. I stayed wrapped around them, the three of us together again, so close and yet worlds apart.

I had been so consumed with revenge it had clouded every thought and action since my death. Now, I realized my murder had never entitled me to the kind of revenge I desired. But I did have the ability to forgive—both Abe and myself.

The space around me filled with dazzling light.

"Annie?"

I recognized the voice immediately. Edla came into view. She no longer wore the blood-stained nightgown she'd died in but appeared radiant and serene. "I told you someone would be waiting for you."

I returned Edla's greeting with a warm smile and my spirit filled with an incredible lightness. I had been living in the land of lost souls too long. No longer would I allow anger to keep me anchored to Earth.

And then he appeared. My da. Still in his youth—no worry, strong, full of hope. I remembered what Edla had said about reaching the Light. The broken shards of the disappointments, the heartaches you carry within you on Earth, leave you instantly and you're made whole again. I touched my left temple. There was no bullet wound, no disfigured face.

I looked past Da for my little angel but she wasn't there. I chastised myself for my selfishness. How could she forgive me for abandoning her?

"She's back on Earth," Edla said.

"So soon?"

Edla nodded. "She gets another chance at life. She's with a family."

My little girl deserved happiness. And so did I. I linked arms with my da and Edla and together we walked into the Light.

# Epilogue

*Jefferson, Texas*
*1931*

On a humid midsummer evening, Ed McDonald stood hunched over a small worktable in a dimly lit corner of his foundry. Slivers of a waning sun slipped through the weathered planks of the building. The clatter of machinery and the whirring from the maze of pulleys hanging overhead had ceased for the day. Flecks of metal glistened on Ed's forearms as he methodically struck his mallet against the chisel. With smooth, even strokes, he carved my name as carefully as he shaped objects out of iron and brass.

The object of Ed's blows was a small piece of Vermont marble. He'd been saving it for this purpose. A simple tombstone rounded at the top, only my name, Bessie Moore, and 12-31-1876 were chiseled inside a diamond-shaped border. The date was wrong, but it was as close as Ed's memory could get. He had been a young boy when I'd died. Now Ed had passed his sixtieth year.

From my place in Heaven, I often watched Ed. He had never forgotten me. He'd married late in life and had two children, a boy and a girl, but he still had room in his heart for me. He was so young when I died on that hill near his town that he hadn't known there was evil in the world until my murder.

His work done, Ed loaded the headstone onto the back of his

stripped-down Ford Model T. He cranked the engine and it sputtered to life. Home was little more than a stone's throw from the foundry, a two-story white frame house surrounded by stately sycamores and oaks.

At supper, Ed didn't mention his plan to his wife, who was as stubborn as he was quick-tempered. She was the reason the project needed to be carried out after dark.

"For heaven's sake," she had said when Ed had first told her of his intentions, "don't let anyone see you. Someone might think you had an affair with her." I'd chuckled over that remark.

Around midnight Ed drove the short distance up North Alley, over the railroad tracks, to Oakwood Cemetery, and up the gently sloping earth to my plot. It stood apart from the others, a magnolia tree my grave's only companion.

Ed kneeled, grabbed the crumbling wooden marker, and pulled it from the ground. For a moment he thought he was doing something sacrilegious. He carried the broken pieces to the truck bed and then placed the new headstone.

He stepped back to survey his work, satisfied with this more fitting tribute for me. Through the darkness the rows of soft white marble, with their angels and crosses, glowed. George Todd had joined me in eternal rest in 1913, and my dear John Vines had passed the next year on the Fourth of July.

Ed wondered why my life had to end so early and so violently, and whether my husband was still alive; if, unlike me, Abe had lived to enjoy old age. Ed believed as a man grew older that he should regret the wrongs committed against others, not the ones done to him.

Ed's thoughts turned to his own mortality. Two strokes had slowed him down. His end was nearing. Placing a new marker was his way of making sure I would never be forgotten. As he left the cemetery he smiled, thinking of the inevitable discovery of his deed and the mystery that would surround it. I did too.

# Afterword

In Elizabeth Gilbert's book, *Big Magic*, she writes about how the creative process is "both magical *and* magic," that ideas are all around us searching for a human partner to notice them and get to work creating.

I chose journalism as my first career, but I always wanted to write novels. I just didn't know *what* I wanted to write. On a day trip to East Texas when my husband and I first started dating, we visited Jefferson, a town I wasn't familiar with even though I had grown up in Irving, a Dallas suburb, only three hours away.

At Jefferson's historical museum, there was a full-page newspaper article in a display case. The story, published in a Dallas paper in the 1930s, was about the murder of a young woman in Jefferson some sixty years earlier. As I stared at the woman's image in the newspaper, I had two thoughts: "Why is she still remembered after all these years?" And, "How did he get away with it?" From that moment Bessie had her hooks in me.

At the time I was working as a television news reporter in Charleston, South Carolina, but I made a vow to research the case when I moved back to Texas. Two years later I got a job anchoring the evening news in San Antonio and immediately started my research. I spent nearly all my spare time reading newspaper articles, court documents, and traveling to every place Bessie lived or visited.

Other than her father's death when she was ten years old, not much is known about Bessie's upbringing. It was reported in newspapers after her murder that she had been "seduced" by a man and had left Canton in shame. She reportedly went to Watertown, but it's unknown when she arrived and whether she had come directly from Canton. From there, she ended up in Chicago at Jennie Williams's brothel, but it is also unknown when she arrived there.

I chose, from deep research, for Bessie's story to reflect a plausible portrayal of a woman during her time who had a lover out of wedlock and what the consequences of that often were. Thankfully, a few mid-to-late nineteenth century prostitutes fortuitously penned their stories (they weren't actually published until the mid-20th century), which shed much light on the reasons why women entered the world's oldest profession and what their lives were like. Bessie's story was the norm, not the exception, for women who had "fallen" and had few opportunities to make a living.

In many ways, Bessie's and Abe's lives represent a microcosm of American life in the mid-1800s, albeit for those on the fringe of society. The two main immigrant groups at that time were the Irish and Germans. While Bessie was born in County Cork, Ireland, Abe was born in Cincinnati, Ohio, but both were children of immigrant parents seeking a better life in America.

While much of the story with Bessie alive sprang from my imagination, many of the events described are true. I'll note the highlights here. A more detailed version is available on my website at www.jodyhadlock.com.

Abe and Bessie reportedly spent time together in Hot Springs, Arkansas, and they were kicked out of their hotel for "inappropriate" behavior. Newspaper articles also noted the incident with Abe intervening in the fight, when he offered his gun to the loser, for which he was taken to jail.

It was common for prostitutes in the north to winter in warmer climes, and Bessie was one of those who did so. Nell Otis was a real madam, but it's unknown exactly where Bessie boarded in New Orleans. Abe followed Bessie there and they traveled together by steamboat to Cincinnati, where Bessie boarded for a short time at a boardinghouse on Race Street before entering Frank Wright's bordello. The couple's relationship was tumultuous and culminated near the end of the year with Abe striking Bessie in front of the cigar boy. Soon after, she went back to Chicago. There was a raid on Jennie Williams's brothel and Bessie's name was printed in the *Inter Ocean*, although the account I used is from September 1876, not December.

There is proof of Bessie and Abe's marriage. A marriage license was issued to them in Danville, Illinois, where they stopped on their way from Chicago to Texas. The couple attracted attention everywhere they went, and a reporter did interview them at the Aetna Hotel.

Bessie's body wasn't discovered until February 5, 1877, fifteen days after her murder, and her corpse was recognizable, causing much debate at the trials over whether she could have lain in the woods that long with such little decomposition.

The motive for Bessie's murder has always been a source of speculation, with the main theories being that Abe wanted her diamonds, which he did covet, and that there was an unwanted unborn child, but the autopsy found that she was not pregnant.

Soon after Bessie's death, it was rumored that her real name was Annie Stone, another prostitute in Watertown, who was the daughter of a shoemaker. That rumor still exists today, but it has been proven that Bessie was Annie Moore, of Canton, New York. I chose to include Annie Stone as a character in my novel in homage to her, and I created her assumed name for her life as a *demi-mondaine*, which was the custom.

When Abe returned to Cincinnati, he took Bessie's trunk with him and paid a baggage man to dispose of it. It's also true that Abe attempted suicide outside Jake Aug's Clubhouse. A reporter for the *Cincinnati Enquirer* happened to be at the newspaper office next door at two-thirty a.m. and heard the gunshot.

John Vines was a widower with two young sons. He, Dr. Turner, and Edward Guthridge traveled to Cincinnati to identify Abe and bring him back to Texas, but the extradition process took much longer than how it is depicted in the novel.

The reporter Lafcadio Hearn, who was of Greek and Irish descent, lived in Cincinnati when Bessie was there, and was a well-known crime reporter, but back then most newspaper articles didn't have bylines, so it's unknown whether he covered Bessie's murder. He did have a damaged left eye, which he was self-conscious of his entire life. Hearn moved to New Orleans in the fall of 1877, where he also made a name for himself as a newspaper writer before moving to Japan, where he became world famous for his writings on Japanese culture, and is still remembered there. There is no record of Hearn going to Jefferson to report on Abe's imprisonment or trials; I included the writer in homage to him.

Thomas Snelbaker and George Ellis were involved in a blackmail scheme against Abe's family and, when that didn't work, they went to the prosecution. Snelbaker traveled to Texas, where he was discredited, but that actually happened at a hearing soon after Abe's arrival back in Jefferson and not at the first trial. Several months after Snelbaker was discredited, he claimed to have found Bessie's diamonds in a pawn shop in St. Louis. Abe had stopped in that city on the way back to Cincinnati after Bessie's murder. But no jewels were ever introduced as evidence at the trials. In fact, the discovery was never mentioned again. Because of this, and the fact that Snelbaker had played both sides of the fence, I decided not to include what was most likely a false claim.

One interesting side note: While Abe was in the Marshall jail, his cellmate for a time was a man by the name of Jim Currie, a detective for the railroad who shot two members of an acting troupe after a performance in Marshall. Ben Porter died from his gunshot wound. The other actor survived but spent a month recovering in Marshall. His name was Maurice Barrymore, the patriarch of the famous acting family, whose great-granddaughter is actress Drew Barrymore.

The phonograph was a new invention in the late 1870s and a newspaper reported on a man who went to the Marshall jail to record Abe's voice. I obviously fictionalized hearing Bessie on the recording.

Congressman David Culberson was not at the first trial because of his duties in Washington, but he was the lead defense attorney at the second trial and credited with Abe's acquittal, partly for his cross-examination of chambermaid Jennie Simpson. Two black men served on the jury at the second trial, which was highly unusual at the time. It was most likely attributed to a March 1, 1880 Supreme Court decision in *Strauder v. West Virginia*, which ruled that barring blacks from jury service violated the Equal Protection Clause of the Fourteenth Amendment.

The events depicting Ed McDonald were either reported on or handed down as family lore. When he placed the headstone on Bessie's grave, it was a mystery who had done so for a decade, until McDonald finally confessed to the good deed.

Not surprisingly, after his acquittal, Abe led a life of crime. If not for the newspaper accounts and court records, his escapades are almost unbelievable.

At first, Abe returned to Cincinnati and was listed in the city directory as a traveling agent for his father's business and living at his parents' home at 264 West Fifth, but by 1882 his name had disappeared from the directory. He next turned up in New York City where he managed a dry goods store for his brothers, Charles and Jacob, but that venture ended in bankruptcy when Abe swindled merchandise for the store.

He then went to work for a company in New York City owned by his cousin David Rothschild that sold bar fixtures and billiard tables. That business failed, apparently through no fault of Abe. David has an interesting criminal story as well. He later opened a bank in New York and became a loan shark. Before the bank folded, he withdrew a large sum of money, which he hid. In 1904, David was sentenced to nine years in Sing Sing prison where he died in November 1908. After his death, his widow finally disclosed where the stolen money was hidden.

Abe next showed up in St. Louis where he came up with another scheme. He would travel to a small town, learn who the most successful merchant was, and then order merchandise on credit under that person's name. At that time, suppliers relied on the merchant credit reports of Dun or Bradstreet (they didn't merge until 1933). Abe would audaciously introduce himself to the merchant he was impersonating, claiming what a coincidence it was that they shared the same name. So when merchandise arrived in the town, Abe was able to claim it for himself and then leave town with the goods without paying for any of it.

Abe worked this ruse all the way west to San Lorenzo, California, near San Francisco, where his luck ran out when a postal inspector finally caught up to him. A deputy US Marshal was assigned to transport Abe back to Missouri but, incredibly, Abe escaped when the train stopped in Little Rock, Arkansas. He made his way to Tuskahoma,

Indian Territory (now Oklahoma) where he resumed his swindling, and this time he included diamonds in his orders.

From there he went to Waelder, Texas near San Antonio, and then to Georgia. By then authorities were on to him again and posted circulars everywhere. Abe became one of the most wanted men in the country.

He escaped to St. Mary's, Ontario, Canada where he was eventually caught and taken to Missouri, tried, and sentenced to three years in a state prison. After finishing his sentence, Abe was being transported to Texas to face charges when he again tried to escape, this time by jumping off a train while manacled to another convict. They made it fifteen miles and found a blacksmith who refused to take off their chains. Less than twenty-four hours later the pair was in custody again.

In Texas, Abe's story really turns bizarre. While waiting in a Gonzales County jail cell for his trial for impersonating and defrauding one of Waelder's merchants, Abe wrote a letter to the British ambassador in Washington, DC, claiming to be a British subject who was "entirely penniless and friendless" and that before he could leave the United States for England, he'd been kidnapped by the Gonzales authorities and was being held illegally on an old forgery charge! Abe never received a response.

He was quickly tried—no more dream teams of defense attorneys—and sent to the Huntsville penitentiary north of Houston in August of 1899. At the end of his three-year sentence, he was discharged on April 2, 1902, nearly twenty-five years to the day after he had arrived back in Jefferson as a prisoner.

It has long been rumored that Abe visited Bessie's grave in the early 1900s. I believe this one is true. When Abe left Huntsville, he went back to New York and it's entirely possible that he stopped in Jefferson along the way. He reportedly laid a bouquet of roses on his wife's grave and asked the sexton why the town had "bestowed such kindness" by giving her a proper burial, to which the sexton had replied, "She was some mother's daughter."

Abe would have walked near the grave of the man who had successfully defended him. David Culberson died in 1900 after serving twenty-two years in Congress. His son, Charles, who attended Abe's trials, more than followed in his father's footsteps, becoming attorney general of Texas, then governor, before reaching the US Senate the year before his father passed.

Back in New York, Abe remarried to a woman twenty-seven years his junior. He and his wife, Mabel, had two children, a boy and a girl, named after Abe's parents, Maier and Rosa, despite being cut out of their lives and wills.

Abe apparently stayed on the straight and narrow for a while, working as a manager at a loan office, but his old habits came back. His final scheme was in 1923 when he went to Baltimore and began selling horse racing tips under the name Murat A. de Rothschild. He mailed circulars offering to send six telegrams to potential clients, each containing the name of a "sure winner" for twenty dollars, to be paid in advance of course. If the bettor's horse lost, Abe would refund the money. Fortunately he was arrested, on July 11, 1923.

Out on bond, Abe and his family went to the beach in Atlantic City, New Jersey on Friday, July 20. Around four-thirty in the afternoon, he waded into the ocean. Strapped to his waist was a belt containing fifteen thousand dollars in cash. Abe never emerged from the water, and his body was never found.

Was it an accident? Was he the victim of a riptide that drowned him and carried his body out to sea? Or, facing more time in prison, was he tired of his life and committed suicide?

In October 1923, his widow, who was also arrested for the racing tip racket, was sentenced to six months in jail. Investigators believed Abe was still alive and had faked his death to avoid prison, but Mabel always insisted her husband had drowned.

The exact circumstances of Abe's death will remain a mystery, but what is not a mystery is whether he killed Bessie.

# Acknowledgments

Throughout the years I spent researching and writing this novel there were many people who guided and supported me, for which I am forever grateful.

First and foremost, Bridget Boland, editor extraordinaire, who challenged me to write Bessie's story from her point of view as an earthbound spirit. When I doubted whether I could do it justice, she gently and patiently mentored me through the many drafts as the story evolved. Without her, you wouldn't be holding this book in your hands.

A world of thanks to those who read early pages of the manuscript: Mark Beauregard, Carol Bernett, Jim Boland, Elyssa East, Denise Fuller, Robin Lee, Carol Matthews, Michael Raymond, cin salach, Meg LaTorre Snyder, Leslie Wells, and my mother, Suzanne. To my stellar writing group: Priya Ardis, Fenley Grant, Jen Geigle Johnson, Jennifer Worsham Looft, Amanda McMurrey, Debbie Ochoa, and Nuha Said.

I was fortunate to be chosen to take part in Aspen Words's "Summer Words" conference where I received insightful feedback on the full manuscript from my workshop leader, the late *Vanity Fair* and Simon & Schuster editor George Hodgman; and from fellow writers Monica Halka, Dipika Rai, Kathryn Diamond Camp, Leah Worthy, and David Rompf, who also suggested the perfect title for this novel.

I'm also grateful to Adrienne Brodeur, executive director of Aspen Words, who always found time to offer advice and encouragement to an aspiring author.

Scott Wolven and Shanna McNair of The Writer's Hotel, another outstanding writers' conference, believed in this story from the beginning.

Four genealogists helped me immensely in my research: Anne Rodda and Dr. Paul MacCotter in Ireland; Elly Catmull at Legacy Tree Genealogists; and Laura Stolk, who found the details about Abe's last scheme and how his life ended.

Thanks also to Linda Casserly, town historian for Canton, New York, who gave me a tour of Bessie's hometown; her research assistant, Steven Sauter; Canton native Connie Sterner; Bryan Thompson, town historian for De Kalb, New York; Paul Hetzler at the Cornell Cooperative Extension of St. Lawrence County, New York; and Paul Finnigan, descendant of Bessie's sister, Hannah Moore Finnigan.

I spent many days in Jefferson, researching at the Jefferson Historical Museum and becoming acquainted with the town's hospitable residents. Several were immensely helpful in my research: Duke DeWare, whose ancestors came by wagon train with the Culberson family from Alabama to Jefferson in 1856; Lisa Lowder, whose research discovered Bessie's true identity; the late Fred McKenzie; Evelyn Mims, and Evelyn's aunt, the late Aree Risley, whose father was Ed McDonald, placer of the mysterious tombstone on Bessie's grave; and the late Evelyn Small, descendant of attorney George Todd.

Thank you to the staff at the Cincinnati History Library and Archives, especially Mickey deVisé; the Cincinnati Public Library; Kevin Grace, head archivist at the University of Cincinnati Library; Chicago's Newberry Library; the Harrison County Texas Historical Research Library, especially Ruth Briggs; the public libraries in

San Antonio, Marshall, and North Richland Hills, Texas, especially Karen Raborn; the State Archives and the Dolph Briscoe Center for American History, both in Austin, Texas; and the New Orleans Historical Collection.

To my publisher, the incomparable Brooke Warner; my project manager at SparkPress, Samantha Strom; and editor Krissa Lagos. To Amaryah Orenstein, who did a phenomenal job copyediting this novel. David Litman, for the stunning book cover he designed. To my publicity team at BookSparks: Crystal Patriarche, Hanna Pollock Lindsley, and Keely Platte; web designer Ilsa Brink; and social media guru Gary Parkes.

Others I'd like to thank for their support: Martha Hall Kelly, Angie Kim, Bren McClain, M.J. Rose, Kevin Short, and my fabulous launch team. Also, Kindred Coffee, especially the late owner, Samuel Iweis, in North Richland Hills, Texas, where I had my unofficial "office;" and to Jill Davis at Joe Pine Coffee in Marshall, Texas, where I spent countless hours working on my manuscript when my husband and I visited his hometown.

Special thanks to Susi Wolf, who performs a one-woman play about Diamond Bessie and loves her as much as I do.

Deepest gratitude to my mother, for lifelong love and encouragement.

To my wonderful husband, Charlie. Little did you know when we visited Jefferson, that it would lead me down this long and winding path. Thank you for sharing the journey with me all these years.

And, finally, to Bessie. Thank you for choosing me to tell your story. May you finally rest in peace.

# About the Author

© Nabor Godoy

After studying journalism at Texas A&M University, Jody Hadlock was a television news reporter and anchor in Bryan-College Station, Texas; Charleston, South Carolina; and San Antonio, Texas. She now lives near Fort Worth with her husband. *The Lives of Diamond Bessie* is her first novel.

jodyhadlock.com

 /jodyhadlockauthor

 jodyhadlock

# SELECTED TITLES FROM SPARKPRESS

SparkPress is an independent boutique publisher delivering high-quality, entertaining, and engaging content that enhances readers' lives, with a special focus on female-driven work.

www.gosparkpress.com

*Dovetails in the Tall Grass: A Novel*, Samantha Specks
$16.95, 978-1-68463-093-6
In 1862, thirty-eight Dakota-Sioux men were hanged in the largest mass execution in US history. This is the story of two young women—one settler, one Dakota-Sioux—connected by the fate of the thirty-ninth man.

*The Sorting Room: A Novel*, Michael Rose, $16.95, 978-1-68463-105-6
A girl coming of age during America's Great Depression, Eunice Ritter was born to uncaring alcoholic parents and destined for a life of low-wage toil—a difficult, lonely existence of scant choices. This epic novel—which spans decades—shows how hard work and the memory of a single friendship gave the indomitable Eunice the perseverance to pursue redemption and forgiveness for the grievous mistakes she made early in her life.

*The Takeaway Men: A Novel,* Meryl Ain, $16.95, 978-1-68463-047-9
Twin sisters Bronka and JoJo Lubinski are brought to America from Germany by their Polish refugee parents after World War II—but in "idyllic" America, political, cultural, and family turmoil awaits them. As the girls grow older, they eventually begin to ask questions of and demand the truth from their parents.

*Child Bride: A Novel,* Jennifer Smith Turner
$16.95, 978-1-68463-038-7
The coming-of-age journey of a young girl from the South who joins the African American great migration to the North—and finds her way through challenges and unforeseen obstacles to womanhood.

*Seventh Flag: A Novel,* Sid Balman, Jr. $16.95, 978-1-68463-014-1
A sweeping work of historical fiction, *Seventh Flag* is a Micheneresque parable that traces the arc of radicalization in modern Western Civilization—reaffirming what it means to be an American in a dangerously divided nation.

*Sarah's War,* Eugenia Lovett West, $16.95, 978-1-943006-92-2
Sarah, a parson's young daughter and dedicated patriot, is sent to live with a rich Loyalist aunt in Philadelphia, where she is plunged into a world of intrigue and spies, her beauty attracts men, and she learns that love comes in many shapes and sizes.

*Trouble the Water: A Novel,* Jacqueline Friedland
$16.95, 978-1-943006-54-0
When a young woman travels from a British factory town to South Carolina in the 1840s, she becomes involved with a vigilante abolitionist and the Underground Railroad while trying to navigate the complexities of Charleston high society and falling in love.